THE HEPCATS OF ULTHAR

AND OTHER LOVECRAFTIAN TALES

BY RICHARD LEE BYERS

As we prowled on into the echoing gloom, I kept imagining I heard the ghouls sneaking up behind us to rip us apart before we even got a chance to talk to them. And now I couldn't even keep my mitt on Mister Speaker. I needed one hand for the flashlight and the other to carry my trombone case.

Eventually, we came to a place where the way widened out into a space like a room with several doorways. Pickman said, "This should be far enough."

I set my flashlight on the floor and, working pretty much by touch, opened the case and screwed the tram together. Then I straightened up and frisked the whiskers a little. If the ghouls liked music, I meant to give them the most righteous riffs they'd ever heard.

And I busted my conk down there in the dark, taking off in a jam that worked in pretty much every tune I knew. For a while I wasn't sure if anybody but Onyx and Pickman heard, but then I sensed my audience gathering around me. They slipped in silently, but the stink gave them away.

I played a while longer, and when I finally lowered the slush-pump, they pounded their mitts. That was encouraging until Pickman ran his flashlight beam around the room and showed them to me. Reet as his horrible pictures were, they hadn't quite prepared me for the real thing, and there were way more ghouls than I had bullets.

One of the dog men, a big one dressed in the moldy remains of what had started out as knee pants and a George Washington wig, glared at Pickman. "Was this supposed to be a peace offering?" he asked. "It was good. We might keep the musician for a while. But it wasn't enough."

"The Horror on the Freighter" originally appeared in *Legacy of the Reanimator: The Chronicles of Dr. Herbert West*, Chaosium, 2015.

"Hate, Courage, and Blood" originally appeared in *NonBinary Review #5*, 2015.

"Vermin" originally appeared in *SNAFU: Unnatural Selection*, Cohesion Press, 2016.

"Kickstarter" originally appeared in *Whispers from the Abyss 2*, 01Publishing, 2015.

"Floater" originally appeared in *Lovecraftian Tales: Stories of Weird Fiction and Cosmic Horror*, Lovecraft eZine Press, 2017.

"Advanced Placement" originally appeared in *Tomorrow's Cthulhu: Stories at the Dawn of Posthumanity*, Broken Eye Books, 2016.

"Leaves" was previously published by the author, 2015.

"Bug Zapper" originally appeared in *Resonator: New Lovecraftian Tales from Beyond*, Martian Migraine Press, 2015.

"The Body Shop" originally appeared in *Cthulhu Fhtagn!*, Word Horde, 2015.

"Hope" originally appeared in *The Fall of Cthulhu*, Horrified Press, 2015.

"The Hep Cats of Ulthar," "IV-F," and "The Bubble Man" appear here for the first time.

DEDICATION

For Mark Jones

ACKNOWLEDGMENTS

Thanks to everyone at Macabre Ink for helping me put this collection together and to the editors who bought those stories that were previously published.

TABLE OF CONTENTS

THE HEP CATS OF ULTHAR

It was dark in the alley, but after the trenches and the Meuse-Argonne offensive, I knew a dead body when I saw one. I moved closer and smelled the blood and the shit. Closer still and I focused it was Margie lying there.

I winced, because of the state of the body—partly shredded, partly smashed, with pieces missing—and because I'd known and liked her. She'd been a cheerful little wren with music in her soul, always stepping and swaying to the beat as she wove her way among the tables.

Then I realized that whoever had done this to her, he could still be nearby, maybe watching me this second. I shifted my trombone case to my left hand and slipped my Harlem toothpick out of my pocket. I thumbed the button, and the blade flicked out to gleam in the moonlight.

I turned, searching the shadows. A pair of blinkers gleamed back at me like it was Satan standing there, and I pointed the knife straight at them.

Then a smallish shape yowled, jumped off the trashcan it had been crouching on, and padded toward me. It was a long, skinny black tomcat with big ears.

Some of the tension quivered out of me. The cat kept squalling.

"It's all right," I told him. "The killer's gone."

The cat went right on fussing. Until suddenly he wasn't just yowling anymore. I could make out a word: "Cop! Cop! Cop!"

For a tick, I thought I was imagining it. I'd blown a little weed between sets, and maybe it was stronger than I'd thought. Then I glimpsed a flicker of motion at the far end of the alley.

It *could* be a pounder heading in my direction, and if it

was, did I want to be caught standing over the body with a switchblade in my paddle? It didn't have any blood on it and neither did I, but little details like that might not keep the man from trying to pin the murder on me. Police work could get fast and sloppy when the victim and suspect were both Negroes. And I could easily have tailed Margie from the speakeasy where we both worked.

I put the knife back in its hideaway and copped a drill between two houses. The black tom bounded along beside me all the way back to the boardinghouse where I was living.

I doubted the saw would like me bringing a stray cat inside. But she was almost certainly copping a nod, I maybe owed the tom a favor, and besides, I was curious. So what the hell.

I found some moo juice in the icebox, poured it into a bowl, set it on the floor of my cubby, and sat on the bed watching the cat lap it up. When he'd had enough, he looked up and me and meowed.

"Don't just make noise," I told him. "Talk like you did before." If he could. Now that some time had passed, it was hard to believe he ever really had.

"*Listen* like you did before," the tom replied, still meowing, but with the words inside the sound. "You have to concentrate."

"Damn," I said. "How is this happening?"

The tom sprang up on the pad beside me. "Where I come from, cats can talk to any human with the knack for hearing us. Scratch my face."

I did. His fur was nice and soft.

"Where do you come from?" I asked.

"Ulthar. A town in another world that some of you humans visit in your dreams."

I shook my head. "I feel like I'm dreaming now."

"No, you don't. That's just a thing humans say when they're bewildered. But you have it in you to be a powerful dreamer. That's the reason you understand me."

"I guess musicians are dreamers." I chuckled. "And drunks. And clipsters. So why are you here in my world?"

He nuzzled my hand. "It's your fault. Well, your band's. I live in a tavern. Sometimes, when everything was quiet, I could just hear your music. I tried to find where it was coming from and wandered into *your* tavern."

"We call it a speak."

"Whatever it is, the jump was confusing, and before I could get my bearings, someone caught me and put me out. I've been waiting for a chance to get back inside."

"And go back home?"

"I hope so."

"I'll sneak you in tomorrow night. Meanwhile, tell me this. Did you see what happened to Margie, the chick in the alley?"

"No, but finding her made me wonder."

"About what?"

"Whether I'm the only thing from the Dreamlands to slip across."

We talked for a while longer, but without me collaring the situation any more clearly than before, which meant I still felt like an icky. I did find out the talking cat's name was Onyx, and that if I partook of a stick, he liked me to blow the smoke in his map. Eventually I caught some cups, and he did the same curled up nestled against me on top of the lily whites.

The juice joint where I worked—the Kadath Club--was a "supper club" where the customers needed membership cards to get in and the panther sweat came in coffee cups. I wasn't happy when I got there and lamped the screaming-gasser parked out front. I had no eyes to talk to the law. But I figured that showing up for work was less suspicious than ducking it, so I told Onyx I'd see him later and broomed on in.

It turned out to be the right choice. The snatcher, a big, square-built Irishman named Boyle, had no idea I'd been in the alley. He didn't suspect me or anybody who'd worked with Margie. But it was routine for him to question all of us anyway, just in case someone knew something.

When he finished with all the questions I might have expected, he asked, "Did you know Donald Williams?"

"No," I said, and it was the bible. I had no idea who that had been. But I had a hunch why Boyle was asking. "Did somebody else die the same way as Margie?"

Boyle glowered. He expected to ask the questions, not

answer them, especially when the man across from him was colored.

I did my best to look and sound all respectful and Tom-o-reemi. "I just want to know because I walk home that way every night."

"Then be smart and stick to the streets. Now get out of here and send in the next dinge."

I sneaked Onyx into the speak not long after. It was easy. People were busy beating their gums about Margie's death and worrying about what Boyle might think or do. I wished I could talk to the tom about what I'd discovered, but I was worried somebody would notice. So I just let him dart onward to find himself a hiding place.

Boyle finally left about that time of the early black when the band needed to start getting ready. I was screwing my axe together when Eddington Pryce—our boss—walked up with a pile of handwritten charts in his hands.

Skinny and pinch-faced with a big white slab of a forehead and thinning hair, Pryce dressed and talked like the biggity blueblood he was, a hincty sort who always had his glasses on and was one salty son of a bitch in general. But he was a Gabriel, too, and somewhere along the way, the jazz bug bit him.

I suspected he wished he could play his trumpet alongside cats like us, but back then you just didn't put ofays and oxfords together on the main kick, and the faces didn't yet have swing bands of their own. So he did the next best thing. He opened a speak, hired a band, and wrote and arranged for us. Which had always been all right by me. He had some chops.

But this evening was different. Scowling as he passed out the sheet music, he said, "You need to perform these songs *precisely* as written. Right down the alley!" Somehow, he never sounded more like a Jeff than when he talked jive.

I glanced through the top chart, an arrangement of "Muscle Shoals Blues." He'd even written down my solo in exact detail.

A couple guys who'd been with the band since before my time exchanged glances in a way that told me they'd been through this before. Shorty, our hide-beater, said, "Boss, if you want it to cook—"

"Do it!" Pryce snapped. "Anyone who doesn't will be fired!"

We went on not long after, and at first it was all right. None of us was a Fats or a Dippermouth, but Boston wasn't the Big Red Apple or Chicago, and as far as the alligators and rug cutters who'd come out to hear us were concerned, we were solid senders. Their mitt pounding made playing fun even if it wasn't as much fun as it could have been.

Gradually, though, the music began to feel wrong, like there was something nasty hiding between the notes or inside the harmony. My tongue felt hot and my feelers smarted as I flipped the slush-pump's slide in and out.

I glanced around the stage. The other cats looked sweaty and shaky. Shorty's eyes shifted to meet mine, and I saw the fear in them.

It was crazy to think Pryce's arrangements were making us sick, but it sure seemed like it. I decided to lay out for a few bars and see if I started feeling better.

I couldn't do it. It was like the music had changed from something we were making to a power that was talking through us like it was a ventriloquist and we were the dummies.

The pains in my mouth and hand got worse, and then the sickness we were feeling up on the main kick reached out to infect the crowd as well. Dancers stumbled, and one fainted. A fat man choked on a bite of steak. A flapper in swinging loops of pearls pounded on his back while a waitress—a gammin' light-skinned peola like all of them, like Margie had been—hovered with a glass of water.

Suddenly, at the other end of the room, Onyx leaped over the counter of the coat-check room and out into the open. As far as I could tell, nobody else noticed. Cecily, the attendant, should have been standing right there, but she wasn't. Maybe she'd passed out, too.

As Onyx dashed along the wall, a shadow appeared behind the counter. It was bigger than a man, big enough to fill the space, and as it started climbing through, it darkened. Or thickened.

Meanwhile, the music stabbed at me. My heart slammed to the beat, and it seemed I couldn't take a breath, although I don't know how that could have been true since we all were playing louder by the second. At one of the ringside tables, a woman let out a high, thin wail, like she had the urge to scream but wasn't sure there was actually a reason.

I was pretty sure there was reason to make a move before I had a real heart attack, the big shadow turned into something I could focus clearly, or it caught up with Onyx. Reminding myself that the tom had said I had the expubidence to be a "powerful dreamer"—whatever that meant—I tried again to break the music's spell. This time, instead of straining to stop playing, I struggled to blast out a sour gutbucket riff that wasn't any part of 'Potato Head Blues', the tune we were in the middle of.

The notes blared out of my horn and tore 'Potato Head Blues' to pieces. The shadow vanished, and over the next couple seconds, the other instruments staggered to a halt. The crowd stared up at the stage. Some looked dazed, some like they'd suddenly been awakened from a nod, and others relieved although they didn't quite know why.

Charles, our clarinetist and leader, a buddy ghee always togged to the bricks with hair fried straight, rapped, 'Honeysuckle Rose'!" He raised the gob stick to his mouth, started the song, and the rest of us joined in, playing something we knew by heart, in the way it felt natural to play it.

We didn't go back to Pryce's new charts, either, and after a couple songs I was worrying less about heart attacks and scary shadows and more about losing my job. But when we finished the set, there was no sign of him. Apparently he'd holed up upstairs in his office.

The other musicians headed for the alley behind the building where it was our habit to nip from flasks, blow boo, and screw whores against the wall. Tonight, they'd likely speculate about what had happened when we were playing Pryce's charts and reassure one another that it couldn't really have been as crazy and dangerous as it seemed.

I peeled off from the rest, looked for Onyx, and lamped his glims shining in a hallway. I followed him into a storeroom full of cases of the real McCoy the blockers ran in from Canada. Onyx jumped up on a stack of the crates and put us more eye to eye.

"What just happened?" I asked him.

"There was sorcery inside the music you were playing."

Even coming from a talking cat, even after what I'd just been through, that was a lot to take in. "You mean like hoodoo? That would make Mr. Pryce the hoodoo man. Which is crazy."

"Why?"

For one thing, he was an ofay, and I thought of hoodoo as a thing we colored folks did, though I'd never put much stock in it myself. For another ...

"Why would he make his own customers sick?" I asked.

"I don't think he meant to," Onyx said. He paused to lick a paw and swipe at his map with it. "He may have been trying to call and control the shadow thing. But the spell went wrong."

"Hm. And why did the spook go after you?"

"Perhaps it recognized me as something else that doesn't belong here. Maybe it thought I recognized it too and knew how to deal with it."

"Do you?"

"No. Like all my kind, I have a nose for magic, but I'm no warlock."

"Is that what we need?"

"Maybe. There's no passage to the Dreamlands left for me to pass through. It closed up."

"I'm sorry about that."

"You should be! Because it means the shadow isn't going anywhere, either, and until it does, it will keep preying on humans. You need to talk to your Mr. Pryce."

I shook my head. "You don't know him. He'd never admit to working hoodoo or being somehow involved in Margie's death, certainly not to the likes of me, even if it turned out he could understand you, too. And if he did, I wouldn't put it past him to try to use you somehow. Maybe knock you to the spook as a bribe."

"Well, you have to do something!"

Did I?

I was sorry for Onyx, stuck where he didn't belong. That didn't make it my responsibility to get him home.

I was sorrier for Margie, dying like she had, but it was the job of killjoys like Boyle to catch the killer. The smart play would be to hop the next train to the land o' darkness and leave them to it. Except that the police were never going to catch the shadow, not when they thought it was a person. The creature would go on killing.

With a muttered "Fuck," I decided I did have to try *something*. I'd always been like that, inclined to step up even when common sense said to turn away. Maybe I liked the excitement. Anyway, I hadn't ended up on the clip side of the big moist because Sam got me. I'd enlisted, and the same stupid instinct was pushing me now.

Unfortunately, the urge didn't come with any bright ideas about what I actually could do. But I mulled it over for a few ticks, and then a thought came to me. "The partner," I said.

"Who?" Onyx asked.

"Pryce doesn't own this place by himself. There's another man, although I haven't focused him in a while."

"Maybe he stopped coming around because he knew bad things were happening."

"Maybe." I snorted. "At least we can ask him about it without accusing him of praying to the Devil."

I claimed I still felt sick from whatever had happened in the club, and Charles gave me the next night off. I used it to track Pryce's partner to an art gallery on Newbury Street. It turned out the joint was exhibiting his paintings: 'The Art of Richard Upton Pickman.'

I didn't recall Pickman ever getting nasty and astorperious with any of the people who worked in the club. But I doubted he'd appreciate one of Aunt Hagar's chillun brooming on into the middle of his party and beefing to him while he was trying to peddle his pictures to other white folks. So I found a side door to tap on, and when somebody answered it, I claimed I had a message for Pickman. The man let me in and, after warning me, "Do *not* let go of that animal," left me to wait with Onyx in a cluttered backroom that smelled of turpentine.

From there, I could look out into the rest of the gallery. Enough to realize that if I did accuse Pickman of worshipping Old Scratch, I might not be the first. And that it might have been hard to turn his show into any more of a bring-down no matter how I buttonholed him.

The paintings were beautiful because Pickman was reet at his job, but horrible enough to turn your stomach because of what was in them. Pale, skinny creatures with doglike maps and long, spidery arms crept through graveyards and sneaked up behind a lone woman on a subway platform. In the picture on the easel in the center of the room, one of the dog men was tearing rotten chunks of meat out of a body in a broken coffin and stuffing them into its mouth.

And most of the folks who'd turned out to lamp Pickman's work didn't like it. They must have had some idea of what they were coming to see, but when they actually focused it, it was just too gruesome. Tall with dark, deep-set peekers, yellowish crumb crushers, and paint stains on his feelers and cuffs, the artist sneered at the squares who flinched, muttered their disapproval to one or another, or collared a broom with a solid zoom back out into the black.

Eventually the man who'd let me in went and whispered to him. Pickman looked in my direction, frowned, and headed toward me.

Though we'd talked a couple times in the speak, I could tell he didn't recognize me. I introduced myself again and then tried to boot him as to what was going on and why I'd come to see him.

At first, it seemed like he believed me. But when I finished, he grinned, shook his head, and said, "You should stop drinking tarantula juice. It's rotting your brain."

"Everything I said is the bible," I replied. "Tell him, Onyx."

"It's all true," said the tom.

If Pickman could hear the words inside the meowing, he didn't let on. "I mean it. You need to dry out before you land in an asylum."

Behind him, a fat woman who'd cut out a few ticks earlier marched back through the front door of the gallery. Underneath the eye shadow, rouge, and lipstick, her round pan was set in a scowl, like the faces of doughboys I'd seen who didn't want to go over the top but had decided that since they had to, they were going to make Jerry sorry they had.

Meanwhile, I was still trying to get Pickman to open up. "Sir," I said, "if you don't believe any of this, then why did you take the time to listen to all of it? On your big night?"

The fat woman stopped in front of the picture on the easel and reached into her handbag.

Pickman gestured to the door I'd come through. "Enough blather. It's time for you to go."

I guessed I might as well final. Whatever he collared, he wasn't going to slide his jib to me. But as I started to turn away, the woman pulled a nail file out of her bag.

I dropped Onyx, shoved Pickman out of the way, and charged out into the front room of the gallery. The woman swung the nail file over her head icepick style. I plowed into her, grabbed for her arm but missed, and we fell down on the floor together.

Scared she'd stick the nail file into me, I kept trying to get hold of her flailing arm. She screamed, and other people came running. A man swung his plate back to kick me in the head, and, tangled up with the woman like I was, there wasn't much I could do about it.

But Onyx sprang onto the foot that was planted on the floor and clawed the man's prop through his pegs. The man yelped, lost his balance, and staggered backward.

Then Pickman was there. He stooped, caught hold of the woman's wrist, twisted the nail file out of her mitt, and waved it back and forth for everyone to see. "Look! She was about to destroy *The Ghoul's Feast!* The Negro stopped her!"

I was pretty sure there were other people in the room who would have been glad to see the painting cut up and who didn't like lamping a colored man put his paddles on a white lady no matter what. Still, after Pickman spieled to them, they didn't have the nerve to act like it. The gallery owner sent the fat woman on her way with the warning that if she ever came back, he'd call the nab. Pickman took Onyx and me back into the storeroom.

"Thank you," he said. "*The Ghoul's Feast* is the best thing I've done so far. I keep thinking that even here in the kingdom of the 'Booboiesie,' as Mencken calls them, some perceptive soul will want to buy it." He snorted. "Perhaps, if the *Herald Journal* reports that an ignorant prude tried to slash it to shreds, the notoriety will help."

"Maybe," I said. "Mr. Pickman, from the things you paint, you *must* know I'm not crazy. Are you sure you can't see your way clear to help me?"

He took a silver cigarette case out of his pocket, scratched a scratcher, lit up a lung-buster, and blew out a plume of smoke. "You have to understand," he said at last, "I'm reluctant to discuss certain aspects of my life. As long as our modern-day Cotton Mathers think I'm painting purely from my degenerate imagination, they're mostly content to shake their fingers and leave it at that. But if they ever realized the truth is more complex, they might break out the nooses and the pressing stones just like in the good old days."

"I won't rat on you."

"I believe you, and now I owe you. So if you really want me to, I'll tell you what's going on in the Kadath Club. Although I think you'd be wiser to find another job and forget about it."

"I think so, too, but I guess I'm just not all that foxy."

He chuckled. "Nor am I. I've always been fascinated by things better left alone; occultism, the secret history of Massachusetts, what have you. That's what drew Eddington Pryce and me together. We met in college, where we noticed one another annoying the professors with questions about the Salem witch trials and pestering the librarians with requests for access to the same restricted books."

Pickman took another drag on his cigarette. "Clearly, we were kindred spirits, but with differences, too. My talent was painting, and his was music. I was lucky enough to possess a modest income and content to live within my means. He came from wealth and had the lavish tastes and grandiose expectations to match.

"That became a problem when his father discovered just how scandalous some of his son's interests and habits were and cut him off without a penny. Eddington couldn't bear the thought of working at an ordinary sort of job and making do with the salary, even if his eccentric course of study had prepared him for one. He had to be the boss, he had to make piles of money, and the enterprise had to be one he found congenial."

"Since he liked hooch and jazz," I said, "that meant opening a speak."

Pickman nodded. "But you need seed money to do that, and he couldn't find investors. So he came to me."

I cocked my head. "Even though you only had a 'modest income?'"

"This is where the story takes a turn most people wouldn't believe. But I suppose you will. Ghouls actually exist, and I've been able to study and paint them because I've cultivated an understanding with them. At Eddington's request, I provided an introduction."

It gave me a chill to hear that the dog men from the paintings really were creeping and crawling around under Boston. But I'd already been through too much to cast a kitten over it. "The ghouls have dough?"

Pickman smiled. "Plenty of people are buried with jewelry or at least the gold in their teeth."

"All right, but why give it to Pryce?"

"Because ghouls enjoy some of the same things we do. They wanted there to be a place where they could drink liquor and listen to live music."

"Wait. These things were *in the speak?* And nobody noticed?"

"Mostly, they hid in the cellar underneath. But some ghouls are born human and change later in life, and some of those can still pass if they bundle up and work some petty magic."

"Jesus! But I dig. The shadow thing is a kind of ghoul that comes up through the cellar and isn't satisfied just to guzzle foam and listen to the band."

"No," Onyx said, jumping up onto a worktable littered with pieces of picture frame. "That doesn't explain how I got here."

"Your friend is right," Pickman said. "There's more to the story. Things were all right for a while, but then Eddington became dissatisfied with the arrangement he'd negotiated. The ghouls drank a *lot* of liquor. Worse, even though they could disguise themselves, ordinary human beings became uneasy without knowing why when they were in the club. Customers left early and subsequently took their business elsewhere. All of which meant the Kadath Club was never going to be as profitable or fashionable as Eddington wanted, as long as his silent partners were hanging around."

"But he couldn't just tell them to beat it," I said. "They wouldn't have come on that tab. They probably would have torn him apart."

"Exactly." Pickman lit a new smoke off the butt of the old one. "But he knew there were things even ghouls are afraid of. If he summoned one and made it his watchdog, they wouldn't come around anymore."

"And he collared how to do that?"

"Unfortunately, more or less. I'm happy just to witness and paint the secret marvels of existence. But Eddington was fool enough to believe human beings can control them. He'd experimented with the ancient spells and corresponded with a cellist in Paris about how to work magic through music. He used the knowledge to summon a creature from another world." Pickman looked at Onyx. "Apparently making a temporary hole that you wandered through as well."

"Did Mr. Pryce know the shadow was going to start killing people?" I asked.

Pickman shook his dome. "He thought he could keep the entity locked in a sort of limbo space where the ghouls would sense it but it couldn't do any actual harm. Obviously, though, it's found a way to break through into our reality from time to time. I imagine the 'charts' Eddington gave you to play represented an attempt to reestablish control, but from your description of what happened, I suspect he's only made things worse."

"Damn," I said. "If he doesn't know how to fix this and you don't, either—"

"I do," Onyx meowed.

Pickman and I both turned our blinkers on him.

"Then lay it on us," I said.

"Ghouls are creatures of your world *and* the Dreamlands. Their tunnels connect the two."

I grunted. "If that means you can truck on home, I'm happy

for you. But it still leaves the shadow killing folks on this side of the fence."

"I told you I'm no warlock," the tom replied, "but I know a witch. If we talk to her, perhaps she can help."

I turned to Pickman. "You like 'secret marvels.' How about letting your peeps dig the range of a whole new world?"

He surprised me with a sigh. "We'd never make it. The ghouls would kill us on sight."

"I thought you were their friend."

"Until Eddington betrayed them. Now they're holding it against me even though it wasn't my fault."

I thought that one over, and wondered again too whether it wouldn't be smarter just to split the scene and head out for St. Louis or New Orleans. Then I said, "Maybe I can calm the ghouls down long enough to listen while we lay our racket on them."

"Whatever you have in mind," Pickman replied, "it's too dangerous."

"Mr. Pickman," I said, "if you don't mind me asking, what are you going to do with the rest of your life if you *don't* make peace with the ghouls?"

His eyes narrowed, and then he said, "Damned if I know. All right, then. Meet me outside the club at ten tomorrow morning."

Hip that I might hop a twig come the early bright, I spent the rest of the black jamming with some cats in a blind pig on Beacon Street, doing the voice with a cute little banter who dug the sound of my tram, and blowing mootah with Onyx. Along the way, though, I made time to visit a pawnshop, where Uncle sold me a .45 Colt hush hush just like the one I carried in the layout across the drink.

For breakfast, I greased my chops with bacon and yellow eyes over easy in a diner, and afterward, Onyx and I made it to the Kadath Club by ten chimes. Pickman was waiting outside with flashlights and a set of twisters to unlock the building.

I kept my hand on the butt of the revolver in my mouse as we crept through the juice joint. None of the regular workers were likely to be around at this hour, but the shadow could be. Or Pryce.

Maybe I shouldn't be worried about Pryce. After all, Onyx, Pickman, and I were just trying to clean up the mess he'd made. But even so, I had a hunch he wouldn't like us sticking our sniffers in.

We made it down to the cellar without anybody or anything jumping us. As the flashlight beams slid around, I saw chairs, tables, and gnawed bones, and smelled a hint of rot. When they'd been coming here, the dog men had been digging up the dustbins of cats who long ago trilled, breaking open their tree suits, and carrying away pieces of them to snack on.

His feeler jabbing, Pickman counted down a row of bricks in the wall and, when he found the one he was after, pushed it. It slid inward with a little scraping noise, and then a hidden door cracked open just enough to show the tunnel on the other side.

"We probably need to hike a fair distance," the painter said. "Otherwise, the ghouls might not approach us for fear of running into Pryce's demon."

I nodded. "I'm ready."

I wasn't, really. As we prowled on into the echoing gloom, I kept imagining I heard the ghouls sneaking up behind us to rip us apart before we even got a chance to talk to them. And now I couldn't even keep my mitt on Mister Speaker. I needed one hand for the flashlight and the other to carry my trombone case.

Eventually, we came to a place where the way widened out into a space like a room with several doorways. Pickman said, "This should be far enough."

I set my flashlight on the floor and, working pretty much by touch, opened the case and screwed the tram together. Then I straightened up and frisked the whiskers a little. If the ghouls liked music, I meant to give them the most righteous riffs they'd ever heard.

And I busted my conk down there in the dark, taking off in a jam that worked in pretty much every tune I knew. For a while I wasn't sure if anybody but Onyx and Pickman heard, but then I sensed my audience gathering around me. They slipped in silently, but the stink gave them away.

I played a while longer, and when I finally lowered the

slush-pump, they pounded their mitts. That was encouraging until Pickman ran his flashlight beam around the room and showed them to me. Reet as his horrible pictures were, they hadn't quite prepared me for the real thing, and there were way more ghouls than I had bullets.

One of the dog men, a big one dressed in the moldy remains of what had started out as knee pants and a George Washington wig, glared at Pickman. "Was this supposed to be a peace offering?" he asked. "It was good. We might keep the musician for a while. But it wasn't enough."

"I swear," the artist said, "I had no idea Eddington was going to turn on you."

"You told him about us," George replied. "You vouched for him. And now we have a ghast loose in this world!"

The other dog men snarled. Spit flew from their muzzles, and some of them started forward on little plates that looked half melted into hooves.

"It isn't loose all the time!" I yelled. "But it might be soon if you don't help us nix it out!"

George swung around to face me. "Can you do that?"

I waved a paddle in Onyx's direction. "He can explain it if you speak cat."

It turned out the ghouls could, and after the tom laid down our hype, most of them huddled with George to talk it over. Their own lingo sounded like sheep bleating. If sheep had claws and crumb crushers like shivs and loved to use them.

Finally George turned back around. "I'll take you and the cat through, but Pickman stays with us. If you banish the ghast, we'll set him free. If not ... well, you can guess."

"We might need him to get our business straight." I eased my hand toward the Colt. I didn't want to pull it, but how could I just take a powder and leave somebody here?

Fortunately, Pickman realized what I was doing and yelped, "Don't! I mean, if this is the way they want it, then this is the way it has to be! Get rid of the ghast, and I'll be fine!"

Well, if that was the way he wanted to play it. I admit, my pins went a little wobbly with relief. I told George, "All right, then. Let me put my axe away, and then you can take Onyx and me where we need to go."

I don't know how much longer we broomed through the tunnels. Long enough for me to worry that the batteries in the flashlight would give out. They didn't, though, and finally George led us clambering up a burrow and through the hole in the floor of a mausoleum. Vines tangled around the iron grille that was the door, but a little sunlight leaked in anyway.

George forced open the door with one sudden shove that snapped the vines, made the hinges squeal, and, for all I knew, broke a lock. It also made me glad all over again that I hadn't waved a hush hush in his pan. He led us on out into an old marble town on a hilltop, with other tombs standing here and there and markers sticking up out of the weeds. The markers had been made in funny shapes or carved with funny symbols. I didn't lamp any crosses or Stars of David, either.

Between the hump with the deep sixes and a shining blue curve of a drink was a little burg with green cottages on the outskirts and cobbled streets and houses with red-tiled peaked roofs in the middle. I was a big-city hipster right down to my bones, but even to me, the place looked pretty.

Shading his peeps like the bright yellow bean upstairs hurt them, George said, "When you're ready, come back here and call me. I'll hear." With that, he turned and dusted back into the mausoleum. Onyx and I watched him cut out and then trucked on down the hill toward Ulthar.

It took until the early dim to get to the center of town, and the way the upper stories of the buildings stuck out over the ground floors threw the narrow streets into shadow. Still, there was enough light to focus that the local people were ragged out like the actors in Fairbanks and Valentino flickers. From the way they peered back at me, I guessed my drape looked funny to them, too, but it didn't seem to upset them any.

Maybe it was because Onyx was with me. Ulthar evidently thought cats were righteous. They were everyplace, prowling, sprawling, and copping z's wherever they liked. One lane fidgeted while he waited for the tabby curled on top of his wheelbarrow to wake up from its nap so he could push his load on to wherever it needed to go.

Every so often, we ran into a cat that was one of Onyx's particular friends, and then they meowed and rubbed against one another. Some of his pals even broomed along with us, until I was walking with a dozen cats padding around my stomps. After that, the other human folks on the street made way for us. I admit, that tickled me a little, especially since many of them were ofays.

Eventually, Onyx and my new guides led me to a tavern that made my peekers widen in surprise. The outside of the place didn't look exactly like the Kadath Club any more than any of the Ulthar's buildings looked exactly like modern American ones. But the basic shape was the same, like the two washers were connected somehow. Maybe that was why, when Pryce was fishing for a ghast, a stray bit of his hoodoo poked a temporary hole to this place big enough for a cat to wander through.

The layout inside was almost the same, too, though the furniture was different, and the patrons were more Robin Hood types as opposed to the jitterbugs I was used to. The air smelled of beer and roast meat, which made my mouth water and reminded me it had been a while since I'd eaten.

Onyx ran and leaped up on the bar, and the fizzical culturist, a flychick with smooth rind the color of café au lait, plaited hair, and a leather apron, cried out in joy and proceeded to simultaneously pet him and scold him for disappearing. Clearly, he was her cat even if she couldn't collar his lingo like I could.

I collared hers, though. Either the people of Ulthar spoke English, or there was some hoodoo in the air that made everybody understand everybody else.

That let me knock her a hard spiel about fetching Onyx home. It would have been just as fair to say he'd brought me here, but he was a pal and let me tell it my way, and as I'd hoped, she ended up giving me a free beer and dish of roast pork and potatoes. I don't usually zoom, but after buying Mister Speaker I was down to fews and twos and had a hunch American dough wouldn't spend here anyway.

While I scoffed my food and guzzled foam, more cats wandered into the fill-mill, until even the locals, who were used to lamping the animals everywhere they turned, realized something was up. They whispered to one another, and then, just as I was tipping back my stein to drink the last drops, a gray cat with a white spot like a teardrop under one yellow eye jumped up on a table in the center of the room and hissed.

You didn't need to talk cat to get the message. People chugged their drinks and took a powder. Hollywood eyes behind the bar gave me a puzzled look when she saw I wasn't finaling, then shrugged and headed up the stairs.

I turned to Onyx. "You cats really do run this town," I said.

"We don't like to rub the humans' noses in it," he purred, "but yes, we do. Come on. It's time for you to meet Calpurnia."

That turned out to be the gray cat that had chased the humans out. I stood before her while Onyx told our story and, copping a squat on tables, benches, shelves, beer barrels, or the bar or else surrounding us in circles on the floor, the other felines listened.

I sounded off when Onyx was done: "So he's home." I waved my paddle at him. "I know how to get back to Bean Town if George doesn't decide my frame looks like too tasty a scarf to pass up. Now we just have to get the ghast back where it belongs."

"Why?" Calpurnia asked.

That surprised me. "It's killing people."

"Not our people," the gray cat said. "We're safer with it on the far side of the wall of sleep."

"The way I collar it," I said, "you have plenty of ghasts in the Dreamlands, and you know how to handle them. So what's one more? In my world, nobody has any idea what a ghast is, let alone how to deal with them. So even a single one is a terror."

"He's right," Onyx said. "Besides, if the ghast returns at all, it should land right back in the Underworld, where neither cats nor humans go. So, please, Calpurnia, don't turn me into a liar. Help me keep the promise I made."

The gray snorted. "It might be kinder to break it. If this Eddington Pryce has the ghast hidden in a shadow plane half a step out of phase with the waking world, I can't snare it from here. The best I *might* be able to do is teach the musician to cast the banishing himself after he returns to his proper place."

That bit of news wasn't exactly a killer-diller. I hadn't liked anything about the little bit of hoodoo I'd experienced so far. Still, I hadn't trucked to a whole different world just to quit now. "Then teach me," I said.

"Sorcery isn't for everyone," Calpurnia said. "It requires learning truths humans shouldn't know. The stress can tear the mind apart."

I shrugged. "If I flip, I flip. How do we start?"

"I talk, and you listen."

With that, Calpurnia started to enlighten me. It came out as screeching, not just meowing, like there was no other way to say what she had to say. Gradually, the other cats answered back, like worshippers in a church service punctuating the preacher's spiel by shouting "Praise Him," "Hallelujah," and "Amen." I suspected they weren't doing it because they wanted to. The message was taking hold of them like Pryce's arrangements had grabbed hold of the other buddy ghees in the band and me.

All that yowling made for an earsplitting racket, but the noise was the least bothersome part of it. As Calpurnia had warned me, the really sad part was simply that she collared terrible truths and was laying them on me straight.

She told me the universe is billions of years old, and millions of races have come and gone before people. There were barrel-shaped things with wings, big worms made of smoke but drilling around on legs, and cones with four writhing boneless arms.

Humans aren't going to last forever, either, because not all the old creatures called off all bets. The strongest are only copping a nod, and when they wake, they'll reclaim the Earth for their own, maybe without even noticing they're squashing us like ants as they get their business straight. One is a dragon that will rise from the Pacific, another is a screaming Hawkins that will blow down from the North Pole and freeze everything it touches, and a third is a king in yellow rags who'll come down from the star where he lives as easily as a person brooms down a staircase.

Calpurnia explained how big the universe is, too. I already

collared that the Earth is just a speck floating in the Milky Way, but now I found out the Milky Way is just one group of stars among countless others.

People don't know anything about how that hugeness works. We think we do because we've studied light and heat and gravity. But there's a dark spider web we can't even see that really holds everything together and a different kind of darkness that will tear everything apart at the end of time.

I could go on, but you get the idea. Everything in the gray cat's spiel laid it out that the world is horrible and that humans beings are too weak, ignorant, and tiny to last for long in it or even to mean anything in the one tick while we're here.

If I'd only heard what Calpurnia had to say, maybe I could have laughed or at least shrugged it off. But I wasn't just hearing it. That wasn't the way her hoodoo worked. It got inside my attic and forced me to lamp the things she was telling me, smell, taste, and feel them, too, in a way that made them impossible to igg.

Even after she and her chorus finally finished, the revelations pounded and tore at me until I could feel my mind giving way. My mitts shaking, I opened my tram case, put the axe together, and started playing 'Hotter Than That'.

The music shrank the ugly knowledge down and built a cage around it. Or maybe it made me feel bigger and more real, and if it did, maybe that feeling was just a lie I was telling myself. But whatever it was, it saved me from going crazy.

Still shivering, I lowered the slush-pump and let the spit spill out through the spit valve. "Damn," I said. "If that's the kind of thing that crawls into Pryce's wig when he studies his hoodoo books, no wonder he's halfway to being a Napoleon. How do *you* stand knowing?"

"I'm a cat," Calpurnia said. "Nothing diminishes me. Now that you have the foundation, are you ready to learn the banishing?"

I took a breath. "Why not?"

"It can be performed with an incantation, but I think it will work better for you if you invoke the powers with your horn."

So that was how we did it. Some of the sharp edges on what she'd taught me before were already going dull and soft in my thinkpad, and I was glad. But enough was left for me to pick up on how to tab issue a spider god on the dark side of the pumpkin to mash me a favor and to command a little bit of the shadow forces at the heart of everything. If I put down all the right riffs, the music would yank the ghast out of its hiding place and shoot it back to the Underworld. Wherever that was. As long as there were no people there, it was copacetic with me.

Shonla, the fizzical culturist, let me catch some cups in the washer and even spotted me breakfast come brightnin'. The cats including me in their secret palaver made me a big man in her pretty brown shutters. I greased my chops, said goodbye to Onyx, and then trumped the hump back up to the graveyard.

George answered my call like he promised and took me back to Boston without trying to eat me. We parted ways in a tunnel near the Boylston Street subway station. He wouldn't lead me all the way back to the Kadath Club for fear of running into the ghast, and I could never have found it by myself.

By then, it was morning in the waking world, and I was hungry again. As I looked for a snack, I passed a newsboy waving the *Herald Journal* over his biscuit and yelling about "murderers and cannibals in the night." The ghast had finally made the papers, maybe because it had killed three people this time around.

That made me think I should get my business straight while the tune of the banishing was still clear in my dreambox. I bought an apple for a buffalo head and munched it while I rode a streetcar back to the speak. Then, as I was stepping off, I remembered I didn't have the twisters to unlock the slammer. They were still in Pickman's rat hole.

Trying to look like an honest cat going about his honest business, I circled around into the alley and then glanced around. As far as I could tell, no one was watching. I used the hush hush to smash a gazer, climbed through, and stood there listening.

I didn't hear anybody—or anything—rushing to investigate the sound of breaking glass. Apparently the fill-mill was as empty as it had been when Pickman and I sneaked in, and I sighed in relief.

I decided the main kick was as good a place as any to try the banishing. I stood center stage in Charles's spot, put my tram together, oiled the slide, and then, eager as I was to get this done and trilly, frisked the whiskers a little. Calpurnia had told me that the spell needed to be in the groove, and I wasn't going to make a mistake because I hadn't warmed up.

When I was ready, I launched into the first part, putting down low, groaning licks in A minor. The room got cold, and after a while, a circle of empty air churned and rippled. I sensed that if I looked hard enough, I could see through and lamp the spidery devil on the far side of the moon, but that was the last thing I wanted to do.

I was glad the spider thing was paying attention to me, though. It meant Calpurnia's hoodoo was working. I moved on to the next section, and then Armstrongs shrilled through the air. The high brassy notes tore my spell apart like I'd ruined the magic hidden in 'Potato Head Blues'. The gazer hanging in the air vanished, and I doubled over like Jack Johnson had punched me in the basket. The mouthpiece of my horn mashed my lips back into my teeth.

I looked up. Pryce was standing on the landing at the top of the stairs with his trumpet in his dukes. He'd been in the speak the whole time, had maybe spent the black here poring over his books of witchcraft, but had only heard me when I started playing.

"Boss," I said, trying to sound like everything was mellow, "oop-pop-a-da! I didn't know anyone else was here."

"No," he said, "I'll bet you didn't."

"I thought I'd do some practicing—"

"Enough!" he snapped. "I'm not an idiot! When you disrupted the ritual of coercion, that could have been instinct, and I didn't really mind because it wasn't working, anyway. But this … don't you think I recognize sorcery when I hear it?"

"All right," I said, "you caught me. But I'm hippin' you, man, I was only trying to help."

He frowned. "Meaning what?"

"I know about the ghast you called out of the Dreamlands. I also know it's off its leash. My hoodoo will send it back where it belongs."

"Whether I like it or not?"

"How could you not like it? It's eating people!"

Pryce sighed. "That's unfortunate. You know I tried to put a stop to it. I *will* stop it as soon as I work out how. But it's not like the thing is killing people right here in the club or its victims are anyone of consequence—"

"Margie worked for you!"

"It's not like the victims are anyone of consequence, and the simple truth is, I need the ghast now that I've broken faith with the ghouls. They'll come for me if it isn't here."

"I've talked to the ghouls. Maybe I can get you straight with them."

He snorted. "My God. You're a regular witch doctor, aren't you? I had no idea. But I'm not willing to bet my life on your negotiating skills. Besides, once I bring the ghast to heel, I have other uses for it."

"Like what?"

"Surely you know there's a rough element in the bootlegging business. Men like Frankie Wallace and Dodo Walsh, who extort money from independent entrepreneurs or force us out entirely. I need a weapon to defend myself. And then I have my parents to consider. They've denied me access to the family coffers, but I suspect they haven't changed their wills. If you *really* want to help me, help me bind the ghast. I promise to make it worth your while."

"Neighbo, Pops. Not even if I collared how, which I don't. And you don't, either. You're nowhere near as reet at this sorcery shit as you think. Let me get you clear of it before any more innocent folks get hurt."

Pryce sneered. "Not a chance."

"Sorry you feel that way." I pulled Mister Speaker out of my hideaway. I meant to get the drop on Pryce, tie and gag him, and then put down the banishing.

Unfortunately, he focused the Colt and snatched the trumpet back up to his chops before I could aim. The horn blared.

The hush hush glowed red-hot and seared my paddle. I yelped and threw it down on the stage before it could burn my feelers to the bone.

Staccato notes stabbed into my dome like nails. I yelped, reeled, and fell down on top of my tram. Then I squirmed on my belly and tried to stand back up despite the pain, which kept on throbbing even after Pryce switched to a different series of riffs.

The towering shadow I'd focused the other night boiled into view in the middle of the room, and then, like on the previous black, it darkened. My blinkers blurry with tears, I realized I was about to meet the thing that scared even dog men, and that Pryce was playing it out of its hidey-hole to kill me.

My one chance was that messing up some other cat's hoodoo seemed to be easier than making your own. I flopped over onto my back and brought the trombone to my lips.

Only a tiny fart of a sound came out, not nearly enough to compete with Pryce's tune as he beat it out. I looked at the slush-pump and found the bent slide and crumpled bell. I'd wrecked the axe when my weight slammed down on top of it.

The form of the ghast was steadier now.

I struggled again to stand up. The pain still wouldn't let me.

The last trace of blurriness dropped away from the creature like it was a figure in a movie that the projectionist had just brought into focus. It looked something like a man or a shaved gorilla, but its map was all chin, too-wide mouth, gray pointed crumb crushers, and all-black glims, with no sniffer or forehead either, and its legs bent backward like a kangaroo's. It made a coughing sound and hopped in my direction.

Then I remembered Shorty's tubs were on the bandstand with me. I floundered around until I had my plates aimed at them, drew up my pins, and started kicking.

The drum kit made a hell of a racket flying off the main kick and crashing onto the dance floor, the clashing cymbal and high hats especially, but the snare and bass drums, too. I felt the noise break the pattern of Pryce's spell, and he stopped playing. The ghast hesitated.

My paddle shaking, I pointed a feeler at Pryce. "*He's* the one trying to keep you locked up," I wheezed.

Whether or not the huge thing collared the words, it seemed to get the idea. It turned and bounded toward the stairs.

The steps were too small and the whole staircase too narrow for it to keep on moving in the way that was natural for it. That slowed it down as it clambered upward, which gave Pryce time to get over being startled.

The trumpet blasted out growls that pounded the ghast like sledgehammers or slashed its scabby hide like razors. Bone cracked, and blood flowed. But the ghast pushed on to the top of the stairs.

Pryce turned to run, and the ghast snatched for him before he could. Its feelers wrapped around his head like a hood.

Then, gnawing, pulling, twisting, and occasionally throwing him on the floor and stamping on him with its hooves, the creature ripped its would-be master apart. It took its time, and Pryce screamed on and on. Bloody pieces of him tumbled over the railing to thump and splat on the floor below.

Meanwhile, my pains faded away. Trying to be quiet about it, I stood up and looked around for Mister Speaker. If the revolver had ever really been red hot, it wasn't anymore, and I had no trouble picking it up.

The foxy play would be to keep right on sneaking, out of the room and out of the speak, and only use the hush hush if the ghast came after me. But the point of everything I'd done was to nix out the damn thing, and it was right in front of me. I drew a bead on it and waited for Pryce to stop shrieking.

As soon as he did, I fired. The ghast jerked as the round punched into its dome. The second bullet hit it in the biscuit, too.

But it didn't fall down. Instead, it lunged, smashed through the railing, and jumped back down from the landing into the room below. The kangaroo legs bent into bobby-pin shapes as its hooves clacked on the floor.

I emptied the Colt into its chest as it hopped toward me. Despite all the damage that Pryce and I had done, it still wouldn't drop. When it jumped up onto the stage, I threw the hush hush at its eyes, then spun a microphone stand at its props.

That made it hesitate. I yanked the Harlem toothpick out of my mouse, thumbed the button, yelled, and rushed it. I stabbed for the heart, once, twice, and again.

The ghast howled, its mitts latched on to my forearms, and

then I couldn't do any more stabbing or much of anything. Its mouth opened wide to bite off the top of my attic the way a person would bite off the end of a carrot.

Then it toppled over sideways, carrying me to the floor along with it, shuddered and gave a little whimper, and stopped moving. After a few seconds, I decided it wasn't going to start again. Either the switchblade had finished it off, or one of its other wounds had finally caught up with it.

And really, that's just about the end of the story.

Once I caught my breath, I decided that even with a dead monster lying around to take the blame, I had no eyes to explain to the pounders what I was doing in the speak with the corpse of my ofay boss. I broomed out of there and didn't stop ballin' the jack till I hit the Big Apple.

When I checked the Boston papers, it turned out I hadn't needed to run that far. The killjoys weren't looking for me. They weren't spoutin' about the ghast, either, so I can't tell you what they thought about it.

Still, before long, I had no reason to regret the change of scene. I was lucky enough to get in with Fletcher Henderson's band at the Cotton Club.

Eventually, the *Herald Journal* reported that Pickman was having another gallery show, so I knew George had set him free as promised. But the painter dropped out of sight in 1927. I figured that either he did something else to make the dog men mad or went to live with them fulltime.

I was grateful I never had another run-in with ghouls or hoodoo. But the time came when I started going back to the Dreamlands the way people generally do, by copping a nod, climbing down the stairs, and passing through the fiery cave.

Which is mellow. Shonla and I became an item, and in Ulthar, nobody sees much difference between white or colored, maybe because everybody has to kowtow to the cats.

Nobody gets old and feeble, either, and I think that someday, when I catch Old Man Mose peeking in my gazer, I may just take a bottle of pills, wash them down with a glass or two of the real McCoy, and go hang my sky piece in the Dreamlands forevermore. But I have a lot more jazz to play first.

THE HORROR ON THE FREIGHTER

In an attempt at self-purgation, I have already written one account of the crimes of Dr. Herbert West and my complicity therein. Should anyone ever read that document, and that document only, he will, quite properly, come away condemning us both.

But he won't see us as the same sort of man. He will loathe West for the fiend he was and despise me for a worm, because my previous confession suggests that while I came to recognize the abominable nature of my associate's experiments, I never once tried to stop them

Until recently, I myself believed that to be true. But, torn to pieces by the terrible, pitiful creatures he reanimated, West has been dead a year, and over time, the knowledge of his destruction has apparently loosened a knot inside my mind. I now remember what was lost to me before.

Such being the case, I am appending this codicil to my original chronicle. I am not fool enough to imagine the new information mitigates my guilt. Nothing can ever do that. Still, I would have the record show that, appearances to the contrary, I was not after all an utter coward.

Dazzled by West's genius and what seemed the promise of his work, I had functioned as his loyal assistant for several years. But I came to my senses when he murdered a traveler named Robert Leavitt to obtain the freshest possible subject for his next attempt at reanimation.

It was by no means the first death in which we were culpable. Two of our previous experiments had embarked on homicidal rampages. But I told myself those were accidents. In the case of Leavitt, no such rationalization was possible, and I belatedly recognized West for the ruthless, reckless fanatic he truly was.

Yet seeing is one thing, acting another. Leavitt's murder planted the seed of betrayal, but after my years of subservience, that seed took time to flower. It was only after West and I relocated from the mill town of Bolton to Boston that I resolved to put an end to his crimes.

Unfortunately, I couldn't do so by reporting them to the authorities. The police would have arrested me too, and much as I deserved it, I didn't want to spend the rest of my life in prison.

That left only murder as a remedy. The question was how to accomplish it.

At first glance, the answer seemed obvious. No one would hear gunshots sounding from West's basement laboratory, and the acid tank would dissolve his body as thoroughly as it dissolved the flesh of his experiments.

Yet on further consideration, I decided this simple plan wouldn't do. By then, West was one of the city's more prominent surgical specialists. If he simply disappeared, he would be missed, and the police might suspect his closest associate of foul play. They might search our home thoroughly enough to discover the gruesome secrets concealed in the cellar.

It would be safer if West was found dead well away from the house, in circumstances that deflected suspicion from me and appeared to render a painstaking search of his domicile superfluous. And I believed I knew how to manage that.

At the start of his investigations, West relied on the chemicals available to any conventional medical researcher. But as the years passed, and he kept falling short of his goals, he tried adding more exotic ingredients to his reagent.

To procure them, he had somehow established communication with a worldwide smuggling network, and when a strange insectivorous plant, cage full of eyeless bone-white scorpions, or jar of toxic crimson fungus arrived, we ventured to the waterfront late at night with a considerable sum of cash to take delivery.

At the time of which I write, the occasion for another such transaction was at hand.

For my purposes, the situation seemed ideal. The note West had received from his contact neither mentioned my name nor specified the nature of the contraband. But it did make it clear that criminals had summoned him to purchase something illicit.

My plan was to ensure West never returned home from that meeting. Instead, sunrise would reveal his lifeless body lying on the docks, and when the police arrived, the most cursory search would discover the incriminating message tucked in his pocket. At which point (I hoped), the authorities would leap to the obvious conclusion: to whit, the clandestine meeting had gone wrong. The criminals had murdered the small, blond, bespectacled surgeon and absconded with his money, while Daniel Cain was home asleep in bed with nary a suspicion that his friend and colleague had become involved in anything illegal.

On the night of the rendezvous, the dank air smelled of saltwater and oil, and a thin mist had blown in from the sea. Blurred by the fog and the dark, the shapes of warehouses, cranes, and ships floating at their moorings were vague and ghostly, the lights mere smears of phosphorescence.

In other words, conditions appeared perfect to shoot a man in the back and then run away without getting caught, and, my pulse ticking in my neck and my palms sweaty, I was eager to get on with it. The hatred I had come to feel for West and my need to be free of him burned in me like a fever, and I could barely keep my hand away from the Colt revolver weighting my overcoat pocket.

But my luck was bad. The hub of trade that is Boston Harbor never really sleeps, and as West and I approached our destination, I kept glimpsing or hearing longshoremen, mariners, and others, close enough that, despite the limited visibility, I hesitated to make my move. Reassuring myself that the right moment would surely present itself after West and I met his suppliers, I followed him on toward the freighter.

Like other vessels in the smugglers' fleet, the ship was a grimy rusted hulk. Barely legible, the painted name *Star of Borneo* was flaking away above the waterline.

Clad in a shabby approximation of an officer's uniform, an Asian man waved for us to come aboard. After my previous encounters with the smugglers, this was as I expected. White faces were rare in their fraternity. All the officers on the ships were Chinese, and the crews mostly so, with a sprinkling of Arabs, Hindus, Africans, and, for all I knew, hands from Borneo and its environs.

Still mute—it was by no means a certainty that he spoke English—the officer led us across the deck to a hatch and the companionway below. This was not quite as expected but still didn't impress me as a cause for alarm. Whatever West was buying, apparently no one had gotten around to bringing it up from the hold.

West and I started down, and the officer dropped the hatch above us. Our steps clanked and echoed. Then I smelled a dry, musky odor, and in the gloom beneath our feet, something hissed like an enormous serpent.

West and I both faltered. Then he said, "Well! I didn't realize ..."

"Realize what?" I asked. "What's down there?"

"Come and see," he replied, then hurried down the remaining steps.

I followed more cautiously and caught up with him at the bottom of the companionway. There, he stood peering at the cage that someone had presumably dragged forth from its hiding place amid the stacks of crated mundane cargo.

A full fifteen feet long, the beast inside was reptilian with a set of fearsome jaws and glaring, beady eyes. It stood on four clawed feet, and a long tail depended from its hindquarters. Yet no one could mistake it for some species of alligator or crocodile. The spiny sail rising from its back and protruding through the bars that ran across the top of the cage precluded that.

I was no paleontologist, but I was a scientist and possessed some familiarity with the discoveries of Cope, Marsh, and others of their ilk. Thus I recognized the creature as an animal that ought not to exist in our modern world, except as a fossil in the Red Beds of Texas, and I gaped at it with a mix of wonder and wariness, the bars that confined it notwithstanding.

"Remarkable, is she not?" said a cultured baritone voice. Startled, West and I turned toward the Chinese gentleman who was just emerging from the stacks of crates. He was tall and gaunt, no longer young but not yet elderly, with a high, bald forehead and the most arresting eyes I had ever seen—and I had looked into the eyes of the reanimated dead. Vividly green, they seemed to catch the ambient light like a cat's.

I knew little of life in China, but from the gaunt man's embroidered silk robe, I might have taken him for a scholar, aristocrat, or government official. Certainly, he looked out of place in his current surroundings.

The mandarin, if that was the proper term for him, executed a shallow bow. "Dr. West," he said.

West bowed in return. As did I, although it already seemed clear that the Chinese gentleman had no interest in including me in the conversation.

"Good evening," said West, and then, after a moment's hesitation, "I'm afraid the message I received didn't include your name."

The aristocrat's lips quirked into the briefest and slightest of smiles. "I accumulate names and titles as a dog accumulates fleas. Perhaps it will be simplest if we simply address one another as 'Doctor'."

"Whatever you want," said West.

The mandarin gestured toward the cage, a motion that provoked another hiss from its prisoner. "What do you think of our friend?"

"I'm astonished, of course," West replied. "The information merely alluded to an uncatalogued tropical reptile, not a creature believed extinct for millions of years. I must know, where did you find it?"

"In the general vicinity of Sumatra," the Chinese doctor said, "but well removed from the sea lanes, is an island with a promontory resembling a skull. The interior abounds in fauna and flora from ages past."

"Amazing," said West. Circling to view the creature from different angles, he stepped closer. The reptile's beady black eyes tracked his movements.

"Please," said the man in the silken robe, "be careful not to put your hand between the bars. She bites."

"Amazing," West repeated, turning back toward the mandarin. "Amazing, but a bit of a problem. I was under the impression I was simply buying the eggs, not their source. Please, don't mistake me. I will certainly purchase the animal. But I need time to arrange—"

The Chinese gentleman raised a long-fingered hand. "No need. You are only purchasing the eggs. The reptile herself is on her way to Limehouse to join a collection of rare and useful animals that I maintain there. I simply exhibited her to you in the hope you would find her interesting. A courtesy, or, if you will, a token of respect for the groundbreaking nature of your work."

West frowned. "How can you know anything about my work?"

"I have many duties within my organization. One is overseeing the activities of our smugglers. Thus I know what you have procured from us over the course of the past few years, and in the aggregate, those items tell the story. You aspire to resurrect the dead."

West's mouth tightened, and I eased my hand toward my revolver. Neither of us liked the idea that anyone else, even a fellow criminal, was aware of our experiments.

Yet there was no sign of threat in the Chinese doctor's demeanor. Smiling that subtlest of smiles once more, he simply stood and waited for West and me to recover from our surprise.

After a moment, evidently reassured, West asked, "Is it really that obvious?"

"Probably only to me," our companion said. "As it happens, my own research somewhat parallels your own. I am endeavoring to perfect a longevity drug. I wonder if you have considered such a project."

West shrugged. "Briefly. But a man can't work on everything at once, especially when he has to work in secret. And, with all respect, a longevity treatment won't save the unfortunate who succumbs to cholera or steps in front of a bus. My reagent will. It represents the greater benefit to mankind."

The mandarin inclined his head a fraction. "Perhaps. What is beyond dispute is that it will provide a formidable advantage to the United States and its European allies."

Behind their spectacles, West's blue eyes blinked. "Excuse me?"

"What force could defeat armies whose soldiers fall only to rise again?"

"I'm not working for the government."

"But you are an American, Dr. West, and when the moment comes to proclaim your discovery, you will announce it to your countrymen. Still, I suppose that needn't concern a man such as myself. Outlaws will be outlaws no matter who rules the world. Shall we conclude our business?"

"If you like." West glanced at me. "Bring out the money."

I reached inside my coat, which is to say, away from my revolver. At that instant, a length of cloth whipped around my neck and pulled tight, cutting off my air. Across from me, a man in a turban lunged from behind a pile of crates, took West from behind, and choked him with a noose.

Thrashing, I tried to work my fingertips under the cloth that was strangling me. When that failed, I remembered the Colt. I fumbled it out of my pocket and tried to point it behind me, but someone grabbed it and twisted it out of my hand.

My ears ringing, my vision darkening, I was sure I was about to die. But when I was on the verge of passing out, the pressure constricting my throat abated. The smuggler who had garroted me grabbed one of my forearms, and the man who had taken my gun, the other.

For the moment, they were holding me up more than forestalling any further attempts at resistance. Similarly immobilized, slumped in his captors' grips, West was plainly as weak as I was.

"The legendary Thugs," the Chinese doctor said. "They live up to their reputation, do they not?"

West sucked in a ragged breath. "Why are you doing this?" he wheezed.

"I was being disingenuous before," the mandarin replied. "The truth is, my organization *does* care about the fortunes of the

United States, Great Britain, and the other colonial powers. That is because we intend to bring them down. Our smuggling and other seemingly mundane crimes are all in service to that end."

"Why?" asked West. "What do you have against America?"

For a second, the aristocrat's jade eyes seemed to burn brighter. "I surmise that you have never traveled in China, Dr. West, or any other land where white invaders have degraded, enslaved, and slaughtered the inhabitants. Otherwise, you would not need to ask."

West managed a twisted smile. "So, after everything I've done myself, I'm going to die for other people's crimes?"

"No," the mandarin said.

West raised his head. "No?"

"I was speaking the truth when I expressed admiration for your intellect and ambitions, and I am loath to remove you from the world. Happily, that will prove unnecessary. You will leave here alive and well with the items you came for, and in the days to come, my organization will continue to meet your needs to the best of its ability. But first, we must make an adjustment."

"Meaning what?"

The gaunt man held out his hand. A Chinese seaman emerged from the shadows and presented him with a syringe. The liquid inside was a murky blue.

"The Azure Whisper," the mandarin said, "dates from the early days of the Xia Dynasty, and the secret of its composition has eluded my every attempt at analysis. There are only a few drops left in all the world, and it is another mark of respect that I choose to use them to preserve your existence."

"What will it do?" West asked. "Paralyze me? Reduce me to an imbecile?"

The leader of the smugglers sighed. "You disappoint me, Doctor. Have I not already promised you will depart unharmed to continue your research? The Azure Whisper renders the effect of certain forms of hypnotic suggestion more permanent and profound. Which is to say, it allows one to tweak the subject's personality, augmenting some traits and suppressing others."

West forced a laugh. "And you really think that will work on me?"

"I do," the gaunt man said, "Men such as ourselves, men of genius and will, often have a streak of cruelty or even perversity in their natures. Consider Tamerlane with his mountains of severed heads and Vlad Dracul with his forests of impaled men. I have every confidence those qualities reside in you, Doctor, and I propose to enhance them. From this day forward, you will care less and less about gracing mankind with immortality and more and more about discovering the most grotesque and macabre results your reagent can produce, without, of course, remembering why or even realizing you are changing. My hope is that, in some small way, the fruits of your labors will damage your country and so aid my cause. Now that you understand, shall we begin?"

The mandarin tapped the syringe to bring the bubbles to the top and depressed the plunger sufficiently to expel the gas. He then advanced on West, who wrenched himself back and forth, straining to break free of the two men holding him, but to no avail.

The Chinese scientist slipped the needle into the side of West's neck. His cries echoing from the bulkheads, West screamed and thrashed.

His agony was so palpable that, out of simple instinctive empathy, perhaps, a strange thing happened: I forgot I had come to hate him. For that moment, he was once again my friend, and I was relieved on his behalf when he finally stopped shrieking and went limp. But my relief was short-lived, because there was worse to come.

West appeared unconscious but was evidently still aware on some level. For the Chinese doctor took his head between his hands, lifted it, leaned in close, stared him in the eyes, and started murmuring.

West didn't convulse as he had before. The drug had rendered him incapable of such exertions. But periodically, his muscles clenched and jerked, and his features twitched and twisted. Tears of blood leaked from his eyes. Plainly, he was in at least as much pain as before, only now it was a pain of the mind and spirit.

The master of the smugglers was speaking too softly, too

intimately, for me to make out what he was saying. But however he was accomplishing his purpose, there was a sick fascination to watching him warp a man's soul into a new shape, and at first, wracked with pity and horror, I could only stare. Then the Thug who had choked me, and who was currently holding onto my left arm, made a tiny sound that hinted at his own revulsion.

The noise reminded me of his presence and by extension of my own danger, for I certainly didn't imagine that the smugglers intended to deal with me any more kindly than they were dealing with West. Did I have any chance at all?

One, perhaps. If the men restraining me were as intent on their leader's performance as I had been; if it had distracted them from their own task. It felt to me as if their grips had indeed slackened just a little.

I jerked my foot up and stamped on one man's toes. Yanked my arm free of his grasp and jammed my elbow back into his midsection. Twisted and gouged at his partner's eyes.

I continued my frenzied assault until I was free and my erstwhile captors had retreated to regroup beyond the reach of my flailing hands. It was plain from their snarls of rage that it would only take them a moment to do so, and then they'd rush me. I certainly had no hope of evading them and all the other smugglers in the hold and making my way off the ship.

So I scrambled to the reptile's cage.

The latching mechanism was sturdy enough to contain an animal of considerable strength, but simple to release. I depressed a handle and swung open the door.

In so doing, I placed myself in a wedge-shaped space between two sets of bars. The living fossil could have circled around and killed me anyway, but I was no longer the easiest target. The two smugglers who were chasing after me were. There was no barrier whatsoever between the reptile and them.

Despite its stubby legs, the creature scuttled forth from its confinement fast as an arrow flying from a bow. The sail on its back rattled against the bar forming the top of the exit.

The reptile snapped and caught my first pursuer—the one in the turban, the Thug—by the leg. It bit down and jerked its head, and its fangs sheared off the limb in a shower of blood.

The Thug fell down screaming, and I felt a pang of vicious satisfaction.

His Chinese companion recoiled. Spitting out the severed leg, the reptile lunged after him, bit into his midsection, and tore out loops of intestines. This time, the beast paused to feed, to snap down the lengths of gut and rip out its prey's stomach and liver, the dying man writhing and howling all the while.

By then, other smugglers were crying out. The two who were holding up the semiconscious West dropped him and scurried toward the companionway. One waved for their leader to follow.

The mandarin gave them a sneer and then fixed on the reptile. Raising his voice, he rattled off words in his native language.

Whatever he said, it seemed intended to attract the creature's attention, and that was certainly the result. The reptile left off rooting in the body cavity of its second victim and turned in his direction.

Still speaking, the Chinese scientist paced toward the beast. He slipped the fingers of his right hand into his voluminous left sleeve.

The reptile lunged and bit. The gaunt man twisted aside, avoiding the jagged, bloody fangs as they clashed shut, snatched a folded black kerchief from its hiding place, and lashed it through the air in front of his attacker's nostrils. The whipping action opened the cloth, and the gray dust inside it darkened the air.

The animal froze and then fell down thrashing. As it rolled, its convulsions snapped the spines supporting the sail on its back and reduced that unique appendage to tatters.

Showing no ill effects from inhaling the poison he'd just administered, the master of the smugglers retreated a few steps and waited for the reptile's death agonies to subside. Once they did, he called out something else in his own language, and, shamefaced, the followers who'd fled came slinking back.

Which is to say, they were advancing on me, and, recognizing there was no escaping them, I pushed the cage door back to its original position and stepped away from it. I didn't want to meet my fate like an animal cowering in a hole.

"All right," I said to the mandarin. "Kill me. I've got it coming."

"So you do," he replied, "and after the inconvenience you have just now caused me, I would enjoy dispatching you with all the tools of the torturer's art. But unfortunately, Herbert West would miss his faithful servant. Your absence would nag at him, and, over time, perhaps even undermine my tampering. So I have a syringe of the Azure Whisper for you, too."

A wild impulse took me, and I charged the Chinese gentleman, but his followers interposed themselves between us. At the conclusion of a brief but savage struggle, the surviving Thug choked me into helplessness.

"I infer," the gaunt man said, "that you do not wish to accompany Dr. West on his descent into atrocity."

"Please," I gasped, "I can't take any more. Even before we came here tonight, I meant to put an end to it."

"But now you'll drown in it," the mandarin said, "with never a thought that you could disobey. *That* will be your punishment."

HATE, COURAGE, AND BLOOD

As David Baum drove the Auburn convertible up the drive, Aldo Nadi studied the long two-story country house at its end. It was aglow with electric light and doubtless provided all the modern amenities wealthy New Yorkers expected when escaping the city for a weekend.

Aldo chuckled. "I was hoping for something more on the order of the castle in Mr. Lugosi's vampire film."

David's mouth tightened. "I keep warning you, Maestro. This isn't a joke."

Well, Aldo thought, at least the money isn't. He'd requested and received payment in advance on the suspicion that even David, who seemed an honorable young man despite his irrational terrors, might hesitate to part with such an extravagant sum after the night passed uneventfully.

David stopped the car in front of the main entrance. Aldo climbed out, dropped the butt of his Modiano on the ground, stepped on it, and stretched. Then he pushed up the sleeve of his white fencer's jacket and wrapped a bandage around his wrist. He used a strap to strengthen his grip on a weapon, and the bandage kept the strap from cutting off his circulation.

Meanwhile, David gave him a worried frown. "I still wonder if some kind of armor—"

"Except for a fencing mask, I've never worn armor in my life. Doing so now would only compromise the skills for which you engaged my services." It would also have made the present situation even more ridiculous.

David had sent the staff away, and silent house *felt* empty. As his student led him into a room with an imposing fieldstone fireplace, Aldo noticed a decanter of brandy and rather wished he could sample the contents. But alas, wanting his condottiere at the peak of his powers, David was unlikely to offer such a libation.

Instead, the younger man opened a cabinet and brought out a rapier.

"This is it," he said.

The sword had the Italian grip Aldo favored. He hooked his fingers around the quillions and drew the weapon from its black leather scabbard. It was surprisingly light for a rapier, and the balance was excellent. He would have little difficulty executing modern techniques, and, smiling, he thought that perhaps it was a pity he wouldn't actually have the opportunity to use it.

Then he noticed the small symbols etched down the length of the straight, double-edged blade. He had no idea of their meaning, and they were merely combinations of lines and curves like any letter or numeral. But something about them made his stomach turn over and his temples throb.

He wrenched his gaze away, and the unpleasant sensations abated. He'd suffered from headaches all his life, and apparently, on this particular evening, squinting at tiny characters had the potential to trigger one. He resolved not to do so again.

"Are you all right?" David asked.

"Fine. Where is our damsel in distress?"

"Already asleep. Sedated."

Aldo frowned. Farcical though the situation was, that aspect didn't sit well with him, and the fact that David's sister had supposedly consented made it only a little more palatable.

"It's the only way," David said. "If the plan doesn't work, I mean. The women who were awake for the ... ordeal were never the same afterward. Some went insane."

"So you said. Are we guardian angels going to hover at her bedside until the dawn?"

"That isn't necessary. There'll be warning signs that it's starting."

So, as the hours crawled by, they lounged downstairs smoking, drinking coffee, and listening to *The Bell Telephone Hour* on the radio. Bored, Aldo pulled on his glove, held the rapier at arm's length, and executed beats, disengages, and coupés against the empty air.

Then, abruptly, the room tilted and spun. If he hadn't already been sitting, he would have fallen. Though he couldn't define why, the furniture on the far end of the room looked as if it were miles away.

Yet the stars beyond the windows seemed closer. Burning a filthy yellow, they swirled around one another, unmaking the familiar constellations and forming new ones.

Aldo told himself he couldn't possibly be witnessing this, if only because the windows didn't permit a view of the entire night sky, just sections of it. He closed his eyes and willed his perceptions to revert to normal.

When his dizziness and nausea faded, he risked another look around. As he'd hoped, the distortions had come to an end.

But the world wasn't entirely as it had been before. Flickering and oozing, amber phosphorescence now stained the rapier blade, proof that something real had happened and was happening still.

Aldo drew a deep, steadying breath. Evidently he was going to have to earn his fee after all.

Five days previously, in the rooms in the Savoy Plaza which he'd converted into a salle, Aldo had watched David fencing foil. For the first few touches, the young man was ahead, and then the prospect of victory turned him fearful of making a mistake. His fellow student rallied to defeat him 10-7.

Afterward, David looked on the brink of throwing his mask, a heinous breach of fencing etiquette. He managed to restrain himself, but trudged to a spot removed from everyone else and flopped down on a bench. There he sat slumped with sweaty head in hand, the picture of disappointment and self-disgust.

During his childhood, humiliations on the piste had often left Aldo feeling much the same. No one had sought to comfort him, and in retrospect, he was glad. It had helped him learn to manage his emotions. But he'd come to believe the American temperament differed from the Italian, and he didn't want to lose one of his most dedicated pupils to frustration.

He walked over and put his hand on David's shoulder. "Cheer up," he said, "you're doing well. It takes several years of training simply to become a mediocre fencer. It took me that long, and I'm 'the God of Fencing'."

He smiled to indicate that he'd quoted Raggetti's accolade with humorous intent. And so he had, more or less. Although if one took the phrase to mean 'the best fencer in the world', his record demonstrated it was true.

David shook his head. "I haven't got years."

"Why not? Admittedly, you didn't start in childhood as one ought, but you're still young. With perseverance ..." Suddenly, a possibility suggested itself. "My God, you haven't agreed to a duel, have you?"

It seemed unlikely, to say the least. The custom was dying out even in Europe, where Aldo had fought the only duel in which he'd ever had the bad judgment to become involved. But David had such an air of despair that the question needed to be asked.

And the younger man didn't laugh off the suggestion. Rather, he said, "It's not the way you're ..." He glanced around at the other students, some of whom were peering curiously in his and Aldo's direction. "I can't explain here. Could we meet later downstairs in the bar?"

The pianist was playing "Blue Monday" and doing a creditable job of it. Aldo took a first sip of his martini and somewhat regretfully shifted his attention from the music to his companion.

"Whatever the provocation," he said, "you mustn't duel. I'd give the identical admonition even if you were an expert fencer, because fencing and dueling are not the same. The former is compounded of courtesy, courage, and skill; the latter, of hate, courage, and blood. Which is to say, excellence in the one is no guarantee of victory in the other."

"But isn't there a trick?" David asked. "Some secret move that won you all those medals and that you don't teach to just anybody?"

Aldo sighed. "You disappoint me. Surely you've assimilated enough to understand that there's a science that at the highest level flowers into art, but no cheap and easy shortcut to mastery."

"I guess I'm grasping at straws."

"Tell me why. Then perhaps I'll see a way to help you."

"It's going to sound crazy." David smiled a bitter smile. "But being thought crazy's the least of my problems. I just have to figure out how to begin ... you know I'm Jewish, don't you?"

"I imagined so."

"Well, I'm sure you also know that, off and on through the centuries, Jews have had it pretty rough over in Europe, and my ancestors always managed to be in the wrong place at the wrong time. We were slaughtered along the Rhine and kicked out of England and France. We lost everything over and over again."

"Tragic. But how is it relevant to your current difficulties? Your family appears to be flourishing on this side of the Atlantic."

"We are. But hundreds of years ago, back when people were blaming Jews for the Black Death, a certain Rephael Baum living in Strasbourg realized the local Christians were gearing up for a massacre. And he decided, not again. Never again."

"So he organized a resistance?"

"God, I wish he had. But he wasn't a soldier. He was a scholar, a mystic, who studied Kabbalah and even stranger things. Things nobody should ever study, and that was where he looked for answers."

Inwardly, Aldo winced. "You're not going to tell me he sealed a pact with the Devil?"

"Not the Devil you're thinking of. Something worse. Maybe Satan is the mask we humans hang on the things that are really out there in the universe, so we don't have to see their true faces."

Aldo scooted back his chair. "Much as I appreciate Goethe and Gounod, I thought we were meeting in order that I might assist you with a genuine problem, not become the butt of a joke or join you on a flight into fantasy."

"Please, Maestro! I warned you it would sound insane, but now that I've started, I wish you'd hear me out."

Aldo hesitated. David actually did appear sincere, and

perhaps it would do him some good if a respected mentor attempted to talk him out of his foolishness. More likely not, but at least Gershwin and cocktails made for a pleasant end to an afternoon of pedagogy.

He pulled his chair back up to the table. "Go on, then."

"Rephael asked the spirit he summoned to protect the family, and it worked. A few days later, the townspeople burned nine hundred Jews alive, but nobody bothered the Baums. Then or since. Instead, we've prospered."

"But I assume from my reading of *Faust* and 'Rumpelstiltskin', there was a price to pay."

For a moment, David scowled, no doubt at Aldo's flippant tone. "An awful one. Do you know the term 'droit du seigneur'?"

"The alleged right of a medieval lord to engage in sexual relations with his female serfs."

"It's like that. When the entity sees fit, it … mates with the young women of our family. It's … breeding us, I think. Over the course of generations, it's gradually replacing our humanity with something else, for some reason we can only guess at."

David so clearly felt shame at this supposed defilement that Aldo felt a pang of pity. But the assertion was sufficiently preposterous that common sense seemed a more appropriate response than sympathy.

"For the product of such a breeding program," he said, "you exhibit a marked lack of freakishness."

"So far," David said, "the changes are on the inside. Dreams. Urges. Thank God, most of the Baums have kept them in check, but I don't know how much longer that will hold true. Anyway, even if we *could* do it forever, what's happening is horrible."

Slightly drawn into the tale despite his skepticism, Aldo said, "You can't be the first Baum to believe so. At some point, someone must have tried to deny your version of Count Dracula access to its Lucys and Minas."

David nodded. "And they always failed. Often the fathers and brothers were killed or left so mentally shattered, they couldn't even recall what they'd encountered. Over time, the family decided the entity must be impervious to earthly weapons."

"That *is* inconvenient."

David glared. "You wouldn't laugh if ... I'm sorry. How could I expect any other reaction?"

"Well, you do have the right to expect politeness. Please, finish the story, and I'll endeavor to contain myself."

"Fair enough. As you can imagine, Rephael wasn't the only mystic the family produced. Down the years, a number of us studied the *Necronomicon* and other forbidden books in an effort to undo what he'd done. Eventually, Howshea Baum, an alchemist, believed he'd discovered the answer. He worked with a sword smith to forge a weapon that *would* be able to kill the thing."

Aldo cocked his head. "In Hans Christian Andersen, that would have led to the triumphant resolution where hero slays dragon."

"It should have. But the visitations continued the same as before."

"Because the sword couldn't harm your incubus, either?"

"That's what Howshea believed; that he'd failed. After the creature got to his daughter, he hanged himself. But I believe the sword *could* work, only the entity is so formidable that it would take an expert fighter to kill it. I *have* to believe it, because the sword is still the only hope we've got."

"At last I see how all this connects to your wish to study fencing."

"Yes. We Baums can sense when the spirit is getting ready to come back. I guess it's the taint in our blood. I've felt it creeping closer for a while, and I thought that if I could prepare myself ... but it's pointless. You say I'm not even mediocre, and by all accounts, some of the men who tried and failed were notably good." He took a breath. "But today I realized there still might be a chance. A *good* chance. Namely, hiring the finest fencer in the world to use the sword on my family's behalf."

Aldo blinked. "I'm sorry, but that's absurd."

"Why?"

"Because while I've done my poor best to listen with an open mind, it's obvious your goblin doesn't exist."

"All the better for you, then. You get paid for doing nothing."

"That scarcely seems—"

"It will work like this. When I sense the entity's about to arrive, I'll drive you to our country house. That's where my sister Edna's staying. You'll spend the night, and if the creature appears, you'll kill it. If it doesn't, then the joke's on me, and maybe I'll look for a good psychiatrist to visit."

Aldo opened his mouth to insist that he couldn't possibly take advantage, and then practicalities caught up with his scruples.

He'd always maintained that money didn't matter. But with the coming of middle age, he found the notion easier to believe when he had some; and currently, he was broke. Worse than that, if the truth be told.

America might be the land of opportunity, but it hadn't turned out to be a country that took much interest in fencing. His lessons hadn't attracted a multitude of students, the nightclubs only booked the occasional exhibition, and his meeting with Louis B. Mayer had come to nothing. On top of which, a night of stud poker with Nikos Dandolos, better known as Nick the Greek, had annihilated his bankroll and obliged him to strew 'markers' in his wake.

He didn't want to close the salle or abandon his admittedly luxurious lifestyle, and perhaps his beloved Rosemary could supply the funds to make such measures unnecessary. In his youth, that would have been fine. He'd lived off a number of women back then. But either he'd changed, or finally met the right woman, because he was reluctant to resort to that expedient anymore.

Such being the case, would it truly be unconscionable to accept David's lunatic commission? The American could afford to pay, and it could scarcely be considered fraud when Aldo had made it clear that he himself didn't credit the Baum family superstition. Perhaps his involvement would even help bring the poor deluded fellow to his senses.

"How much are you offering?" he asked.

Aldo sprang up from the couch and tightened the strap securing the rapier's grip to his wrist. As he did, he couldn't help reflecting that the blade might indeed prove incapable of harming the creature from Hades, or beyond the sky, or wherever it actually came from. If so, confronting the thing would be tantamount to suicide. With a scowl, he thrust such thoughts away, just as he'd always refused to contemplate failure before a match.

David rose from his armchair. "Do you believe now?" he asked, his voice shrill and breathy.

Aldo inclined his head. "I owe you an apology. But now is not the time. Does your connection to the entity provide a sense of its precise location?"

"No. I just know it's close."

"Then I need to place myself in proximity to Edna."

Aldo started for the doorway that led to the staircase, pacing quickly but warily. He didn't want the spirit to pounce on him from ambush.

Before he could exit the room, the lamps flickered and dimmed, their light turning the same dingy yellow that had previously fouled the stars. Behind him, David gave a strangled cry.

Aldo whirled. Nothing was attacking his companion, nothing visible, anyway, but David's features twisted in pain. He raised his shaking hands and beat at his temples.

"Tell me what's wrong!" Aldo said.

But David could only manage a whimper. He staggered, fell to his knees, and then his body stretched, the spine and limbs lengthening. His skin paled to alabaster stained by the filthy light. Even his clothing changed, the drape-cut suit tearing itself and shifting color to become a cloak of yellow tatters.

The transformation only took a few seconds, and then the creature that had been David raised its masklike face. The eyes burned like black stars in an otherwise featureless ivory sky. No, not quite featureless, for faint yellow symbols wrote themselves on the smoothness, then erased themselves to make way for others. They hurt Aldo's head like the etchings on the sword. Only this time it was worse, because he sensed that if he looked too long, he might begin to understand them; and that would be unbearable.

He shifted his gaze, but only slightly. A duelist couldn't

afford to look away from his opponent. Meanwhile, the incubus clambered to its feet to tower over even his lanky frame, its head nearly brushing the ceiling.

"You are not a Baum," it said. The brassy tenor voice sounded like a trumpet. It didn't seem to issue from the place where a mouth should have been, or from any particular direction.

Aldo sneered as he'd sometimes done at an opponent, in hopes of rattling him. "No. Your victims finally got past their shame and consulted a professional, which is unfortunate for you. Unlike the poor wretches whose bodies you've borrowed, I'm quite capable of using this sword to kill you."

"I have no 'victims.' I take only that which is rightfully mine by the terms of the pact. More importantly, it is not yet time for my reign. Stand aside and you can live out the rest of your days as humans have always done."

"What do you mean, your 'reign'?" What are you? Why are you doing this?"

In truth, Aldo was less interested in the answers to those questions than he was in keeping the gaunt figure talking. Every moment gained thereby was an opportunity to study the way the incubus carried itself. It bore no discernible weapons, but judging from David's stories, it was dangerous even so.

"I am a Scion of Carcosa," the entity said. "An echo, a reflection, a shadow cast too soon while my progenitor is still at zenith. I must go into exile to ensure the stability of the throne, and so I must secure my own kingdom. But the way to Earth is too long for me to make the journey in all my physicality. The solution is to breed a vessel capable of holding my essence permanently and completely. Now that you know whom you face, will you step aside?"

"Actually, I'm even less inclined to do so than before."

"Even though you could not slay me without also murdering the very youth who called on you for succor?"

"He'd willingly die to rid his family of you."

"Then come and perish, if you must. My mate awaits me."

The Scion stepped forward. It advanced without any semblance of a combative posture, arms swinging at its sides, and once again Aldo found himself fearing that the rapier would be powerless against it. Rejecting the thought, he poised himself to take advantage of the creature's apparent vulnerability with an explosive lunge.

But that was the wrong approach. Fencers could afford boldness. With their lives at stake, duelists needed to proceed cautiously. When the Scion stepped into the distance, Aldo essayed a shorter attack, one that made him less vulnerable to a counterattack. If his point reached target anyway, good; but his true intent was to test his adversary's responses.

A long yellow tatter whipped up and knocked the sword aside, the impact clanging as if steel had parried steel. Then the strip of cloth riposted, the action flowing like a viper's strike.

Though startled, Aldo automatically retreated and parried. When his blade intercepted the tatter, the serpentine muscularity went out of it. It flopped back down towards the floor, a mere strip of cloth again.

But an instant later, a different tatter lashed its ragged end at Aldo's sword arm. Once more caught by surprise, he snatched his hand back barely in time to avoid a contact that he suspected would have maimed him like a cut from the toothed edge of a saw.

He made another retreat and scrutinized his opponent. All the tatters that made up the cloak were writhing sluggishly. The motion reminded him of dozens of worms crawling over one another, or of a sea lily filtering specks of nourishment from the current.

Pushing down the revulsion the sight inspired, he feinted to the inside line and disengaged to the outside. Undeceived, the Scion knocked aside the true attack and riposted to the face. Aldo parried in his turn.

As the exchanges continued, it became clear that the creature could only utilize one tatter at a time, and thank God for that. Had it been capable of striking with several at once, no swordsman could have withstood it. Even as things stood, Aldo found himself hard-pressed because he couldn't predict which tatter would attack next, or the instant at which the Scion would let one strand fall limp and lash out with another.

But damn it, he *should* be able to predict it. Every combatant had his favorite sequences of actions, and every fencer learned to discern them. Aldo fought defensively for the nonce as he probed, observed, and analyzed.

When he'd discovered what he needed, he eased forward in preparation for an advance lunge, the initiation of a phrase that should enable him to score with the third intention. Then the Scion screamed.

The trumpet-like blare was inhumanly loud, and Aldo was sensitive to noise. He faltered, stumbled off-balance, and a tatter struck at him. He wrenched himself aside and kept it from ripping open his throat, but it cut through his jacket and sliced his chest as the incubus pulled it back.

Shrieking again and again, the Scion attacked relentlessly, and, jolted by every new burst of sound, it was all Aldo could do to stay alive. *Don't hear it!* he commanded himself. *Nothing exists but your weapon and your opponent!*

Somehow, the admonition worked. Though the screams didn't stop, they dulled and lost their ability to pain him, although not before they'd scraped his nerves raw.

Trembling, he struggled to recall the sequence of actions he'd had in mind mere moments before.

Then distance, or at least his perception of it, warped into ambiguity. *Was the Scion five feet away? Six? Seven?* Memory supplied the answer, but vision couldn't. Even though the incubus was currently standing still, its position seemed to shift from second to second in some unfathomable fashion.

Fencers lost bouts when they lost awareness of distance. Duelists lost their lives.

Aldo sidestepped, circling, no longer blocking the doorway.

The Scion turned, keeping him in view. Despite his apparent attempt to abandon the fight, it evidently intended to kill him and so to deny him the opportunity to stab it in the back.

Aldo waited until he had it in the proper attitude. Then he bellowed, extended the rapier, and ran at it.

Startled by the sudden aggression, the creature scrambled backward into the doorway, and while the ceiling was high enough for it to stand up straight, the lintel wasn't. The back of its head thudded against the obstruction, and apparently that broke its concentration. It stopped screaming, and Aldo's sense of space snapped back into place.

He lunged and extended the rapier at the incubus' heart. A tatter flailed at the feint. He dipped the blade under the parry and thrust it into his adversary's thigh.

The Scion staggered. While it was off-balance, he pierced the other leg, and that dropped it to its hands and knees. He pressed his point against the side of its neck.

"Surrender!" he gasped. "Or I'll kill you!"

The incubus remained silent long enough for him to steel himself to administer the coup de grâce. Then it said, "I yield."

"Swear to leave the Baums in peace. No, swear to leave this entire world in peace. Swear by whatever a demon like you holds sacred."

"I swear it by the Unnamable and the Hyades. By the Pallid Mask and the Yellow Sign."

Given the blank whiteness of its countenance and the amber symbols that flickered in and out of existence there, Aldo decided the Scion might truly have given an oath it considered binding. In any case, it was either accept the creature's pledge as genuine, or slay it and David both.

"Go," he said.

David's limbs shortened, and his face blurred and bulged as its proper features restored themselves. Wriggling, the torn mantle knit itself back into a London Drape, albeit one worn with bloodstained trousers, while the lamps flickered and then shone white.

David cried out and thrashed.

Aldo gripped his shoulder. "Easy!" he said. "It's over!"

The younger man cast about, and the absence of any looming monsters evidently reassured him enough to notice lesser details.

"You're hurt!" he said.

Aldo had forgotten. He stripped off his crimsoned jacket and yanked open the equally gory shirt beneath, scattering buttons in the process, and was relieved to find his wound purely superficial.

"You are, too," he said, "but fortunately, neither of us

mortally. Some first aid, a call to the local physician, and we'll be fine."

"What happened?"

Aldo hesitated. "What do you remember?"

"I sensed the creature was near. After that, nothing."

Aldo decided the list of horrors that likely haunted David's nightmares was extensive enough without adding possession and an approximation of incest to the tally.

"I suspect your link to the thing interfered with your cognitive functioning and prevented you from retaining the memory. Happily, it didn't hinder you in the moment. You attacked the apparition bravely even though I was the one with the rapier, and the distraction helped me dispatch it. Now tell me, are there any bandages handy, or should I tear those antimacassars into strips?"

He hoped it was the former. He'd had enough of tatters.

AUTHOR'S NOTE

The phrases "hate, courage, and blood" and "courtesy, courage, and skill" are direct quotes from Aldo Nadi's autobiography *The Living Sword*, my source for information about his life and a sense of his personality. I tried hard to get them right, but apologize to the great fencer's shade for any errors of fact or interpretation.

IV-F

The rock music was shelved at the front of the store, where posters of the Beatles, the Beach Boys, and Bob Dylan decorated the walls. Scrawny and curly-headed with a moustache so blond and wispy it was nearly invisible, Paul walked right by it to the back of the shop, and started grabbing records from the Classical section. Pretty much at random, as far as Gerry could tell.

"What are you doing?" Gerry asked.

"The old records are cheaper," Paul replied, tucking another one—Franz Liszt's organ music—under his arm. "And they don't care. So the money goes farther."

"*My* money goes farther, you mean."

Paul sighed. "Don't be like that."

"This doesn't make sense. Why don't these friends of yours want to get paid in cash?"

"You agreed, no questions."

"That was before it started getting weird."

"Look, man, it's up to you. You can get a letter from a doctor. You can show up drunk or stoned or shove some Ivory soap up your ass. But you know what? The guys who try that stuff get drafted anyway. Now me, I got my IV-F. You can get yours, too. But you have to trust me."

Gerry hesitated. He knew that Paul truly had gotten medical deferments for himself and half a dozen 'clients'. It was just funny that not a single one of those guys would talk about how he did it.

But really, did it matter? The important thing was to avoid going to Vietnam. Gerry had watched the coverage on the news—the firefights in the jungle, the dead GIs zipped into body bags, the native people who might be friendly or might be Communists just waiting for the chance to kill Americans—there was no way to tell. It all scared the shit out of him.

He hoped that didn't make him a coward. He liked to think that if the war made sense, like when his dad fought in World War II, he would have been willing to go. But everybody knew it didn't.

Unfortunately, Gerry had to work and could only go to UMass Boston part-time, and part-time didn't qualify you for a student deferment. He didn't want to abandon everything and run to Canada. So that didn't leave many options.

"I do trust you," he said. At least he wanted to. "It's just ..."

Paul grinned. "Hey, man, I understand." He reached inside the shabby James Dean jacket that was a size too large and brought out a pewter flask. "This will settle your nerves."

Gerry unscrewed the cap and took a swig. Bourbon.

"Thanks. I've got a joint when we get someplace safe to smoke it."

"Not a good idea. Grass can make you paranoid, and you don't need that tonight."

Paul pulled more records from the rack, then paid for the ones he'd taken. After that, he led Gerry back out into the cool autumn air and on up the sidewalk.

The record store was on the edge of a North End neighborhood given over to students and the tenements in which they lived. The Turtles sang 'It Ain't Me Babe' through a second-story window that someone had cracked open.

As the song faded behind them, the night grew darker. Gerry realized it was because there were fewer and fewer streetlights—or anyway, ones that worked—and fewer and fewer lights shining from the buildings to either side.

He could still make out the shapes of those buildings, though, their gables and gambrel roofs. They were older than the tenements. Old and dilapidated enough that the city should either declare them historical landmarks and restore them, or just condemn them and knock them down.

He and Paul turned down an alley so narrow there was barely room for the two of them to walk side by side. Litter cracked and rustled beneath their feet.

Paul stopped in front of a door framed by boarded-up windows and pulled an old-fashioned house key from his hip pocket.

"In here?" Gerry asked. "Seriously?"

"It's against the law to help somebody dodge the draft. What did you think, they'd have an office in the Pru?"

"I wasn't expecting this."

"Trust, remember?" Paul unlocked the door, then exchanged the key for a penlight. "Come on."

Revealed a bit at a time by the penlight's pale glowing circle, the inside of the house was filthy and, except for cobwebs and mouse droppings, seemed to be empty.

Paul led Gerry down the cellar stairs. For a moment, Gerry thought the basement was just as empty. Then, sliding back and forth, the light picked out the circular hole—a well?—in the middle of the floor, and the tarnished brass bell bolted to the wall.

Paul crossed to the bell and gave it a clang.

"Now we wait," he said.

"For what?" Gerry asked.

"For them to signal back."

That took a couple minutes. Then another bell rang, one clang, a pause, then two more. The sound came up the hole.

"Down we go," said Paul. The light shifted, revealing the first of what was presumably a series of rusty iron ladder rungs inside the well.

Gerry shook his head. "No way."

"Don't chicken out now. The other guys I brought here are glad I did."

"Still ..."

"They've got tunnels in Vietnam, too. The Viet Cong dig them, and the Army sends our guys in to fight them. Which ones would you rather go into?"

Gerry had heard Walter Cronkite report on that part of the war, too; on the tight, lightless spaces, the ambushes and booby traps; the snakes, scorpions, and poison gas. It was hard to imagine anything worse.

He swallowed. "You go first."

"No problem," said Paul. "I was going to anyway." He put the penlight in his mouth and then, the shopping bag of LPs dangling on his forearm, started down the ladder.

Gerry groped his way down after him. One rung gave slightly when he set his foot on it, and, scared it was about to rip out of the wall, he clutched the gritty, corroded bar he was holding with all his strength. But the loose rung held, and after a moment he swore under his breath and continued the descent.

At the bottom of the well, a brick tunnel ran away in two directions. The passage stank, a rank smell that reminded him of cages in a zoo.

"This way," Paul said. He headed left.

His mouth dry, waiting for something to happen, Gerry trailed after him for several yards. Then the penlight went out, plunging the tunnel into total darkness.

Startled, Gerry froze. At the same instant, a scuffing, scuttling *rush* sounded at his back.

Instinct made him flatten himself against the wall. That way, maybe the things racing toward him would pass right on by.

But that wasn't what happened. The ambient stink thickened, and then hands clamped shut on his forearm and yanked him into the center of the tunnel. An instant later, another pair of hands grabbed his other arm. He thrashed, but his captors were too strong for him to break free. Someone pulled a sack over his head.

After a moment, light glowed through the weave of the burlap bag. Gerry realized Paul had *deliberately* switched off the penlight and now turned it on again.

Then Paul spoke, his voice coming from right in front of Gerry. "Everything's all right! I promise! It's just that it would freak you out to see them."

"I don't understand!"

"You don't have to. Just trust that my friend Charles will take good care of you. Isn't that right, Charles?"

The voice that answered was like none Gerry had ever heard, guttural one moment, a sort of rasping tenor the next. "It is if you brought something good from up in the city."

"Music." Paper rustled. Paul was handing off the shopping bag. "Have you got something for me, too?"

"Here."

Something rattled like dice in a cup. "Huh. Not much this time around."

"Not every box has gold in it," Charles said.

"I know," Paul said. "I wasn't complaining. Should we get on with it?"

Gerry's captors marched him forward. One turn and then another suggested that he wasn't in just a single tunnel, but a whole network of them.

Charles and the guys who had hold of Gerry chatted back and forth. They all had the same kind of voice, soft but harsh, snarling from deep to high and back again, and they were speaking a language he didn't recognize. It sounded as much like some kind of animal noise as it did human speech.

Gerry turned his head toward the faint smear of light still penetrating the sack. "Please!" he said. "You can keep the money! Just let me go!"

"I know it's scary," Paul replied, "but try to be cool. They like courage. It can make a difference in how they treat you."

Voices and footsteps echoed in the tunnels, and eventually the echoes changed. Gerry realized the sounds were bouncing back from walls that were farther away.

It meant the passage had opened out into a larger space. Where he could hear more people moving around, and a coppery smell competed with the stink.

"Shit!" Paul exclaimed. "What happened?"

"The Sharp Teeth," Charles answered. "There are lots of them, and they want Copp's Hill all to themselves."

"I'm sorry, man."

"If you're sorry, get us guns."

"I'm working on it. For now, can we get Gerry started?"

Gerry's captors marched him to the right. Then Paul turned the penlight off. Gerry flinched when complete darkness returned, even though the trace of light leaking through the sack had never revealed anything other than itself.

Someone pulled the bag off his head, and then the guy

holding his right arm let go.

"Put your hand out," Charles said. "Feel around."

Trembling, wondering if he was about to fall victim to some vicious prank, Gerry stretched out his arm. First, his fingers found a broken piece of wood, smooth on top but with splintery edges. Then, on the makeshift platter, scraps of what felt like cold meat.

"Eat," Charles said.

"It's all right," Paul said. "I did it. So did everybody else."

Gerry put a piece in his mouth.

The meat was raw, tough, and tasted nasty. He gagged when he tried to swallow.

"He has to start out with fresh," said Paul.

"It's fresh enough," Charles said, then put his hand on hand on Gerry's shoulder and made him gasp. "Keep eating. We can't help you unless you do."

On his second try, Gerry managed to swallow the morsel and keep it down. He grimaced and groped for another.

When he finished, his captors slipped the bag back on his head, and Paul turned the light back on. "His physical's in three days."

"He'll be ready," Charles said.

"Okay, Gerry, I guess this is it. I'll be back to pick you up."

"What?" Gerry cried. "You can't leave me here!"

"I have to," said Paul. "The thing they do takes time. Hang in there." His sneakers squeaked as he walked away.

Gerry tried to tear himself free and run after the noise. Hands seized his right arm, and his captors held him as easily as before.

When he stopped struggling, and all trace of the penlight was gone, they let him go and pulled the sack off his head.

"Sit," Charles said. "Relax. Get used to being here."

Gerry sat down on the dank dirt floor. Charles and the others padded off.

After that, all Gerry could do was listen to the bestial speech of the tunnel people and the vague sounds of them doing whatever they were doing. Well, that and think about escaping. But how, when he was right in the middle of them, and, even if he could somehow slip away, had no idea how to find his way back to the ladder?

Suddenly, Charles's voice grated from out of the dark. "Have you calmed down? We need you calm for the next part."

His pulse ticking in his neck, Gerry asked, "What is it?"

"We're going to ask the Messenger—the Prince with a Million Faces—to speed things up for you. What you have to do is stand where I put you. It would be dangerous to move."

Gerry didn't understand much of that, but he hoped Charles meant that no one would hurt him if he cooperated. He stood up, and the tunnel man took him by the arm and guided him along.

"Can I ask something?" Gerry said. "How do you and your friends see in the dark? Is it night-vision goggles?"

Charles chuckled. "It's night vision, anyway. Stand here." He released Gerry and stepped away. Then came the soft sounds of other tunnel people drawing near.

Gerry shivered. For all extents and purposes, they'd had him surrounded since the moment he'd arrived, but now he was the focus of everyone's attention.

A steady rapping began. One of Gerry's captors was banging on a snare drum while walking around him counterclockwise. His intuition told him that all the tunnel people were pacing in the same circle.

Next, chanting began in time to the beat. Sometimes it was a single voice, sometimes all of them, but always declaiming in the tunnel people's snarling, hissing private language. Most of the time, Gerry couldn't pick out individual words, although they repeated 'Nyarlathotep' often enough that he came to recognize it.

In time, the rotation of the circle infected the space around him. Everything spun as if he were drunk.

Suddenly, pain throbbed in his teeth, gums, and the hinges of his jaw. It pounded down his body, punishing his shoulders, elbows, and knuckles. He staggered and cried out

Then, however, the sensation changed. Though it still hurt, it was also exhilarating. It filled him with the need to move, and he somehow knew that now that would be all right. He stumbled forward to claim a place in the circle. He sensed that even if the tunnel people had started out pacing, they weren't just pacing anymore. They were dancing.

He capered along with them, doing a frenzied version of the dog, the monkey, whatever felt right, feeling higher and higher by the moment. Until a thunderous drumroll signaled the end of the celebration, and, exhausted, he flopped back down on the floor.

Someone brought him a cup of water and more raw meat. This time, the food tasted marginally better and was somewhat easier to chew.

Afterward, he slept until a noise like wolves howling jolted him awake. Disoriented, he cried out and scrambled in the opposite direction.

"Easy!" Charles said. "This is how we mourn. Someone died of the wounds the Sharp Teeth gave her."

Gerry's burst of panic subsided. Now his thoughts felt heavy and slow.

"I guess you guys really do need guns."

Charles grunted. "We need something. Sit. Listen. This will help you, too."

"How?" Gerry asked, but Charles didn't answer. Apparently he'd already moved off.

There really wasn't anything to do but listen to the quavering cries. For a long while, they wore on Gerry's nerves, and then, for a time, he had the feeling they were on the brink of conveying something secret and profound. He never did understand them, though, and eventually he simply stopped hearing them. He dozed, and dreamed about a man without a face.

When he woke, the wailing had stopped. Someone brought more meat.

It had a riper smell than his previous meals, and for a second, he thought that really ought to make him queasy. But it didn't, and when he tried it, it actually tasted okay, and he didn't have any trouble chewing it.

More sleep and more dreams. Charles roused him with a nudge.

"Time to earn your keep," the tunnel man said.

"What do you mean?" Gerry asked. "Paul already gave you those records."

"And I gave him gold," Charles replied. "Our trades are complicated, and your work is a part of them."

"What kind of work?"

"Work that will help get you where you need to go."

Gerry rose and noticed he was standing in a stooped posture. He supposed that made sense considering that he'd slept on the ground. Although he wasn't bending forward because his back ached. It just felt more comfortable this way.

"Put out your hand," Charles said.

Gerry obeyed, and Charles put something unexpectedly heavy into his fingers. Examining the article by touch, Gerry discovered it was a folding short-handled shovel of a kind he associated with soldiers in the field. Although the tunnel man might not have intended it, it was an unpleasant reminder of what he was trying to avoid.

Charles took him by the arm. "This way."

As they set off, Gerry heard others joining them. Apparently he and Charles were part of a larger work crew.

They hiked through the darkness for what felt like an hour or two, the tunnel people whispering back and forth. Then Charles said, "This is the place. Find the wall on your right."

Gerry stretched out his arm and took little shuffling steps until he touched it. At some point, the brick walls had given way to earth.

"Dig a side tunnel," Charles said. "Slant it upward."

"When I can't even see what I'm doing?"

"It won't be that bad. And you don't want the others thinking you refuse to do your share. They're not as friendly as I am."

Gerry sighed, gripped his shovel with both hands, and jammed it into the wall at chest level.

At first the labor was just as hard and unpleasant as he'd expected. Dirt spilled out of the wall and into his shoes. Dust stung his sightless eyes and choked him.

Gradually, though, the grit in the air stopped bothering him. His arms grew stronger, or, more likely, he was finding the right technique. At any rate, a moment arrived when he no longer minded the digging, not even when he had to crawl right up into his cramped little hole to make further progress, and every jab and scoop of the shovel brought dirt pouring into his face. It actually all felt pretty natural.

Eventually, he heard one thump and then another.

Then Charles called, "Come out!"

Gerry clambered back down his unfinished burrow. Someone took the shovel from his grasp.

"This makes it easier," Charles said.

Then came rasping, snapping sounds. Gerry realized two of his fellow diggers had reached something made of wood or metal and had slid those prizes down their tunnels, and now Charles was prying the containers open.

Gerry wondered how his companions had broken through to wherever ahead of him. Maybe they had better equipment, although he didn't know what that would be. He hadn't heard the clatter of a jackhammer or the sound of any other power tool.

An enticing aroma wiped such speculations from his mind. His mouth watered, and his stomach rumbled.

"It needs to go back to the family," Charles said. "But not every bit of it. We deserve a little treat."

Someone pressed a strip of meat into Gerry's hand. It had a film of grease coating it and was chewy like jerky underneath. It was also delicious, as tasty as anything he'd ever eaten.

When he finished gobbling the snack, Charles guided him a few steps farther down the passage. "Bend over," the tunnel person said.

Gerry did. Charles took his hands and put each of them on something knobby with what felt like scraps of slimy leather on top of the bumps.

"Let me grab my end," Charles said, "and then we'll pick it up."

Seeking the best grip, Gerry fumbled around. And, by feel, identified the ragged, rotting feet attached to the ankles.

Shock pierced the dullness induced by the Messenger's ritual. He realized what the containers must be. What the tunnel people had been feeding him ever since his arrival. His stomach squirmed, and for a second he was sure he was going to puke.

But he didn't dare. His captors might turn on him. He had to keep going along with whatever they wanted, and hope that somehow it really did keep him out of the Army. And never, ever talk about this to anyone.

He struggled to push his newfound knowledge aside, to pretend he'd never discovered it, and to be the muddled, acquiescent prisoner of a minute ago. Somehow, he managed well enough that when Charles told him to pick up his end of the corpse, he was able to make himself take hold of it and help the cannibal carry it.

Back in the family's home, he slept once more.

A faint clang woke him.

Moments later, another bell sounded closer to hand, one note, a pause, and then two more. With a surge of elation, he realized Paul had signaled from the cellar and Charles had given the countersignal.

Charles's voice came out of the murk. "Come on, Gerry. Time to go."

The cannibal led him back into the maze of passages and eventually tugged the sack back over his head. Not long after, a hint of light penetrated the cloth. After so much time in total darkness, even that was enough to make him squint.

Gerry!" Paul called. "My man!"

Charles gripped Gerry's shoulder. "Good luck," he said. "Don't take the hood off until I'm gone." He padded back down the tunnel.

Paul waited a few seconds, then pulled the sack off and shined the penlight at Gerry's face. That was almost like looking at the sun. Gerry hissed and twisted away.

"What the fuck!" Paul exclaimed. "What the fuck!"

"What's wrong?" Gerry asked.

"Nothing!" Paul snapped. "Just don't look behind you!" He started shouting: "Charles! Get back here! What the fuck, man?"

After a moment, Charles's voice growled back down the passage. "It just hit him harder than it did you or any of the others. He must have an ancestor who was a changeling."

"Is he going to be all right?"

"Yes. Gerry, for the next few days, you just want to avoid the wrong kind of stimulation. Stay aboveground and don't eat meat."

"Why?" Gerry asked.

But Charles didn't answer. Apparently he'd said all he'd intended to say and gone on his way.

Paul drew a deep breath. "Okay. He explained, and everything's cool."

"What's everything?" Gerry asked. "What are you talking about?"

"I'll show you." Paul took a small mirror from the pocket of the James Dean jacket. "But you have to promise not to go nuts."

"Just do it!"

Paul held the mirror in front of Gerry's face. Then he shined the penlight up under his chin to illuminate his features from below.

That left parts of Gerry's face in shadow, and grime covered nearly all of it. But he could still see that the lower half now stuck out an inch or two, like it was trying to grow into a dog's muzzle. His teeth had enlarged, and each one was pointed. So were his ears, while his eyes were so bloodshot the 'whites' looked entirely red.

He cried out and recoiled.

Paul grabbed him by the arm. "Listen to me! It's temporary! You weren't with the ghouls long enough for the change to stick!"

Ghouls? Gerry thought. *Freaks? Monsters?*

Blind or not, how could he have spent days among them and still imagined they were just a bunch of crazy human beings living underground? Maybe the vagueness produced by the Messenger's ritual was to blame, or maybe it would have been too frightening to acknowledge the truth.

"You'll change back in a day or two!" Paul persisted. "But first you're going to your physical!"

"My physical," Gerry repeated. For a few seconds, he'd forgotten all about it.

"Yeah, and you're going to fail it! Your spine is curved. Your heartbeat, temperature, and blood are all abnormal. Trust me, it's going to be funny watching the doctors try to figure out what-all is wrong with you. And after they cut you loose, you're free!"

Right. Free. Gerry would probably have nightmares about this experience for years to come. But he'd be tossing and turning as a civilian, not some poor draftee shipped off to die in Vietnam. Now that the worst was over, that was what he needed to concentrate on.

"All right," he panted. "Let's get up the ladder. How long do I have before I'm supposed to be—"

Back down the tunnel, racing footsteps thumped. He and Paul pivoted toward the sound.

The penlight picked out a hunched, running figure with almost canine jaws and mold-spotted skin. Jagged claws projected from the fingertips, and the bare feet were so stubby and rounded they looked like hooves.

Just shadows in the gloom, but similar in shape, two other creatures were pounding after the first.

Gerry realized what must be happening. The ghoul in the lead was Charles, and the ones chasing him were members of the Sharp Teeth tribe.

Abruptly, Charles whirled. He snarled and raked at the nearer pursuer with his claws.

That ghoul stopped to fight him. But the other swung wide and bounded toward Gerry and Paul.

The humans bolted. Paul shrieked once as the monster evidently caught him from behind. Liquid spattered against a surface, something crunched, and the penlight's glow went out. An instant later, Gerry tripped on an uneven spot in the floor and fell headlong.

Even as he scrambled back up, he knew his situation was hopeless. Blind, he'd never reach the ladder.

But then his eyes ached, fiercely but only for an instant, and afterward, he could see. The brick-walled tunnel flowed into view, like a scene in a movie fading in.

At his back, something roared. He spun around. Paul's killer was jumping up from the mangled form to rush him.

Gerry dodged. One foot slipping out of a shoe that no longer fit, he narrowly avoided his attacker's initial claw-slash.

The ghoul whirled back in his direction. Gerry's fingers throbbed, especially the tips, and he stabbed them at the monster's midsection. It was only when they plunged in deep that conscious thought caught up with his instincts and he realized that he now had talons of his own.

He scrabbled with them, up and down and back and forth, ripping the ghoul's insides. The creature flailed, clouted him across the face with its forearm, and floundered clear of his hands.

Terrified that he hadn't hurt it badly enough, that it would come back on the attack if he gave it the chance, he sobbed, sprang after it, and carried it down beneath him. He tore at it some more, swiped away both crimson eyes, but it wouldn't stop thrashing until he lowered his head and bit its throat out.

Dazed, he slumped on top of the body. Something touched him on the back. He yelped and jerked around.

Charles leered down at him. The ghoul had gashes on his left shoulder and all the way down his chest but had evidently killed his own opponent.

He gestured at the body under Gerry's knees. "Good work."

Gerry suddenly couldn't bear touching it. He scrambled to his feet.

"Please," he said, "help me get out of here. I won't tell anyone about you. Nobody would believe me anyway."

"It's too late," Charles replied. "Feel your face. Look at yourself."

His hands trembling, Gerry did. His muzzle was as prominent as Charles's. His arms were too long and skinny, and the pale skin looked rubbery.

"The change has gone too far," Charles said. "You have to stay with us. But don't worry. We'll make you welcome. You can fight, and we need fighters."

For the next minute or two, Gerry couldn't think. There was just a sort of whine in his head as he and Charles skulked back the way they'd come.

Then it occurred to him that in spite of everything he'd

endured, he'd ended up drafted after all, and that started him laughing. He laughed and laughed and couldn't stop, until even his ghastly companion was eying him askance.

VERMIN

A wail made Adalric spin around.

Stefan and Pierre were dragging a Muslim woman from her house. A little boy started after them, and she shrilled at him to go back inside. The jabber prompted Pierre to slap her, and Adalric scowled. The blow seemed unnecessarily brutish even if she was an enemy of Christ.

His hauberk clinking, the young knight strode toward the two foragers and their captive. "What are you doing?" he demanded of Stefan. It was easier than asking Pierre. Adalric's recently acquired French was better than his recently acquired Turkish, but not a great deal so.

Setting forth from Bavaria, he'd somehow ended up in nominal charge of a small band of pilgrims who, though often wayward and undisciplined, at least all spoke the same German as himself. But the Turks had annihilated the majority of Little Peter's followers almost as soon as they arrived in Anatolia, and the surviving 'Tafurs'—penniless men—had clumped together as circumstance allowed.

They had little choice. None of the great lords leading the Crusade cared to welcome into their own companies such men, who were generally regarded as rabble. Though they were happy to dispatch them on dangerous errands through unfamiliar territory.

His square face peeling with sunburn, Stefan had the grace to look momentarily sheepish. Scrawny, with a rotten-smelling mouth missing several teeth, Pierre glowered at the interruption but left it at that. It was questionable whether the Frenchman truly respected Adalric's authority, but he had sense enough to be wary of proper weapons and armor and a man trained to use them.

"She has money hidden away," Stefan said. "Look at her."

The woman's dress did have more embroidery than seemed common in this dusty desert village. But it didn't matter.

"We're here for food," Adalric said. They were seeking provisions for the Christian army starving beneath the walls of Antioch. "We need to collect it and get away."

"This won't take long," Stefan said.

"She won't even understand what you're asking her."

Stefan leered. "Oh, I'll make her—"

A horn blatted through the morning air. No one had taught the bugler to blow proper signals, but the repeated blasts conveyed urgency. The Tafurs looked wildly about as if they imagined the villagers they'd been robbing were rising up against them, but that wasn't the problem. The sentry atop the tower was watching the approaches to the town, not what was happening inside it.

"Back to the fortress!' Adalric shouted. Some men ran. Others flung themselves onto the half-loaded wagons as the drivers shouted and snapped the reins to set the mules in motion.

Forgotten in the confusion, one cart remained. Adalric scrambled onto the bench. Emboldened by the Christians' hasty departure, a villager in a brown robe threw a stone, and it clinked against his mail.

As his conveyance rumbled and clattered through the streets, Adalric tried to count the Tafurs riding in the other wagons or pounding along on foot. Some were missing. Though he'd attempted to keep them close, the better to control them, a few had plainly sneaked off to loot unsupervised. It was only what he'd expected, but damn them anyway!

The bugle kept blaring, though with longer pauses between notes. The sentry was getting winded. Finally the man himself came into view, atop a keep that was unimpressive to anyone who'd seen the castles of the Rhine and Constantinople—or Antioch for that matter—but which was nonetheless the tallest structure in the village, poking above the sandstone wall surrounding it.

Adalric raced through the gate and, left to his own inexperienced devices, might have driven his mules broadside into someone else's cart. Fortunately, the animals had sense enough to balk on their own initiative and brought their wagon to a jolting halt while their teamster was still fumbling with the reins. A crate bounced out the back and smashed open.

Rising from the bench, Adalric looked up at the sentry.

"What's wrong?" he shouted.

The trumpeter tried to answer but was so out of breath as to be inaudible to anyone at the foot of his perch. Realizing as much, he pointed with one jabbing hand and flailed the bugle back and forth with the other. The brass horn flashed in the sun.

"Close the gate!" Adalric bellowed.

Faramund turned in his commander's direction. A man-at-arms by trade, with a long straw-colored beard and pox-scarred cheeks, he was one of the few Tafurs whom Adalric actually trusted.

"By my count," he called, "we still have people outside."

"By mine, too," Adalric answered. "But I think we're running out of time."

They dashed to the gate and began the process of securing it. Just as they slid the massive bar squeaking through the brackets, hooves pounded outside.

Adalric hurried up the stairs leading to the wall-walk. Keeping low, he peeked over the parapet.

Mounted archers rode around and around the fortress that had likely been their own just a day before. They numbered at least fifty, more than his band of ill-equipped peasants could hope to best in open combat.

If the Turks had only stayed away until afternoon, the foragers might have gotten away clean. Curse the luck! Curse—

Adalric took a breath. It was no use railing against misfortune. Or wondering why God rained adversity on those who fought in His name while lavishing every advantage on the miserable heathens who contended against them, although it wasn't what Little Peter's sermons had led him to expect, to say the least. The Tafurs would simply have to cope with the situation as it was.

Perhaps it wasn't *all* bad. The foragers couldn't defeat the Turks on a battlefield, but they might be able to withstand a siege. The modest size of their stronghold would actually help. Its walls weren't too long for a small force to defend.

Still making sure to keep his head down, Adalric considered the orders he needed to give.

Meanwhile, a Tafur straggler with a dead chicken dangling from his hand blundered into the open space surrounding the fortress. At once, a mounted archer twisted in the saddle, nocked, drew, and loosed. The Tafur pitched forward with the shaft in his chest.

In the darkness, the fort was like a gray fist with an upraised finger. Standing where a narrow, rutted street gave way to the ring of clear space surrounding the stronghold, Zeki squinted at it, striving vainly to spot some weakness that had hitherto eluded him.

His sergeants had urged him to stay behind cover even after dark, but he wasn't worried. The last three days had shown that all the expert archers were on his own side, which made it all the more galling that he had thus far failed to dislodge the wretched infidels from their stolen refuge.

Behind him, someone coughed. Zeki turned and then hesitated when he beheld, not the subordinate he might have expected to interrupt his ruminations, but a stranger.

The newcomer was stooped, perhaps not a hunchback but on the verge, with long arms and big hands. He wore a striped aba, the sleeveless coat of a Bedouin, and a kufeya held in place with an igal of camel wool. The headwear shadowed a dark-eyed saturnine countenance with a grizzled mustache and beard, so bushy as to essentially conceal the mouth.

"You need to stay back," Zeki said, trying not to sound brusque. There was no reason to take out his ill humor on fellow Muslims. "My men and I have commandeered the area until such time as we storm the citadel and destroy the Franks."

Perhaps the stranger grinned. The hair covering his lips made it impossible to be sure.

"How is that going?" he asked.

"That's a matter for soldiers," Zeki snapped, no longer caring if he was rude.

The Bedouin raised one of those big, long-fingered hands. "Forgive me, Captain. I don't mean to pry. It's simply that, like every good man, I yearn for the day when the Faithful will drive these savages into the sea."

"I appreciate that—"

"So I offer what help I can, which is more than you might suppose. My name is Ibrahim, and, appearances to the contrary, I'm an educated man. In my youth, I studied in Dar al-Ilm, the great library of Tripoli. You see me clad as a nomad because I now travel seeking wisdom unrecorded in any of its hundred thousand books."

Zeki cocked his head. "I don't entirely understand."

Ibrahim spread his hands. "Perhaps we could explore the subject more fully indoors? The night grows cold."

Well, why not? It was indeed getting chilly, and Zeki wasn't accomplishing anything as he was. Perhaps the stranger had stumbled across a manual on siege-craft while wading through his hundred thousand volumes, and could provide some sound advice. Stranger things had happened.

Zeki led the self-proclaimed scholar into the house in which he'd taken up residence, which he'd selected for the view the windows afforded of the citadel. The woman who lived there served them hummus and raki, the latter white from being mixed with cold water. Then she, her husband, and their three children left their guests to their deliberations.

Ibrahim sipped the lion's milk and sighed. "Delicious. And now, Captain, would you care to tell me how a capable soldier like yourself comes to find himself barred from his own stronghold?"

Zeki's cheeks grew warm. It was the last story he wanted to tell ... or then again, perhaps it wasn't. Everyone else in the village knew it already, and maybe it would be a relief to unburden himself.

"Well," he began, "I'm like you. I want to help rid our country of the Franks."

"While playing a hero's part in the jihad?"

Zeki's face grew warmer still. "I wouldn't put it like that, exactly."

"Please understand, I'm not criticizing. A soldier is supposed to want to fight the enemy."

"I agree. But my father doubted my ability—" Zeki pushed away the thought that events had proved his father right "—and he serves the Governor and is highly placed enough that Yaghi-Siyan actually knows him. When it became clear the invaders meant to march on Antioch, he prevailed on our lord to station me here, in theory removed from any danger."

"That must have been frustrating."

"It was." Zeki sipped his anise-flavored drink. "And when I received word the Franks had foraging parties ranging far from the city, I was eager to find and destroy one. But I'm not an idiot, however it looks! Yes, I took most of my men on patrol, but I didn't leave the fortress unattended."

"So what happened?" Ibrahim asked.

Zeki took another drink. "As near as I can make out, the Franks must have observed the village without being spotted in their turn. They figured out there were only a few soldiers left in the fortress, and that night they sent horsemen wearing turbans to gallop up to the gate. In the dark, a person could mistake them for riders returning from the search, and one of them spoke our language and pleaded to be let in. Somebody obliged, and the infidels killed him, and his comrades too. Then, in the morning, they began stealing what they came for, beating and otherwise mistreating people while they were about it, even though no one was resisting. Until their sentry sighted my patrol returning and, knowing their wagons couldn't outdistance our pursuit, they retreated back into the stronghold. Now they're inside, and I'm outside." He sighed. "Farcical, is it not?"

"Embarrassing, certainly. Until you dislodge them."

"I'm trying. But the Franks' commander knows something about resisting a siege. More than I know about mounting one, if the truth be told. My training focused on maneuvering mounted archers on the battlefield." He took a breath. "But I *will* get back inside. I may not know much about sieges, but I've seen the engines an attacking force brings against a stronghold. The village carpenter couldn't manage a tower on wheels, but I've got him working on a battering ram, with a roof to shield the men swinging it back and forth."

"I trust he knows how to contrive an apparatus that can punch through the heavy reinforced wood of the gate and withstand burning oil."

Once again, Zeki was uncertain if the wanderer was mocking him. "Do *you* know how?"

Ibrahim shook his head, his bushy beard swishing across the front of his aba and the brown cotton tob beneath. "I'm not a siege engineer, either. But I *can* offer assistance if you're willing to accept it."

Zeki frowned. "Why wouldn't I be?"

"I told you I seek wisdom in the trackless spaces of the world. It is there one hears the jinn and afrit whispering in the wind."

"You're talking about sorcery?"

"I understand if that perturbs you."

"Do you? The Prophet said magic is one of the seven noxious things."

"Certainly, it is knowledge that weighs on the mind. But if a man uses it in the service of Allah, it is not a sin."

Zeki snorted. "I doubt my imam would agree."

"It is your decision, of course, but I implore you to consider carefully. Is it not your duty to retake the fortress as expeditiously as possible? Don't those who suffered abuse deserve to see the infidels punished?"

Ibrahim didn't add, *Don't you want to avenge your humiliation?* But the thought hung in the air between them.

"Consider, too," the scholar said, "that if working magic *is* a sin, it will be my sin, not yours."

Running his finger around the rim of his cup, Zeki considered. He didn't want to be the sort of sophist who rationalized his way past the clear intent of the teachings of the Quran. But he also didn't want word of the current fiasco to reach his superiors—or worse, his father—before he managed to put matters right.

Besides, though sorcerers existed—they must, for wise men

said that they did—they were plainly rare. Zeki had never in his life encountered the genuine article, whereas he had witnessed countless mountebanks performing on street corners and in bazaars. In all likelihood, Ibrahim was simply one of the latter, seeking a reward for ineffectual posturing. If so, it could do no harm to watch the show. "What exactly would you do?" Zeki asked.

"Have you taken any prisoners?" Ibrahim replied.

"Well ... yes. A few Franks wandered off from their fellows and failed to get back to the fortress before my riders caught up to them. We took three alive for questioning—I speak a little of their language—but they didn't say much that was helpful."

"That's all right," Ibrahim said, rising. "They'll help us now. Please, take me to them."

The only proper manacles and cells were back inside the fortress. The Turks had made do by tying the infidels hand and foot, dumping them on the earthen floor of a derelict house, and setting a guard to mind them. The soldier came to attention when Zeki and Ibrahim entered. The Franks eyed them with a mix of apprehension and defiance.

Ibrahim looked over the three, then focused his attention on the sweaty, shivering man whose bandaged thigh was bloody where an arrow had pierced him. "I'll have this one," the sorcerer said. "It will be merciful. Otherwise, the festering in his wound will kill him slowly."

"Do you mean—"

"Surely it lies within your authority to execute an infidel who committed outrages against the innocent. And if I'm merely carrying out the order, then everything is as it should be."

With no more preamble than that, Ibrahim turned toward the prisoners and chanted in a language Zeki had never heard before—if, in fact, it was speech at all. Some of the syllables were less the tones of human language than clicks, buzzes, and hisses, as if the stranger were imitating a menagerie of vermin. Meanwhile his body bobbed up and down, first straightening and raising his hands to the extent his crooked back would allow, then bowing so low his sweeping gestures nearly brushed the floor.

Gradually the oil lamp dimmed and the gloom thickened and rippled, suggesting shapes the eye couldn't quite define but which were repulsive nonetheless. A cold wind moaned, carrying the stink of something fetid. Zeki somehow knew that if he opened the door, he'd find the same wind was not blowing outside.

The guard caught his captain's eye. Then he touched the shagreen-wrapped hilt of his scimitar.

His mouth dry, Zeki almost nodded. But he didn't, because so far, Ibrahim was only doing what he'd promised: raising a power the officer hoped could be directed to destroy the enemy and avert his impending disgrace. He shook his head instead.

Writhing, struggling to worm their way backward despite their bonds, the Franks cried out to their Savior, Virgin, and saints as the magic unfolded. Then they started begging Zeki for mercy.

He wasn't sure why they humbled themselves to him at that precise moment. As far as he could tell, no new uncanny phenomenon had appeared. Then it occurred to him that they could see Ibrahim's face and he couldn't.

The sorcerer stooped over the prisoner with the wounded leg. Zeki couldn't see what he did next; saw only his bowed head and broad, curved back. The Frank screamed, thrashed, and bucked to the extent he was able. It appeared to Zeki that something in addition to the man's bonds was holding the infidel in place.

His shrieks and struggling subsided after a few moments. Ibrahim rose and turned around. The sorcerer's hands were wet and red, and the Frank's corpse had holes stabbed or torn in its chest. Zeki couldn't make out the exact nature of the wounds through the soaked, shredded clothing, and he had a squeamish suspicion he didn't want to.

"Come," Ibrahim said. "I should use the power quickly, before any of it slips from my grasp."

The foul wind dying behind him, the surviving prisoners cursing and weeping, the sorcerer then passed back out of the door. Zeki gave the guard the no-doubt-inadequate reassurance of a clap on the shoulder and followed.

Ibrahim only went far enough to place himself in the center of the street. Then he murmured the start of another incantation. Though recited in the same ugly mockery of language as its predecessor, the new one differed in that it possessed meter and rhyme. Or perhaps Zeki was simply learning to pick out those features from the clicking and croaking.

As the sorcerer declaimed, little forms came scuttling to converge on his position. For a moment, Zeki imagined the darkness itself was stirring as it had before. Then he discerned that the shapes were scorpions drawn from their haunts in the village and possibly the desert beyond.

Ibrahim reached down, and some of the creatures crawled onto his bloody hands. Zeki winced to imagine them nipping, stinging, and scurrying up under the sorcerer's sleeves. Although apparently they didn't do so.

Still reciting, Ibrahim lifted his fingers to his beard. Some of the scorpions hopped off to cling and burrow amid the tufts of hair.

Meanwhile, more arrived to form a seething pool that washed over his sandaled feet, until he pointed in the direction of the fortress, whereupon the creatures scuttled in that direction. The ones crawling on the magus' body jumped down to join the procession.

Ibrahim slumped like a man who'd been working hard. "They shouldn't have any trouble slipping under the gate," he said. "With luck, the Franks might not even notice their arrival."

Now that the worst was presumably over, Zeki tried to steady himself and focus on practicalities. "Your vermin may make the infidels miserable, and that's good. But I doubt this will prove a decisive blow."

Ibrahim chuckled. "Patience, Captain. We're just getting started."

Crouching, Adalric surveyed the clear space around the fortress. Someone in the village had spent the day hammering and for all he knew, had been constructing new scaling ladders. If so, the enemy might be organizing even now to make another run at the redoubt, in the hope that darkness would help them accomplish what they'd failed to achieve in the daylight.

A while ago, Adalric's vigilance had faltered. First, dread seized him as if he'd glimpsed something horrible abroad in the night—even though, of course, he hadn't. Then fear gave way to dizziness, and though nothing about its appearance changed, he *felt* the black sky open like a sinkhole. Knowing the impulse was insane, he nonetheless clung to a merlon lest he fall upward.

The fit had passed quickly. He hoped it had just been a manifestation of weariness and not the first symptom of some looming fever. His little band of fools and reprobates needed his leadership if they were to hold out.

Hold out. He sighed. He'd deemed himself clever when he'd devised his scheme to neutralize the garrison, then plunder the village with impunity. Yet now the Tafurs found themselves trapped, quite possibly for months, until either Prince Bohemond and his fellow commanders somehow took Antioch and had men to spare to search for missing foragers, or Turkish reinforcements arrived in the village in sufficient numbers to negate the defensive advantage that the fortress' walls afforded.

Well, that was the nature of sieges, and there was no use lamenting it. At least, between the provisions the Turks had laid up in the keep and the additional food the Christians had extorted from the town, the occupiers had sufficient to last them for a while. They *didn't* have a well of their own—the only one Adalric had spotted was down in the marketplace—but there was a cistern more than half full of water. Hunger and thirst wouldn't drive them to surrender anytime soon.

Down in the courtyard, someone gave a choked little cry.

As Adalric spun around, he was certain he was going to see that the Turks had somehow gotten inside the walls. But the enclosed space appeared empty. At first glance, he couldn't even see the man who'd made the noise. Perhaps no one had. After all, his senses weren't entirely trustworthy tonight.

Then he noticed the sentry on the far side of the wall was looking across at him waiting for orders. That meant the other Tafur had heard the sound, too.

Adalric raised his hand, signaling the man to stay where he was and continue keeping watch. Then, still keeping low and holding his kite-shaped shield for maximum protection, he darted toward the steps leading downward.

The shield jerked as an arrow thudded into its leather covering. He wondered if the damnable Turks could see in the dark like owls.

He wished he could. At first, scrambling down the steps, nearly losing his balance for an instant, he still couldn't see whoever had cried out. But as he reached the bottom, he spied a fallen man jerking and shaking.

As he hurried forward, the stricken Tafur came into clearer view.

It was Pierre. His breeches were open and wet, his manhood exposed. Evidently he'd come outdoors to piss.

Mostly concealed by his shuddering body, something was moving on the far side of him. A small dog perhaps, or a cat, or conceivably even an enormous rat. Then it clambered onto Pierre's belly, its eight legs scrabbling for purchase, pincers clicking, sting curled over its back, and Adalric discerned it was none of those things. Rather, it was the largest scorpion he'd ever seen.

He gawked at it—and then it charged him.

He retreated. Long legs should have opened the distance faster than short ones could take it up again, but that was only barely so.

Still, he managed to snatch his broad-bladed sword from its scabbard. He cut, the low stroke whizzing mere inches above the ground. The scorpion hopped backward, and the attack fell short. Then the two combatants hovered out of range of one another. Adalric was considering how best to dispose of his adversary—and perhaps, in its fashion, the creature was doing the same.

But when the knight caught the faintest of rustling sounds at his back, he knew he'd guessed wrongly. In reality, the one scorpion had merely done its best to hold his attention while its twin crept up behind him.

Adalric spun and cut. The sword struck off a pincer and tumbled the onrushing scorpion across the ground. He pivoted, struck a second time, and once again the first arachnid dodged the slash. But at least he balked it and kept it from closing to striking distance.

He wrenched himself back around, cut down at the second scorpion just as it was righting itself, and all but split it in two. It hung on the blade for a moment before dropping away when he whirled once more.

The first scorpion was gone. Gasping, Adalric peered this way and that but couldn't tell in which direction it had fled.

Still watching for it, he inspected the fallen Pierre. The Frenchmen was still breathing, albeit in gurgling, slobbering wheezes through swollen lips. The attacker's sting had punched through his worn-out shoe to pierce the flesh inside.

Adalric was no more a physician than anyone else in his ragged company, and he wouldn't have been eager to perform the chore at hand even if he had been. But it was his responsibility.

He bellowed for help, strained to pull off the shoe—the foot within was swollen just like Pierre's lips—and started sucking out the venom.

Zeki took another gulp of raki. He knew he was drinking too much. But although the magic had ended some time before— the shadows had stopped shifting, and the swarm of scorpions had scuttled off toward the fortress—he couldn't seem to leave the alcoholic beverage alone. He wasn't even bothering to mix it with water anymore.

Seated across from him, little more than a silhouette in the red glow of the dying embers in the hearth, Ibrahim chuckled.

"What?" Zeki asked.

"Now," said the sorcerer, "the campaign has truly begun. I suggest you double the number of archers keeping watch and impress upon your entire company the importance of being ready to fight at a moment's notice."

"Why?"

"From this point forward, conditions within the stronghold will deteriorate. Deserters may seek to slip away. The entire pack of infidels might even burst forth in a desperate attempt to escape. Whoever emerges, you'll want to ensure that their act is suicidal."

As the sky outside the narrow window brightened, Adalric took stock of himself. Discounting the frazzled feeling attributable to worry and fatigue, he didn't seem to be ill. He'd heard of men who'd sucked poison from another's wound, only to fall sick themselves because they swallowed some or it had entered their blood through sores or broken teeth in their mouths, but apparently that misfortune hadn't befallen him.

So far, Pierre was still alive. Adalric hoped he'd recover, but had no idea what more—if anything—he could do to help him. His task now was to keep the same fate from befalling anyone else.

Except for Pierre and the sentries on the walls, his men stood assembled in the hall of the keep with their miscellany of scavenged weapons. There was even one peasant still making do with the hayfork he'd carried away from home when Little Peter's exhortations fired his pious zeal.

The scorpion Adalric had killed lay atop a table for their inspection.

He waved his hand at it. "That one won't give us any more trouble, but there's another. We need to find and kill it." He repeated the same message in his halting French.

"But what *is* it?" Stefan called.

"You see what it is," Adalric replied. "A scorpion."

"It seems … unnatural."

It seemed that way to Adalric as well. But he didn't *know*, and it would be counterproductive to say anything that would unsettle the men worse than they were already. "Nonsense. It's a bigger scorpion than any we've seen before, but remember, we're newcomers in these lands."

A Frenchman asked a question, Adalric laboring to decipher the meaning.

"What if there's more than one left?"

"That's unlikely. Surely the Turkish garrison didn't live side by side with a whole swarm of the creatures."

A German raised his battle-axe to attract his captain's attention. "What—"

"Enough!" Adalric rapped. "Our quarry may be big for

a scorpion, but it's still little compared to a man, and I easily killed its fellow. It was only able to sting Pierre because it took him by surprise, and we're going to watch one another's backs so it can't sneak up on any of us again. Now stop whining and split into two groups!"

Muttering, the men obeyed, predictably dividing into a German search party and a French one. Since Faramund spoke only German, it fell to Adalric to lead the latter. He judged that it was likewise his responsibility to search the darkest, most claustrophobic part of the fortress, to prove that he meant it when he claimed there was nothing to fear.

Accordingly, he led his group to the steep, narrow steps descending into the blackness of the dungeon. With a twinge of reluctance, he set his kite shield aside, the better to manage a lantern. Then he headed down, and his companions followed.

When he reached the bottom, the lantern's yellow glow washed over three common scorpions eating the carcass of a rat, their jagged, segmented mouthparts scissoring. Short from head to tail, longer, and longest, the trio plainly represented different breeds of their odious kind, but they appeared content to share the meal, and Adalric wondered if, like the two arachnids he'd fought in the courtyard, they'd worked together to bring down their prey.

Evidently deciding that if they were hunting scorpions, they were hunting scorpions, four of the Frenchmen shoved past Adalric to assail the vermin. He winced as wild swings and stabs clashed weapons on the floor, no doubt dulling them.

A Tafur screamed, dropped his mace, and swiped at his greasy black hair. His hands dislodged a pale little scorpion, but instead of tumbling to the floor, it dropped down the back of his tunic. By the time his comrades got the garment yanked up and the creature brushed away and crushed, he had half a dozen swelling bumps on his torso to match the one in his scalp.

The Frenchman whimpered. Adalric took his head between his hands and looked him in the eyes. "I know it's painful," he said, "but a normal scorpion can't kill a man. You're going to be all right."

"It wasn't one of the ones eating the rat," the Tafur replied in a high, breathy voice. "It jumped on me from the ceiling or the wall. Why did it do that?"

"The commotion frightened it," Adalric said. "Go upstairs and rest." He raised his voice: "The rest of you, search the cells!"

The hunt soon rousted out several more common scorpions, prompting him to wonder just how many the fortress harbored. Up until now, he'd seen his refuge as small, but he was starting to appreciate just how many dark corners and hidden recesses it contained. *There could be scores—*

He scowled to chase such fears away. Small pests weren't the problem. The one big scorpion was, and surely it couldn't evade them for long. They'd catch it before the morning was through and, rid of the distraction, refocus on the real menace: the Turks beyond the walls.

As it turned out, the big scorpion wasn't hiding in the dungeon. Leaving Faramund's party to search the aboveground portions of the keep, Adalric led his men to the stable.

The outbuilding smelled of grain and leather. The company's several riding horses and the mules that drew the wagons stood in the stalls. One of the latter heehawed a greeting—or perhaps a demand for breakfast.

Adalric directed the search of the stable with the same cautious thoroughness as before, and when it revealed more common scorpions, the men assailed them viciously. Then horses whinnied, and donkeys brayed. The Tafurs looked frantically about.

The surviving enormous scorpion was advancing from the far end of the building, where it had evidently hidden during the night. Or at least Adalric assumed this was the same creature— but if so, it had grown in just the few hours since their previous encounter. The arachnid that had eluded him had been, at most, the size of a small dog. This one was as big as a boarhound. Its claws and stinger were poised, mouthparts gnashing, and multiple pairs of round black eyes staring.

Tafurs cried out and crossed themselves. Someone threw a hand-axe that glanced off the scorpion's segmented shell, leaving a scratch but nothing more.

"Spread out!" Adalric said. "Attack from all sides!"

Peering over the top of his shield, he stepped forward to meet the creature head on. *Someone had to.*

His advance provoked the scorpion into scuttling faster. But before it could close, it listed drunkenly to the left, and then the legs on that side of its body buckled beneath it. It heaved itself up again, attempted to walk, and then all eight legs gave way.

With a roar, the Tafurs charged. It sought to fend them off, but clumsily, as if its pincers and sting had grown too heavy for it. Its shell crunched as weapons smashed and stabbed through to the flesh beneath.

When it was certain the scorpion was dead, some men cheered. Others fell to their knees to give thanks to God. The noise drew Faramund and his Germans.

Faramund gave Adalric a nod. "Nicely done."

Adalric moved close enough to reply without the men overhearing. He didn't want them to feel he was belittling their victory. "It wasn't difficult. The scorpion was sick."

Faramund shrugged. "The important thing is, this particular problem is over."

"Right," Adalric agreed. Even though the taut, edgy feeling inside him had yet to go away.

The pole hung on the horizontal, slung from several ropes. Zeki gave it an experimental push and found that even a single man could easily swing it in its cradle. That confirmed what his eyes had already told him.

"It's too light to break open the gate," he said.

The carpenter spread his hands. "My lord, it's the heaviest pole I had to work with."

Zeki indicated the peaked roof built atop the ram. "And this doesn't stick out far enough. An enemy on the wall could still hit one of the men underneath."

"Captain, if you had specified exactly … shall I begin again?"

"If you can't make a proper ram, what good would it do?" Zeki took a breath. "I apologize. I know you did the best you could." He handed the villager a little drawstring bag of clinking silver dirhems and walked back outside, where the bright heat of the day was giving way to twilight.

Ibrahim was waiting for him. "I infer from your expression," the sorcerer said, "that the carpenter failed to produce a serviceable device."

Zeki sighed. "As you predicted."

"If you recall, I also explained that it doesn't matter if your troops can't get inside. Our strategy is to force the infidels out."

'*Our*' strategy. Zeki resented the implication they were now co-commanders. Especially since the more repulsive aspects of last night's conjuration had heightened his suspicion that the wanderer's magic was something a pious, sensible man should shun.

Yet Ibrahim truly had worked a marvel, even if aspects of it were unsavory, and it was now plainer than ever that Zeki *needed* a marvel to avoid becoming a laughingstock in Antioch. So he buried his distaste beneath a smile and said, "I'll ask you what you asked me when we first met: how is that going?"

The hair covering the scholar's mouth stirred. For an instant, Zeki imagined leftover scorpions crawling around in there. But Ibrahim's next words suggested he'd prefaced them with a sigh forceful enough to puff out his mustache.

"Not as well as I might have hoped," the sorcerer said. "The Franks went on a scorpion hunt. They didn't find all the creatures I sent to plague them, but they killed some."

Zeki nodded. "At least you have some left. Enough to still make a nuisance of themselves, I hope."

"Yes, but the situation is more complicated than that. I watch through the scorpions' eyes and compel them to do my bidding. That taps my strength. I made two of the creatures grow to enormous size, and that takes even more power. Indeed, the giants need recurring infusions of magic simply to enable them to walk, let alone threaten the Franks. Nature didn't intend their frames to support the weight that this enlargement imposes on them."

Zeki frowned. "Are you telling me you ran out of strength?"

"To my sorrow, yes, and at a key moment. One of the giants stood a fair chance of killing the infidel captain before his followers slew it in its turn. Instead, it collapsed, and the Franks overwhelmed the poor thing with little more trouble than farmers slaughtering a goat."

"Then your effort has run its course?" Zeki wasn't sure if he felt disappointed or relieved.

The tufts of hair under the sorcerer's nose stirred again, this time as he laughed. "Hasbinallah, no! Please forgive me if I worried you. I was merely trying to explain that I require new vitality to continue."

Zeki swallowed. "Does that mean you want to kill one of the remaining prisoners?"

"Both, I think. Perhaps then I won't run short of power again."

"I ... don't know if I should allow that."

Ibrahim's cocked his head. "Why not? You were being just, were you not, when you condemned the first infidel to death? Aren't the other two guilty of the same crimes?"

"You told me the first one was going to die anyway."

"Painfully, and it seemed merciful to spare him. But as a soldier, surely you would agree that war does not always afford us the luxury of kindness."

Ibrahim hesitated. Last night's ritual had reeked of the unholy, but it hadn't hurt anyone on his side, and if allowing it was a sin, well, it was a sin he'd committed already. Perhaps a victory on behalf of Islam would balance the scales.

"Very well," he said. "Execute the prisoners." *Execute* seemed a more righteous word than *murder.* Or *sacrifice.* "Work your magic one more time."

Adalric roused with a start to find himself beside one of the wagons parked outside the stable. An instant before, or so it seemed to him, he'd been near the doorway into the keep. Evidently he'd crossed the courtyard sleepwalking, or in a stupor approximating sleep.

He scowled and knuckled a gritty eye. If he was going to doze off, he might as well seek his bed and sleep properly. God knew he needed it, and surely the trouble with the scorpions was done. Both big ones were dead, and dozens of the common sort as well.

Yet he couldn't rid himself of the suspicion that, just as

strange perils had crawled from the darkness last night, they might arise tonight as well. His imagination might simply be running wild, however, and if he didn't want to alarm the men when they'd finally calmed down, he needed to patrol the fortress himself.

He gave his head a shake and headed back across the courtyard.

At the periphery of his vision and low to the ground, a shadow shifted ... or perhaps not. When he pivoted in that direction, nothing was moving anymore.

He suspected his eyes were playing tricks on him, but he needed a closer look to know for certain. He adjusted the strap that ran from his shield to loop around his neck, made sure his sword was loose in the scabbard, and stalked forward.

After two paces, he perceived he was advancing toward the cistern, a rectangular hole in the ground with a low brick ledge around it. A bucket on a rope sat ready to hand to draw the water forth.

Adalric still couldn't see any further movement. But he squinted, because something about the murky shapes before him was off. Was there a spot where the brick barrier humped up higher than it should?

He took another step. The bulge became a scorpion the size of a man's head. It had been crouching motionless atop the ledge, but now the sting poised above the cistern began to flick. It was flinging venom into the water.

Underneath Adalric's coif of mail, the hairs on the nape of his neck stood on end. He and his fellow Tafurs had rid the citadel of the enormous scorpions, yet here, inexplicably, was another deliberately poisoning the water supply. Surely no vermin would undertake such a thing unless guided by a man's intellect ... or a demon's.

Whatever accounted for it, Adalric had to stop the contamination. He drew his sword, shouted for help, and advanced.

The arachnid neither fled nor assumed a defensive posture. It just kept on flicking. Was it so intent on the task that it hadn't even noticed him? Or was it trying to hold his attention while another scorpion sneaked up on him like the creature last night?

He glanced behind him. Nothing was there but one of the sentries, scurrying down from the battlements in answer to his call. Reassured, Adalric turned back toward the scorpion.

The sentry, a Frenchman, shouted something. It took Adalric an instant to translate it to "Watch out!" By then, the ground was grumbling, and dirt was sliding under his boots.

He whirled, and a scorpion the size of a donkey heaved itself from the burrow where it had hitherto lay hidden. One set of pincers hooked around his shield to seize him.

Appalled, he didn't consciously shift the shield, but a lifetime of training, cutting at the pell and sparring with other men-at-arms with swords of wood or whalebone, did it for him. The action kept the claws from closing on his body.

Unfortunately, it didn't stop the pincers from grasping the edge of the shield itself. The alderwood crunched and splintered, and the scorpion jerked on its prize, staggering Adalric. He reeled and fell into the burrow from which his foe had just emerged, a low space like a shallow grave.

Legs splayed to straddle the pit, the scorpion tried to reach him with its unencumbered set of claws. With his shield immobilized and his sword all but useless in such close quarters, Adalric dropped the blade, snatched the dagger from his belt, and met the groping claws with stabs. Each counterattack balked them, but only for a moment. Meanwhile, dirt spilled down the edges of the grave, blinding and choking him.

The scorpion grasped the shield with both pairs of pincers and tried to wrest it away. Adalric clung to the hand strap, switched back to his sword, and stabbed upward, shouting with each thrust, half in fury and half in terror.

His weapon jolted against the scorpion's body. With the shield blocking his vision and dust blurring his eyes, he couldn't tell if any of his strokes penetrated the creature's shell.

A piece of the shield crumbled in the arachnid's grip, exposing more of Adalric to its attacks. He struck across his body at the pincers that now sought to close on his shoulder. They jerked back, but then the arachnid's sting whipped down, pierced the shield, and stopped a finger-length above his chest.

It yanked free and struck again. The repeated blows clattered like hail on a roof and were steadily smashing the shield to pieces. Though still fighting as fiercely as before, Adalric braced for the death stroke that was likely imminent.

Then pincers and sting lifted away, and, legs skittering around the hole in which he lay, the scorpion changed its facing. Something, probably the sentry rushing to his aid, had distracted it.

Adalric gathered himself to take advantage, and then a smaller but still unnaturally large scorpion, likely the one that had been poisoning the cistern, hopped down by his feet and seized one of his ankles in its claws. The pressure *hurt*. If not for the reinforced leather of his boot, it would surely have cut flesh and broken bone.

Adalric drew up his other foot and stamped. His heel slammed home just above the gnashing mouthparts, in the center of the four sets of black little eyes. Shell crunched, and although the creature still gripped him even in death, the pressure abated. He'd have to settle for that.

Adalric scrambled to his knees and thrust his sword at the remaining arachnid's underside, driving the blade into the seam between two pieces of shell.

The scorpion froze for an instant, then scuttled backward away from the pit, nearly jerking the hilt from his hand. He hoped he'd hurt the creature badly.

Grinning, he scrambled out of the burrow before the scorpion could straddle it anew, and his momentary elation turned to rage. A decapitated body sprawled on the ground, gore pooled around the stump of the neck, while the scorpion held the severed head in one set of claws. The sentry had indeed succeeded in saving his captain's life— but only at the cost of his own.

Adalric realized the bugle was blaring. The remaining sentry was sounding it. Responding to the call, Tafurs charged out of the keep, then faltered when they beheld the scene before them.

"It's wounded!" Adalric bellowed. "Flank it and kill it!" He ran at the scorpion; partly to encourage them, partly because he hated it. His strides shook the carcass of the smaller arachnid loose from his ankle.

The scorpion dropped the sentry's head. Its pincers snatched and, not trusting the scant remains of his shield to block the attack, Adalric dodged. The claws clacked shut on empty air, and he cut at the place where they swelled from the limb behind them. The sword didn't shear them off entirely, but when he drew it back, they dangled uselessly.

A moment later, Faramund lunged, chopped with his battle-axe, and maimed one of the scorpion's legs. Another man rammed a spear into its side.

We're killing it, Adalric thought. Then something clanked on his helmet and knocked it askew. It wasn't the scorpion. Its sting and remaining set of claws were busy assailing other foes. He cast about; arrows were whistling down from overhead.

The Turkish bowmen could arc shafts over the fortress walls. But how did they know to loose at this particular time and at this particular section of the courtyard?

Only newly risen from his sickbed, Pierre gasped as an arrow pierced into his shoulder. Other men cried out in consternation.

"The Turks are shooting blind!" Adalric shouted. "We'll be all right, but we have to kill the scorpion!" He cut at the head and hacked off one of the mouthparts. An instant later, an arrow plunged down and punctured one of the rearmost eyes. The vermin flailed its claws.

"Kill it!" Faramund roared. He struck a second blow with his axe.

Heartened, other Tafurs resumed attacking, and after a few moments, the scorpion fell. The segmented tail was the last part to stop moving, flipping back and forth in diminishing arcs.

"Now, get under cover!" Adalric cried.

Once inside the keep, he checked on everyone's condition. Fearsome though it had been, the huge scorpion had only killed the sentry, while the shower of arrows had only found Pierre, who appeared likely to recover.

"We were lucky," Faramund said.

Perhaps so. But Adalric didn't *feel* lucky. And he wondered just how enormous the *next* freakish scorpion would be.

Ibrahim stared at nothing, presumably looking through the eyes of one of the vermin in the fortress. Zeki wondered if a man could simply walk up to the sorcerer and kill him while he was in his trance.

Then he glimpsed a tiny scorpion crawling on Ibrahim's foot. Zeki suspected it was playing watchdog. That didn't mean it could read a man's thoughts, but he still felt a ridiculous impulse to somehow convey to it that he'd merely been speculating and didn't intend its master any harm.

The sorcerer turned in his direction.

"How did we do?" Zeki asked.

"Not as well as I expected," Ibrahim replied. "We got some venom into the cistern, but the scorpions only killed a single Frank. The archers hit another, but in all likelihood not fatally."

"That's not good enough! Especially when we're running short of arrows."

"I promise you, Captain, in the end, it will all work out. If we simply continue applying pressure, the enemy will inevitably break."

"Go on, then. Work more magic."

"Tomorrow night. After I renew my power."

Zeki frowned. "We're out of prisoners."

Ibrahim waved at the street behind them. "Walk with me, young sir. There's no need for simple soldiers to overhear deliberations that might distress them."

"Keep watch," Zeki told one of the sergeants. Then, with a pang of trepidation, he followed Ibrahim into the dark.

"Like every village," the wanderer said, "this one surely has one or two troublemakers as well as old, sick people who live in constant misery. If they fly off to Paradise as martyrs, won't everyone be better off?"

"You can't be serious!"

"You and your men need not take an active part. I can gather the harvest myself."

"That's not the issue! You're talking about slaughtering our own people!"

"Only a handful, and as you and I have already agreed,

in war a soldier must occasionally commit a small wrong to achieve a greater good."

Zeki hesitated. "Even if that were true, how can you be sure the new deaths would give you enough power?"

The hairs around Ibrahim's mouth stirred. "To explain," he said, "I must take you deeper into my confidence than I originally intended—or that may be comfortable for *you* to hear. But if you insist?"

"Yes."

"As you wish, then. You have likely assumed that I'm simply taking the lives I reap and burning them like wood in a fire. But the truth is more complicated. The lives are offerings to something strong and old—think of it as a jinn, if you like—and as I continue ingratiating myself, it grows increasingly generous in its turn. Once it fully accepts me as its imam ... excuse me, *vizier* ... cleaning out your fortress will be child's play. Why, together, you and I will raise the siege of Antioch."

"You sound like a blasphemer, and mad as well."

"Because I believe the Old One would favor me to that extent? You doubt because you haven't seen the signs." Ibrahim brushed his mustache and beard to the sides of his face, revealing the wet, protruding mouthparts twitching beneath.

Zeki cried out and snatched for the hilt of his scimitar. Then something pinched his calf. He looked down, and a black scorpion, long and skinny like a needle, scuttled up his leg.

"Please don't slap at it," Ibrahim said. "Magic has increased the virulence of its venom twentyfold."

Heeding the warning, Zeki simply stood and trembled. Even when the scorpion writhed inside his clothing.

"It won't hurt you," Ibrahim said, "as long as you don't attempt to betray our holy cause. So I implore you to forbear. Let me win us our victory, save you from disgrace, and make you the hero you yearn to be."

Adalric surveyed the men assembled before him in the hall. Sleep, a meal, and the return of daylight had steadied them, but fear still lurked in many a haggard face—and perhaps even in the stink of their unwashed bodies.

"We now know," Adalric began, "that our situation is more desperate than we first supposed. The Turks are using witchcraft against us. We have to decide what to do about it."

"Keep a guard on the cistern," Faramund said. "The larder, too. Kill the giant scorpions whenever they turn up."

"That's one option," Adalric said. "But for all we know, the water supply is already unsafe. Even if it isn't, it seems likely the sorcerer, whoever he is, will work magic against us night after night, with the curses growling steadily stronger and the scorpions ever larger. I doubt we could hold out for long."

"We might not have to," Faramund said. "Bohemond's men could show up to raise the siege tomorrow."

"Because of the love the prince bears for King Tafur's followers?"

Faramund snorted. "Fair enough. There's not much chance of it, is there? But do we have another choice?"

Stefan pushed to the fore of the assembly. "Maybe it's time to think about surrender."

Some of his fellow Germans snarled, "Fuck that!" and "Coward!" —but only some. A moment later, after the suggestion was translated for the Frenchmen's benefit, perhaps half of them expressed similar sentiments in their own language.

Stefan bore his comrades' scorn without flinching. "I don't like the notion, either," he said, "but how long can ordinary men last against witchcraft?"

"The warlock works his magic at night," Adalric said. "That's when the scorpions grow and do his bidding. If we make a move before sunset, he may not be able to harm us."

Stefan sneered. "'May not.' That's not reassuring coming from someone who's been wrong about everything up to now. You said we'd raid the village and get away before the patrol returned. We didn't. You claimed we'd be safe in the fort. We aren't. When the first big scorpion appeared, you told us it was a natural creature. Now you admit you were mistaken about that, too."

"I do admit it," Adalric said. "Since we came here, I've been wrong more than once. In my defense, I can only say that in war, nothing is certain, and that I don't see how anyone could have predicted the Turks would use witchcraft against us. They never did before, even at the massacre outside Civetot."

He took a breath. "But it doesn't matter if I'm shrewd or stupid. It matters that we came on this journey vowing to do the work of God. We assumed that meant killing the Turks who prey on pilgrims bound for Jerusalem. But we've found a greater evil even than that. We've come face to face with Satan himself. We can't surrender to *him*. We have to defy him with our last breath."

Faramund smiled a crooked smile. "Yes," he said, "if only because, if we serve ourselves up to a devil worshipper, he's likely to do even worse than make us renounce Jesus and slice off our foreskins. Better to fall in battle than be tortured to death on Hell's altar."

The Tafurs muttered back and forth. Then they drew themselves up straighter, and one of the Frenchmen called, "We're with you, Sir Knight!" Either Adalric's words had swayed his followers, or their innate grit and faith were buttressing their resolve.

Stefan grimaced. "So be it, then. But if we won't surrender and can't stay in the fort, what do we do?"

"The only thing left," Adalric said. "Throw open the gate and try to break through the Turks. Some of us will die, but with God's help, some may survive to carry warning of the warlock back to Bohemond."

Some in this instance meaning one or two—and only if God was finally inclined to provide His ragtag soldiers with a miracle.

The Turkish soldiers surrounded the fortress in groups of three or four, wherever cover could be found. Though it was unlikely an infidel archer shooting from the battlements could hit a vulnerable foeman at this distance, it was nonetheless prudent to deny them the opportunity.

Zeki prowled from one position to the next inspecting the arrangements. He was sure the sergeants checked periodically to correct any deficiencies and did so with a keener eye than his own. But he wanted a distraction from the creature nestled between his shoulder blades.

He suspected from the occasional twinges and constant itching that the scorpion had hooked the tiny claws at the end of its legs into his skin. Perhaps his back was bleeding, but if so, the rectangular iron plates of his lamellar armor, the padding underneath, and the tunic under that would hide the blood, and anyway, no one could help him even if it were visible.

He just had to endure the discomfort as best he could—and, worse, his gnawing dread of the creature's sting. If he could only bear up, all would be well. The Franks would surrender or perish, Ibrahim would relieve him of his hideous minder, and in due course the world would hail him as a hero.

Except, he thought as entered another house that afforded a view of the stronghold, it wasn't that simple.

Ibrahim stood revealed as a monster in service to a greater monster. How, then, could Zeki believe anything he said about his intentions regarding the war in general, or his unwilling collaborator's ultimate fate in particular?

He couldn't, and even were it otherwise, how could he allow the sorcerer to murder innocent people to achieve his ends? *It was his duty to protect them!*

If he didn't at least try, then what would it matter what his superiors or even his own family thought of him? Forever after, *he'd* know he truly was the incompetent weakling he'd always feared being, a cringing dupe who could be controlled by a vermin riding him like a horse.

"Captain?" Murat asked.

Startled, Zeki jumped. "Yes?"

"You walked in," the burly, black-bearded sergeant said, "and then you didn't say anything. Is something wrong?"

"No," Zeki replied, "I was just thinking. What's your appraisal of our situation?"

"Well," Murat said, "nothing has changed since last night when we loosed those volleys of arrows. Honestly, sir, I advise against any more blind shooting, whatever your friend the scholar recommends. We don't have enough—"

Without warning—or at least he prayed the scorpion didn't sense his intent—Zeki threw himself backward and slammed his shoulders into the wall.

An instant later, he felt a stab. The scorpion was still alive. The padding under his armor had protected it.

He pounded it again, and it responded with more stings. Zeki was surely a dead man now. All that remained to him was to make sure his killer didn't survive, either.

He bashed it, and it scuttled onto the top of his shoulder. Apparently the repeated impacts had alarmed it at last. It scraped the side of his neck as its pincers and head emerged from under his layers of armor and garment.

Screaming, he grabbed it, ripped it all the way out, and dashed it to the floor. Then he stamped on it repeatedly, reducing it to scraps and slime before realizing that Murat and the other soldiers were gaping at him in astonishment.

"That ... was a big one," the sergeant said.

"It's killed me," Zeki gasped. Then he realized that, although the stings were burning and throbbing, he didn't feel consciousness slipping away.

"Let's take a look," Murat said. He helped Zeki remove his armor and tunic and then inspected his back. "They're going to hurt, that's certain. But they don't look any worse than other scorpion stings."

Zeki surprised himself by laughing. "The son of a dog didn't really make the venom deadly. He thought me coward enough that the mere threat would paralyze me."

"Who, sir? Your so-called sorcerer?"

"Yes. Ibrahim put the scorpion on me. How much do you understand about him?"

Murat hesitated. "Again, if I'm to speak honestly, I know you put great stock in him. But some of the men claim to sense evil hanging over the village since he arrived. I just thought he was a lunatic or a fraud."

"I wish you had been right," Zeki said. "You *were* right in thinking I never should have trusted him. But he truly does command magic, and not for the glory of Allah, whatever he claims. If we don't stop him, he'll do terrible things with it."

The sergeant frowned. "If he is what you say, *can* we stop him?"

"I hope so. He mostly casts his spells at night. That suggests he's weaker during the day. Perhaps we can even catch him sleeping."

Murat grunted. "That sounds sensible. Do we arrest or kill him?"

"Kill."

"Yes, sir, and how many men do you judge that will take?"

Murat smiled wryly. "We do still have a fort full of infidels to deal with."

Zeki's instinct was to lead his entire force against Ibrahim, but he did need to keep the Franks contained, and if he suggested otherwise, Murat would think he was crazy. He might believe it anyway, but if so, he was willing to humor his poor deluded captain if it meant disposing of a troublemaker whose presence undermined morale.

"If there are only a few of us," Zeki said, "we can sneak up on him more easily. Let's say four of the men, you, and me."

"You, sir? You've just gotten hurt."

"I can stand it. It's my fault Ibrahim gained a foothold here, and my responsibility to deal with him." He swallowed away an excess of saliva, perhaps another manifestation of the venom in his system. "Help me put my armor back on."

Despite the cloth underneath, the weight of the lamellar plates chafed his stings and made them hurt worse. He tried not to let it show as Murat gathered and instructed the soldiers who would accompany them.

In due course they set forth, and people who spied them hurried indoors. Apparently Zeki and his companions had a grim cast to their expressions—or at any rate, something about their mien conveyed they'd embarked on an ugly business.

When Ibrahim's temporary lodgings came into view, everything was quiet. Zeki blinked away a momentary blurriness, likely another symptom of his poisoning, and he and his men prowled up to the little house.

He took a breath and threw open the door. No one was in the front room, and he and his soldiers spread out to search the rest of them. Moments later, the man who'd entered the kitchen cried out, and everyone scrambled in his direction.

Ibrahim wasn't there, but the widow who'd been taking care of him was. She lay face-down in a pool of blood with two ragged wounds in her back and her head torn halfway off. Scorpions swarmed over the corpse, partaking of the feast their master had left them. A soldier turned away and vomited.

Zeki's jaw tightened with an anger directed in equal parts at the sorcerer and himself. "I should have gotten here sooner."

Murat frowned. "You couldn't know this was going to happen."

"I knew Ibrahim links his mind to the minds of his servants. I should have guessed that when I killed the scorpion, he'd understand I was about to lead men against him and seek to gather the power to withstand us."

"While the sun's still up?"

"Evidently he can invoke his jinn in the daylight if he has to. We need to find him before this gets any worse."

They strode back outside. Zeki considered the village with its low, huddled buildings and narrow tangled streets. Ibrahim could be hiding anywhere. He could even have fled into the desert. Zeki tried to decide how best to direct a search—and then, away to the south, someone screamed.

The soldiers ran toward the sound and as they rounded a bend, two more corpses appeared—a man's and a little girl's, each ripped like the widow's. Behind them the door of another house stood ajar, revealing the gloom within. A smear of blood led up to it and over the threshold, as though Ibrahim had dragged yet another victim inside.

If so, perhaps he'd intended that unfortunate for a lengthier, more formal sacrifice—a ritual more pleasing to the Old One— in which case, the villager might still be alive.

"We have to get in there now," Zeki said.

He led his squad toward the front door. They were a few paces away when a scorpion the size of a horse lunged forth to meet them.

Ibrahim had alluded to enlarging scorpions, but the words hadn't prepared Zeki for anything like this. He froze for what would likely have been his final moment, except that the arachnid with its splayed limbs and upraised sting had difficult negotiating the cramped confines of the doorway. As it thrashed its way into the open, he broke through his shock and came on guard.

He blocked a sweeping sting attack with his shield and riposted with a scimitar cut that fell short. Meanwhile, claws clacked and men cried out to either side. He realized there had been more scorpions lying in wait along the sides of the house. But he couldn't spare so much as a glance for them or for the soldiers they were assailing, lest his own foe dispatch him in that instant.

A soldier rushed past him on the left and struck at the arachnid that had come through the door. Until then, Zeki hadn't realized he had a partner in his portion of the battle. The looming terror of the scorpion itself had consumed every iota of his attention.

The soldier's blade clashed on shell. The scorpion pivoted, bringing its pincers to bear. Zeki lunged and cut at the creature's flank, at the spot where the stub of a head fused with the body.

The scimitar sliced deep but not deep enough. The scorpion still caught Zeki's ally in both sets of claws. The pressure snipped him to pieces and dropped them thumping to the ground.

Screaming, Zeki struck a second time. The arachnid fell, a moment too late. Its tail whipped in spasms, wasting its venom on the dirt.

Zeki cast about for someone he *could* help.

The brown scorpion on his right crouched over a pair of corpses.

The yellow one on the left lashed its sting up and over, spiking it right through Murat's helmet into the top of his head.

The sergeant whimpered. His eyes rolled up and his knees buckled, dumping him on top of the previous man whom the arachnid had slain.

Zeki couldn't fight the two surviving scorpions alone. Panting, sweating profusely—fear, the venom afflicting him, or a synergy of the two—he backed up.

Seemingly in no hurry, the giant vermin moved to flank him. Perhaps they meant to toy with their prey. Or, more likely, the shadow framed in the doorway was holding them back.

"It didn't have to be like this," Ibrahim said. Even speaking normally, his voice now hinted at the inhuman clicks and buzzes his sorcery required. "I truly would have made you a hero and rid our land of the infidels."

Terror was supposed to dry a man's mouth, but Zeki still needed to spit away more excess saliva before replying. "At what cost?"

"In your lifetime, relatively little. In a generation or two, the nature of your faith will change, and ultimately, strengthened by the devotion of multitudes, the Old One will return from exile."

"All because of the help you provided? We don't need it!"

"Possibly not—but someone, the Governor, the Sultan, or one of the Emirs, will *want* it—and will quickly come to depend on it. My influence can only grow from that point forward."

"It will never happen. Your ambush killed the soldiers lying here, but I have fifty more."

"Even if you could make it back to rally them, it wouldn't matter. I explained that with every offering, my patron grows more generous, and even undertaken on the fly in the daylight, these last few proved remarkably efficacious. Let me show you."

Ibrahim stepped farther into the doorway. He was indisputably a hunchback now. He'd discarded his kufeya, and his beard and, indeed, every hair on his misshapen head had fallen out. As a result, the wet, scissoring mouthparts, grown even more prominent, were entirely visible, as were the several pairs of round black eyes. Each set of bloody pincers was bigger than his skull.

Zeki flinched back a step.

"Now you understand what an ingrate you were." Ibrahim waved the scorpions forward. "Kill him."

The arachnids moved in. Zeki saw no way to evade both of them. He raised his scimitar.

Behind him, a door creaked open. "Here!" a bass voice called.

Zeki bolted for the house that offered survival. He lunged through the door, and a stout old villager with a mole at the corner of his mouth slammed it shut. The door clattered and jolted on its hinges as the scorpions struck at it. The tip of a claw punched through.

"Get out!" Zeki gasped. He dashed to the back of the house and swarmed out a window into an alley that was as yet mercifully free of pursuers.

If he kept ducking into houses to throw them off, he might just make it back to the troops surrounding the fortress, after all.

Astride his roan stallion with the gate at his back, Adalric regarded his fellow Tafurs. The other five accomplished horsemen were likewise in the saddle. But most of the company were on foot, just as they'd tramped all the way from their homes in Christendom—and as many, if not all, would die today.

"We're ready," he called. "When the gate opens, run. Don't stop for anything unless you're one of Faramund's party. They have a special errand." He turned to the rider on his left.

"Spying from the top of the keep," Faramund said, "we spotted the paddock where the Turks are keeping their horses, and the shit-eating sons of bitches are cavalry to a man. If we interfere with their mounts, they may lose the will to chase us. Failing that, we might at least delay them long enough to give us a good head start. So my fellows and I will throw some spears, set a fire, chase the horses out of the pen, something. Whatever looks feasible when we get there."

"If anyone gets separated, Antioch is to the northwest." Adalric pointed. "That way. May God be with us." He took a fresh grip on the round shield he'd found in the citadel's armory and nodded to the men charged with opening the gate.

They started to slide the bar back, and then voices clamored from outside. Some of the cries, he thought, were Turkish soldiers shouting orders, although he failed to catch the gist. Others were people wailing for help or emitting wordless shrieks of terror.

The men opening the gate looked up at their commander to see if he would countermand his order. Faramund turned to him as well.

"Did someone come to rescue us after all?"

"I don't know," Adalric replied.

He could dismount, ascend to the battlements, and look around in an effort to determine what has going on outside—but he begrudged the time it would take. His men were ready *now*. By the sound of it, the enemy was dismayed and distracted *now*. He shouldn't let the moment slip away.

"We're still going out!" he shouted. "But watch me when we do! If I change the plan, I'll signal! Otherwise, do what I told you before!"

The men on the gate pulled it open as fast as its bulk would allow. Adalric kicked his stallion into motion. Shouting the names of Christ, the Virgin, and various saints, his fellow Tafurs rushed out behind him.

A few arrows flew at them. One whizzed through the space between Adalric's horse's neck and his own torso. But despite the cover of which they'd availed themselves, he could tell most of the Turks were turning away from the fortress. Some at least were abandoning their positions and advancing into the village.

"They're running away!" a Tafur cried.

"It's a miracle!" another shouted.

It wasn't. The Turks had turned to contend with an immediate threat. But that didn't mean Adalric shouldn't seize the opportunity that afforded. In all likelihood, it was another company of Crusaders attacking the Muslims, and if the Tafurs joined in, they and their allies could grind the enemy between them.

He brandished his lance over his head. He was about to sweep it forward to order a charge, when a Turkish archer scrambled from behind a barricade constructed early in the siege and ran straight at his Tafur foes. He was more terrified of something at his back than he was of them.

An instant later, the something climbed over the barrier and scuttled in pursuit. It was a coppery scorpion with a thick body the size of one of the Tafurs' now-abandoned wagons. Its pincers snapped shut on the archer's head, and blood squirted out around the edges. The arachnid dropped the corpse with its pulverized skull and crouched over it with mouthparts gnashing.

Adalric's stallion balked, and he would have reined it in if it hadn't. His men likewise froze, their martial fire chilled like his own.

Faramund spurred up even with him. "The attackers aren't Bohemond's men!' the man-at-arms declared, and Adalric resisted a mad impulse to laugh at the most unnecessary statement anyone had ever uttered. "The Turks' witchcraft has turned against them!"

"Apparently so," Adalric said, and then a little girl raced out into the open. No doubt she was running away from one enlarged scorpion, and when she discovered her flight had brought her into proximity with another, she froze. Abandoning the body of the man it had just killed, the boxy arachnid pivoted in her direction.

Adalric had to spur his horse three times, but then it charged. As the scorpion neared the little girl, he thrust his lance into its flank.

The creature wheeled in his direction. His steed danced backward in an effort to evade it, and he yanked the lance from the puncture it had made.

The scorpion's sting whipped in a horizontal arc. Adalric caught the stroke on his shield, but the bludgeoning force of it all but knocked him out of the saddle. As he struggled to recover his seat, pincers reached for him.

Faramund galloped in and plunged his lance into one of the round black eyes. An instant behind him, other Tafurs stabbed and swung their weapons. Someone managed a mortal blow, and the arachnid fell down thrashing.

Faramund turned to Adalric.

"What were you *thinking*?"

Adalric hesitated because he wasn't sure himself. During their time trapped in the fort, he'd come to hate the scorpions, but there was more to his fury than that.

"She was a child."

"We've seen scores of dead children since we set out—and are apt to see plenty more. But anyway, you saved her. Now let's get out of here and leave the scorpions and the Turks to one another."

Feeling like a fool, Adalric said, "I don't think we should."

"What are you talking about? The Turks are the enemy! Muslims who resorted to witchcraft to try to kill us! Whatever befalls them now, they brought on themselves!"

"The soldiers, perhaps, but the scorpions are likely to kill the villagers, too."

"Again, filthy Muslims! Our task is to fight for Christ!"

"If you're fighting for our Lord, don't you see the Devil in the scorpions? They're more his servants more than any ordinary Turk could ever be!"

"Whatever they are, if you try to lead the men against them, they won't follow. Not when they have the chance to escape with their lives."

"If so, I won't blame them." Adalric turned toward the other Tafurs, many of whom had indeed hung back, staying clear of the most recent battle. "Brothers! Demons are killing women and children! I believe God intends us to put a stop to it! If you agree, help me! If you don't, Faramund will lead you back into the desert!"

With that, Adalric trotted his horse toward the nearest street. After a moment, he glanced back. He was afraid to, fearful he'd see that no one at all had chosen to join him in his folly. But he needed to know what he had to work with.

The sight behind him made him weak with relief. Many Tafurs were fleeing, but a score were courageous or crazy enough to accompany him. Faramund cantered up to ride beside him.

"I thought," Adalric said, "you were going to march the other half of the company to Antioch."

"You pointed them in the right direction," Faramund replied, "and I can't have people saying you spat in Satan's eye while I turned tail. Look there!"

As they negotiated a dogleg in the street, the scene ahead came into clearer view. Several Turks stood in a line shooting at another scorpion with a body the size of a cart, this one slate gray with a tail that switched from side to side. The front of the creature bristled with shafts that had seemingly done only superficial harm. A scissoring mouthpart snagged the fletched end of one such arrow and snapped it in two.

Adalric groped for the proper Turkish words.

"Make way!"

Startled, the archers looked around. One drew, but the man next to him grabbed him, prevented him from loosing, and shoved him to the side. The rest of the Turks moved of their own volition, clearing a path up the center of the street.

Adalric spurred his steed into a gallop. Faramund and the other horsemen pounded after him. Presumably the Tafurs on foot were bringing up the rear.

The creature balked when it realized opponents were running directly at it. Perhaps, given the choice, it would even have fled—but if so, the same power that had grown it to monstrous size compelled it to stand fast. Pincers reached and, guiding his stallion with his knees, Adalric urged his mount to the right. The claws clashed shut, off-target.

His lance plunged into the spot where the arachnid's stubby head emerged from its body, deep enough that the weapon wouldn't readily come out again. Hoping to recover it later, he let go and rode on down the creature's flank.

Behind him, shrieks rang out, a man and horse screaming together.

Adalric turned his stallion. The scorpion had grabbed a Tafur and his steed, thrown them to the ground, and was indiscriminately pinching both. The effect reminded Adalric of playing with clay as a child and pressing two lumps into one.

He drew his sword, rode forward, and cut at the arachnid's rearmost leg. When he crippled that one, he moved on to the next.

The scorpion scuttled backward, maneuvering into a position from which its sting could threaten him. He caught the banging impact on his shield.

Then the giant faltered, shuddered, and flopped over on its side. Someone had slain it—or near enough. Several Tafurs kept hacking, hammering, and stabbing anyway.

Adalric pulled his lance out of the carcass and walked his horse back to the Turkish archers.

"That—charging the scorpion—was brave," said the man

who'd kept his comrade from shooting. "I don't know if I could have done it."

Adalric grunted. "Thanks to you people, we've had some practice killing the things."

The bowman spat. "Don't blame us! Given a choice, we would never have tolerated a sorcerer. It was our captain!"

"Where is he now?"

The Turk waved his hand. "If he isn't dead, somewhere in that direction. He was trying to lead the entire company against Ibrahim. He said that if we could kill him, the giant scorpions would lose their strength. But everything was confusion, the creatures attacking from every side, and we couldn't stay together."

"Stick with us." Adalric turned to the Tafurs, a couple of whom were still doggedly assailing what was now manifestly a carcass. "Enough of that! Apparently, if we kill the warlock, this all stops! He was last seen in the southern part of the village, so that's where we're going! Form up!"

They pressed on. Bodies lay scattered about with scorpions feasting on them, both the common sorts and the unnaturally large ones. Still, a number of the houses to either side were closed up tight.

Adalric hoped some of the villagers were still alive inside. But if so, they surely couldn't hide for long. Plainly, this Ibrahim's sorcery had grown vastly more powerful, for the plenitude of oversized scorpions was staggering. It put Adalric in mind of a dam bursting. *If someone didn't contain the flood of abominations, who knew how far it would spread?*

Periodically, one or more of the arachnids attacked the Tafurs and their newfound allies. The Turks expended the last few arrows in their quivers on threats that appeared at a distance. Scrambling to envelop, the Crusaders fought the creatures that got in close. They did so ferociously, conceivably grateful that their current adversaries were merely cat and dog-sized—not big as oxen or wagons. Still, they faltered when they caught sight of the marketplace with the well in the center.

Possessed of a black body and a sand-colored tail and limbs, the biggest scorpion yet to appear had knocked down most of the market stalls as it rampaged back and forth, tearing people apart. Now, though, it was restricting itself to a smaller area, the better to protect the even more hideous creature sheltering behind it, from the Turkish soldiers struggling to get at him.

Clad like a desert nomad in a striped sleeveless coat with a robe beneath, their target was a hunchback with enormous pincers in place of hands, a shifting, jutting puzzle of a mouth, and several pairs of round black eyes. Ibrahim, surely, so given over to magic that he'd come to resemble the vile servants he commanded.

Adalric hoped that if he and his men rushed onto the battlefield, they could swing around the scorpion before it had a chance to react. He spurred his horse onward, and the surviving members of his command streamed after him.

The giant creature shifted toward him, and he glimpsed his reflection in its eyes. It started forward, and some of the Turks who had engaged it scrambled to hold it back. Long as a sword, the scorpion's sting flicked and stabbed one in the chest. As the Muslim staggered, venom swelled his body so the edges of his armor cut into his flesh. His bulging lips split lengthwise.

Adalric kept circling. Intent as he was on reaching Ibrahim, it took him several moments to distinguish a frantic voice from within the general cacophony, realize it was calling to him, and then decipher the Turk's imperfect French. The man was shouting, "Above you! Above you!"

Adalric looked up. A twin to the prodigious scorpion before him was perched on a rooftop to his left. Just as he grasped what he was seeing, the creature leaped down among the Tafurs. The jump smashed several men beneath the scorpion's double-clawed feet.

Pincers snapped shut around the head of Adalric's horse. The arachnid yanked the dead or dying stallion toward its mouth. Adalric kicked his feet out of the stirrups and threw himself clear, landing hard on his hands and knees. His hauberk rattled. He gasped in a breath and, planting the butt of his lance as if it were a staff, clambered to his feet.

Meanwhile, the scorpion's pincers snipped Pierre's fighting arm off at the elbow. The Frenchman stared at the stump as it spurted blood. He was still staring when the claws came back, clamped onto his torso, and pulverized it.

Adalric charged. Even without the impetus of a running horse behind it, his lance punched deep into the scorpion's body—perhaps he'd found a thin spot in the shell. The arachnid wheeled in his direction, and Adalric retreated, drawing his sword.

He never got a chance to use it. Pincers snapping, sting whipping, the scorpion attacked so relentlessly, it was all he could do to block it with his shield and dodge. But while it was fixated on him, Faramund and others scored on it, and after several moments, the vermin fell convulsing.

Adalric pivoted and cried out in elation. The Turks had killed the other scorpion—albeit at a heavy cost, as the shredded bodies strewn before it attested.

Unprotected at last, Ibrahim still stood at the far end of the marketplace. Someone found a final arrow to loose, and it streaked towards the sorcerer's chest.

Ibrahim shifted one of his pairs of claws. The arrow struck the armored extremity and glanced away.

Then we'll kill you with our swords, Adalric thought, and as if that had prompted them, the Turks surged forward. Faramund and another mounted Tafur pounded past their leader. Adalric ran after them, even though it was unlikely he'd get close enough to strike a blow before the sorcerer fell to the foes who would reach him first.

Ibrahim cried out in an inhuman rasp, and then his body expanded. For an instant, Adalric imagined he was witnessing some manner of witchy suicide and the attendant death throes, for his mind balked at the notion that any living thing could enlarge so violently without tearing itself apart.

But Ibrahim didn't disintegrate. Not when the lashing, lengthening tail and extra legs which sprouted from his sides tore his garments to tatters; nor when, in a matter of moments, his body loomed as large as any of the houses surrounding the marketplace.

Entirely a scorpion now, with only the shape of the head hinting at the humanity he'd cast away, Ibrahim scuttled forward to kill the men who'd been rushing in to kill him.

One pair of pincers snapped shut on two soldiers at once. Faramund galloped past the claws, slashed at one of the colossal scorpion's legs, ducked, and charged on underneath the body. Adalric judged it was a maneuver intended to flummox Ibrahim and keep him from striking back. But the transformed warlock scurried, spun around, and so put the man-at-arms within reach of his pincers. Ibrahim snatched rider and steed together, hoisted them into the air, and silenced their screams with a final squeeze.

The Turks quailed. Shouting, a young man who was apparently their commander ran forward to rally them. Short, skinny, and mild-looking, he was nothing like the mighty adversary Adalric had been imagining since the siege began. But something in his exhortations or his simple willingness to stand in the forefront steadied his men.

Casting about, Adalric realized his own troops were also in danger of breaking. He brandished his sword over his head.

"We can kill it," he bellowed, "just like we killed the others! Hit it when it's looking elsewhere, and defend when it turns in your direction!"

The Tafurs held and, insofar as their untrained desperation permitted, fought as Adalric had bade them, chopping at the scorpion's legs as if they were felling trees. Their tactics might be prolonging the battle, but weren't accomplishing much more. Unfazed by any trivial hurts he might be suffering, Ibrahim reached again and again, claws cutting and pulping anyone he caught.

Perhaps the solution was to strike at a more vulnerable spot in the giant's anatomy, but people were already swinging and jabbing at every portion within reach. Adalric ran to one of the houses bordering the marketplace, climbed onto the roof, and then discerned that in the moments this had taken him, Ibrahim had scuttled farther away.

Adalric waved his sword and shouted the Turkish word for 'captain'. The enemy commander looked up.

"Push him back this way!"

The Turkish officer hesitated, but then he shouted, "Charge!"

Scimitar extended, he ran at the titanic scorpion, and his men pounded after him.

Claws spread to punish their recklessness, but at the same time, reflexively perhaps, Ibrahim gave ground. His retreat carried him back toward Adalric's perch, and the knight leaped.

He landed on the scorpion's rounded back and immediately started to slip off. He twisted, threw himself down, and sat astride, his legs splayed by the creature's bulk, then peered about to determine whether Ibrahim had noticed him. It appeared not. The monster arachnid was too busy killing the men on the ground.

Adalric had intended to make his way up the creature's body to the head, but he now feared that if he tried, the violence of Ibrahim's movements would buck him off. Praying that scorpions had vital, cleavable spines, he raised his sword and cut repeatedly.

Like his comrades attacking Ibrahim's lower parts, he only inflicted shallow wounds. The arachnid's natural armor was too hard and thick. Yet suddenly instinct screamed that he'd caused sufficient discomfort to draw his foe's attention.

A glance assured him that Ibrahim's pincers were incapable of reaching around to pluck a man from his back— but then he looked behind him.

The tail with its bulbous segments was swinging up, and he felt a surge of hope. Because scorpions sometimes stung themselves to death. *Perhaps he could make that happen now!*

Heart pounding, he waited until the sting plummeted at him. He dived forward, and shell crunched.

He'd expected his frantic evasion to toss him off Ibrahim's back, but he stayed put, more through luck than agility. No doubt the scorpion would shake him off momentarily, when its death spasms began.

But they didn't. His whole life, people had told Adalric that scorpions could perish of their own venom—but evidently it wasn't true. The sting whirled up for another stroke and, feeling defeated, cheated, he half wanted to let it pierce him and be done.

Then he noticed the ragged breach in the shell and the

puncture beneath. Effectively poisoned or not, the wound was more severe than the petty cracking and chipping which his own attacks had produced.

Adalric wrenched himself around, scrambled forward, and once more managed to stay atop the scorpion. He thrust his sword into Ibrahim's wound and yanked it out, wondering how many more times he could do so before the sting found him.

He stabbed three times in all. Then the scorpion's back heaved and flung him into space. He slammed down with all his weight on one twisted foot. His ankle snapped, and he pitched forward onto the ground.

He rolled onto his back. To his amazement, Ibrahim was toppling. It seemed such a glorious outcome that he almost didn't care if the creature crashed down on him. As appeared likely, for there was no time for a lame man to struggle to rise and hobble out of the way.

But he didn't have to. The scorpion's body thudded down behind him, and he lay safely amid the feebly-kicking legs.

Zeki surveyed the surviving soldiers. There were more Turks left than Franks, and their superiority with regard to gear and deportment was apparent. Perhaps he could take the infidels prisoner or kill them. Arguably, it was his duty. But he doubted anyone had the stomach for such a confrontation, least of all himself.

The stings on his back throbbing, he walked over to the Franks' leader. Though younger than expected, the knight was broad-shouldered, brawny, and capable-looking, the sort of officer who had often inspired Zeki's envy. But he didn't feel that way now. Perhaps he was too tired, or too numbed by the terrors he'd endured.

A man who knew about setting bones had wrapped the Christian's ankle, and someone else had brought him a stool to sit on. Judging from his glower, those kindnesses hadn't filled the knight with gratitude.

"One of your archers told me," he said in broken Turkish, "that you unleashed the sorcerer and brought all this down on our heads."

Zeki resisted the urge to look away from the other commander's flinty gaze.

"I believed Ibrahim's magic was a weapon like any other. When I understood otherwise, I tried to make amends."

The Christian's expression softened. Now he simply looked as exhausted as Zeki felt.

"I suppose you did at that. What happens now?"

"Obviously, I can't let you to strip the village of food. But we can have a truce. You and your men can go away."

"Under the circumstances, that will do." The infidel snorted. "It will be strange to go back to the war as if this nightmare never happened."

"Well, we needn't forget quite yet. Sup with us tonight and depart tomorrow."

THE BUBBLE MAN

The Bubble Man knew all the standard tricks, and performed them with never a fumble. He made chains of bubbles that looked like caterpillars. He assembled bubbles into clusters and blew them inside one another, using a straw and the smoke of a hand-rolled cigarette to make the interior forms visible. One such, I remember, was a cube, a seeming impossibility in his realm of curved, fragile soap films.

If skill were all that mattered, he would have done as well as the caricaturist, the juggler, or the other buskers performing at various points along the boardwalk. Yet the tourists rarely stopped to watch him for more than a few seconds, or dropped money in the beat-up old straw hat at his feet when they moved along. Nor did he often find a volunteer when he proposed putting someone inside a bubble. People winced and held onto their children to make sure they wouldn't step forward, either.

All that may make it sound like I'd paid a lot of attention to him, but I really hadn't. Home from the University of Florida for the summer, I was too busy working in my family's shop selling Coppertone, stuffed 'pygmy alligators', and postcards with palm trees and beautiful girls in bikinis on them to the customers who wandered in. But based on what I had seen, I assumed the Bubble Man's unsavory appearance and manner accounted for his unpopularity. His long greasy hair and dark shabby suit made him look like a tramp, while the muttering made him seem a little crazy. It wouldn't have surprised me if the police dragged him off to a psychiatric facility or just dumped him over the county line to bother other people.

They didn't, though, and so what happened, happened.

My sister Beth and I were on our lunch break, drifting down the boardwalk. Petite and black-haired, pretty in a sharp-featured way, Beth hated spending her vacation from high school working for my parents and her displeasure often shone through, making her snippy with customers and with the world in general.

I hadn't said so because it wouldn't do any good to start a fight, but I didn't think she had much of an excuse to be that way. She'd escape the family business soon enough when she went off to college, like I had, and would do so with my parents' blessing. They realized theme parks like Disney were going to change Florida tourism for good, and were all for us kids doing something different with our lives. They just wanted us to contribute to financing our educations. But Beth couldn't see past the fact that her friends Amber and Lynn were running around having fun while she was stuck behind a cash register.

She was complaining about the unfairness of it all as we sucked down what was left of our Cokes, and, having heard it all before, I was only half listening. I was more aware of the hot sun beating down on us, the saltwater smell of the Atlantic mixed with that of frying meat wafting from a food stand, and the music of the steel drum trio playing up ahead.

My friend Roger headed up the group. He wasn't even Jamaican, let alone a Rastafarian, but with his dreadlocks and red-yellow-green-striped knitted cap, he looked the part, the better to charm tips out of the tourists.

Generally the music and his cheerful Caribbean act— complete with fake accent— combined to do the job pretty well. But when Beth and I came close enough, I saw the drummers hadn't drawn the usual crowd. Hardly anyone had stopped to listen.

It was obvious why. Hoping to leech off the trio's success, the Bubble Man had relocated from his usual spot to perform just a few steps away. It wasn't helping. People were avoiding him, and the entire patch of walkway on which he was operating, the same as always.

Shuffling awkwardly, trying to caper in time to the music but failing, he drew out a huge elongated worm of a bubble and coiled it around himself. As he did, I noticed something I hadn't before. Ordinary bubbles glint pretty much any color depending on how they catch the light. His had a persistent blue tinge to them, pretty but somehow nasty-looking too, like they could poison a person who touched them. I guessed he must add dye to his bubble soap.

Just as I was thinking that, Roger stopped drumming, and the music stumbled into silence as, surprised, the other members of the trio stopped a few notes after. Glaring, Roger stalked toward the Bubble Man.

"This is *our* spot!" he snapped, the phony Jamaican accent vanished along with his usual joshing manner. "Go somewhere else!"

The Bubble Man waved his bubble maker through the air, a ring on the end of a handle, and more blue bubbles tumbled out. It could have been the kind of mute placatory gesture a child would make. *Please don't be mad! Look at the pretty things I made for you!* But it didn't feel that way to me. Silly as the notion seemed, it felt like he was warning Roger off.

However Roger took it, it simply angered him. He cocked back his fist.

I darted forward. Partly I didn't want to see a pitiful vagrant beaten up—even an obnoxious one—and partly, I didn't want a friend to go to jail for assault. So I jammed my way in between the two of them.

Up close, the Bubble Man stank like he hadn't washed either himself or his clothes in a while, and might even have pissed his pants a time or two. Some of the bubbles he'd blown floated around my head, sparkling.

"You don't want to do this," I said.

"Yeah," Roger said, "I do."

"You'll get in trouble, and for what?"

Roger sighed and lowered his fist. "It's not our fault people don't like him. We need to make tips, too."

"I'll take him back to his own spot." Though I didn't really want to touch him in all his grubbiness, I took hold of the Bubble Man's arm and led him away. He didn't resist, and Beth didn't follow. Instead, she gave me an eye roll, telling me that it was up to me if I was stupid enough to put my hand on such a lowlife and risk catching a disease, but she wasn't coming anywhere near him.

The Bubble Man muttered something. Thinking it might be "Thank you," and it would be nice to hear that, I asked him to speak up.

He raised his voice just enough. "I don't choose."

"What?"

"I don't choose. It chooses." He shifted his arm in a feeble attempt to free himself from my grip, and I let him go, hoping he wasn't planning to turn back around. He shuffled on down the boardwalk, strewing bubbles left and right like a shy king tossing coins to the peasants.

I was busy that afternoon opening boxes, checking the contents against the paperwork, and putting the new plastic sunglasses, baseball caps, coconuts with funny faces, and other merchandise out on the spinner racks and shelves. By the time Dad cut Beth and me loose, I'd forgotten all about Roger's altercation with the Bubble Man.

Beth grabbed the phone, hoping she could find Amber or Lynn and that they'd drive over to rescue her. I wandered back up the boardwalk, intending to get some fried shrimp at the food stand which sold them.

By then, it was dusk going on full dark. The swimmers and sunbathers had left the beach, and the rental paddleboats were back at their dock. A fair number of the entertainers and merchants had packed it in.

That didn't mean the whole boardwalk was shutting down, though. The animals on the carousel—some the usual horses, others seahorses, porpoises, and gators to remind the tourists they were in Florida—went up and down and round and round to the calliope strains of 'By the Beautiful Sea'. A kiddie roller coaster still clattered along its track.

Still, sections of the boardwalk were devoid of traffic, and, with the kiosks closed up, had only the occasional light on a pole to push against the gathering gloom. I was just entering one such dark stretch when a shadow lunged out from behind the bait-and-tackle shop fifty feet ahead.

It was Roger. I could tell from the lanky frame, the dreadlocks bouncing around his head, and the fact that he had an arrangement with Mr. Villiers, the bait shop owner, who allowed him to stow the steel drums inside at night for safekeeping.

"Roger?" I called.

His head snapped around in my direction, and he waved his arm in a way that said, *Go back!* Then he ran on across the boardwalk and up the slope that climbed away from the ocean.

A moment later, a low shape pursued him. A big dog? I didn't know what else it could be, but at a distance, in the dimness, I couldn't quite make sense of it. The proportions were wrong, and fast as it was, it didn't run like a dog. It *scuttled.*

I hesitated for a long second after the pursuer disappeared. Roger had warned me off, and my glimpse of the thing chasing him had rattled me. But he clearly needed help, so I sucked in a breath and ran on up the boardwalk.

When I came up even with the bait shop, a couple bubbles were floating on the night breeze. I would have missed them if they hadn't been shining blue—I assumed with the light of the merry-go-round turning up ahead—and they popped a moment after I spotted them.

I looked around for the Bubble Man and didn't see him. That didn't mean he wasn't lurking somewhere nearby, but if Roger was in trouble, there wasn't time to search.

I charged up the slope through sea grape and sand spurs and past a couple dwarf oaks, my feet sinking and slipping in sand. Night finished swallowing the world, and I couldn't see any sign of my friend—or of the scuttling thing, either. I stopped running and shouted Roger's name.

I got an answer, but not in words. A voice screamed ahead and to the left. Just for a moment, and then the wail cut off abruptly.

I rushed in the direction of the sound but, after blundering around for twenty minutes, couldn't find any trace of Roger, or of the creature either. Neither could the police, when I went back to the boardwalk and called them.

Afterward, when an officer with a round ruddy face named

Halloran sat down and listened to a more detailed version of my story, I let the pursuing beast be a large dog. I doubted Halloran would take me seriously if I expressed my feeling it had been something else. Unfortunately, he was skeptical even so.

"Are you sure you saw your friend?" he asked. "You said it was dark."

"Yes."

"And then you saw bubbles. But not this Bubble Man himself."

"Yes. But he must have been there, and I told you, he and Roger had a fight just this afternoon."

"I understand. But did you ever see the Bubble Man with an attack dog? Or any kind of dog?"

"No."

"You say you think he's living like a vagrant. How could he have a dog unless he took it around with him?"

"I don't know."

"Son, are you sure you weren't drinking? Not even one beer?"

"No!"

Halloran shrugged. "Okay, but you see why I'm asking. We'll search again when it's light, and have a talk with the Bubble Man whenever he turns up."

I imagine they followed through, but nothing came of it and as far as I know, they didn't do much more, even when it became apparent Roger really had disappeared. I suspected that in their eyes, he wasn't much better than a vagrant himself, a drifter apt to move on without notice as the mood took him. Plus, he was black, and in that time and place, the police cared less if people of color came to harm.

Meanwhile, I tried to make sense of what I'd seen. It occurred to me that if the scuttling creature hadn't been a dog, maybe it had been an alligator. If so, then the Bubble Man had been nearby coincidentally, but bore no responsibility for Roger's fate.

But I couldn't convince myself that things had been that simple—or rather, that natural. Surely a gator would have left behind some trace of human prey, even it was only a splash of blood.

Eventually, I hiked down the boardwalk to find the Bubble Man. I didn't know what I hoped to accomplish. If he'd hurt Roger, it didn't seem likely he'd admit it. But I owed it to my friend to make at least a token effort.

The Bubble Man was performing his tricks for a fat, sunburnt husband in Bermuda shorts, his wife in a wide-brimmed sun hat that hadn't kept her from getting burnt as well, and their equally pink and peeling little girl.

The sight of him was almost enough to make me second-guess my suspicions yet again. With his stooped, puny frame and downcast eyes, his mumbling and shabby clothes, he seemed as pathetic as he was repulsive, and incapable of hurting anyone.

After a moment, he spotted me and bared his gapped teeth in a smile. Apparently he remembered I'd intervened when Roger had been about to deck him, but didn't realize the drummer had been my friend or that I suspected he was to blame for his fellow busker's disappearance.

He dipped his wand in his pan of liquid soap and swept it through the air to produce dozens of blue bubbles. For a second, they just looked pretty but vaguely nasty at the same time, as his bubbles usually did. Then I saw the vistas caught inside them as if they were snow globes. I could make out detail even though the views were tiny.

Reptile men rode lumbering dinosaurs across a desert of black sand that glittered in the light of two suns in the sky.

Creatures that were a mix of monkey and spider clambered on trees huge as sequoias that occasionally swatted at them with silver-leafed branches, like human beings slapping at mosquitos.

Something swam in glowing magma, the jagged ridge along its back breaking the surface like a shark's fin.

I gasped and recoiled a step. The woman in the sun hat gave me a puzzled frown, and I realized she didn't see the same things I did. The dozens of scenes inside the bubbles were something their maker had shared with me alone.

Still, the tourists sensed something strange, or maybe the Bubble Man's look and manner just put them off as they usually did. Tugging on her father's hand, the little girl whined, "I want to go", and the family moved on.

Unnerved, I had the urge to do the same. But the bubbles weren't hurting me—indeed, the vistas inside were fading, and surely this phenomenon was what I'd come to discover. So I stayed put and asked, "What was that?"

"Other worlds," the Bubble Man replied, pride in his croak of a voice. "Other times, even."

"Are they real?"

"Yog-Sothoth is the Blue Knight of the Crossroads. Offer to it, and it will open the paths." The Bubble Man's pride gave way to wistfulness. "You have to offer a lot." Then pride returned. "But it gives you so much more!"

I didn't follow all that, but took it to mean the visions were real.

"More than just seeing?" I asked.

"You can go in, but it's dangerous. It's safer to call something out. Not safe, but safer."

"Is that what happened to Roger? Did you call something out?" *Something that carried its victim back to its own proper place, and that was why no one could find a body?*

The Bubble Man opened his mouth to answer, and then a belated wariness checked him. "I don't know what happened to Roger."

"Are you sure? If you were afraid he was going to come after you, no one could blame you for protecting yourself."

He touched a tobacco-yellowed fingertip to his lips in the manner of one conspirator admonishing another not to speak so freely where just anyone might overhear. I kept on coaxing for a while, but couldn't persuade him to say anything more. Finally, annoyed at my persistence, he walked away.

Afterward, I didn't know what to think. Though I considered the possibility of hypnotism and the power of suggestion, deep down I believed the Bubble Man truly had shown me something uncanny. But he hadn't proved he could do more than produce illusions, nor had he admitted he was responsible for Roger's disappearance.

Even if he could summon monsters to do his bidding, and

one of them had made away with Roger, what could I do about it? Halloran and his fellow policemen would never believe the story, and I wasn't some TV marshal or private eye ready to bring bad guys to justice wherever I found them. I was just a regular person.

So, feeling cowardly because I wasn't taking some sort of action, I dithered—and meanwhile, the Bubble Man started doing things he hadn't done before.

No one else suspected he commanded any sort of magic. But everybody who worked on the boardwalk soon learned that Roger had threatened him hours before his disappearance, and that the police had questioned him afterward. So they suspected foul play, and the Bubble Man went from being someone they simply looked down on to being a person they feared.

When he realized, he took advantage. He panhandled spare change from the rest of us and ate at the food stands without paying. His manner was hangdog as ever, but still, people hesitated to say no—or at least, most did.

I was coming back from a break when I heard my sister screaming inside our family's shop.

"That isn't yours! That isn't yours!"

I hurried to the doorway. Beth and the Bubble Man were playing tug-of-war with a new straw hat from off the shelf. The sales tag bobbed around at the end of its string.

"Beth," I said, "don't!"

Ignoring me, she wrenched the hat away from the Bubble Man and looked inside it, presumably because he'd tried it on. Her face screwed up in disgust. "It's ruined!" She threw it over the counter in the general direction of the wastebasket.

The Bubble Man peered past her at the ratty old hat he'd abandoned on the floor.

He couldn't retrieve it without going deeper into the store again, and Beth wouldn't tolerate that even if she had to touch him to prevent it. She pushed on his chest and sent him reeling backward, and kept shoving until she had him outside. She then shot me a glare that told me how useless I was for failing to help her throw him out and stalked back into the shop.

The Bubble Man stared after her. Gradually his mouth

twisted into a snarl entirely different than his usual demeanor.

"Please," I said, hoping he still felt grateful to me, "she's my sister."

He shook his head. "I told you. It chooses. And it doesn't like what she did." With that, he shuffled away.

Afterward, I could no longer tell myself that maybe he wasn't really a killer after all. The sneer and his words had burned any common-sense doubts away. Nor could I find any excuse for further inaction. Roger was gone, and nothing I could have done would have brought him back. But my sister was still alive, and I had to protect her.

I tried first by telling my parents they shouldn't make her come to work on the boardwalk when she didn't want to. But they wouldn't have believed the real reason, and the weak justifications I offered instead failed to persuade them.

Next, I called Halloran and told him about the Bubble Man's panhandling and petty theft. Even if he wasn't involved in Roger's disappearance, I insisted, he was a troublemaker and needed to be removed. Unfortunately, I'd lost all credibility with the policeman during our previous interactions, and I could tell he didn't intend to do anything, either.

Much as I wracked my brains, I couldn't think of any other recourse, or rather, none that a sensible, law-abiding person would use. When I gave up, I waited until I was in the shop by myself, reached into the space under the cash register, and took out the Luger my father had brought home from World War II. It still worked, and I'd fired it on occasion.

I tucked it in the back of my pants, covered it with my shirttail, and waited until the shop closed up for the night. When it was full dark, I prowled down the boardwalk.

My plan was to catch the Bubble Man alone, take him up the slope into the scrub, shoot him, and hide the body in a patch of palmettos until I could move it someplace no one would ever find it. It wasn't a brilliant plan, but I was counting on the fact that no one cared enough about my intended victim to call the police after he disappeared—and even if anybody did, Halloran and his fellow officers wouldn't care much, either.

I found the Bubble Man after just a couple minutes,

performing his tricks alone in the dark. The bubbles shone blue even though he was too far from any light source for them to reflect any ambient glow.

That bit of strangeness made me shiver and nearly persuaded me to turn around. Reminding myself Beth's life was at stake, I reached for the Luger instead.

The Bubble Man gave me a big goofy smile that changed to wide-eyed astonishment when I brought out the pistol. "Why?" he asked. Evidently his perspective was so different from normal people's that he truly didn't understand.

"You want to hurt my sister," I said.

He shook his head. "Not me. The Knight. I explained, didn't I? I'm almost positive I did."

"Go up the hill," I said. "We'll talk about it where it's really private."

"No," he said. "I won't."

That threw me off my game. I'd assumed that if I pointed a gun at anyone, even a crazy man with magical powers, he'd do what I told him to. That was the way it worked in movies and on TV.

Because it wasn't working in real life, I had two choices. I could give up—or shoot the Bubble Man right here and carry the body into the scrub.

I realized the latter was feasible. No one was watching, and with luck, no one would notice a pistol shot or two over the music of the carousel, the shrieking of the children riding their little roller coaster, and the other sounds of the night-time boardwalk.

If I was going to do it, it should be now, before some third party happened along. But I'd never shot a gun at anyone before—never tried to really hurt anybody, let alone commit murder—and, my hand shaking, I balked.

That gave the Bubble Man the chance to dip his wand in his pan of soap and sweep it down the length of his body. Glowing blue bubbles tumbled out of the ring with unearthly vistas inside them.

Fear for my own safety jolted me into action. I pulled the trigger, and the Bubble Man stood unharmed behind the dozens of shining spheres he'd created. Thinking I'd simply missed, I took aim and fired again. The second shot didn't hit him, either.

He waved his off hand at the bubbles. "This is the Blue Knight itself. Its flesh made manifest. It protects me."

I thought I understood how. The bullets didn't reach him because the bubbles pulled them into the worlds inside. Now that the possibility had occurred to me, I even perceived their readiness to provide passage through space and time—not a suction, exactly, but a sense of openness.

That should have persuaded me to save my ammunition. Instead, scared, I fired the remaining rounds in the Luger as fast as I could—and to no greater effect than before

Meanwhile, a speck appeared inside one of bubbles and raced forward. It grew larger in the process, but came on so fast that my eyes didn't have time to make sense of it before it exploded through the curved gleaming membrane between worlds.

I'd wondered if the thing that took Roger could have been a gator, and now I saw the actual beast was built long and low like one. It was more like a centipede, though, with a dozen legs on either side. The head tapered to a tentacle or prehensile proboscis that coiled and writhed and had a ring of growths like lobster claws sprouting around the base. Apparently those were sensory organs. They pointed at me, and the similar protrusions on the creature's flanks and back did too.

I nearly bolted. But this thing had run down Roger. It could run me down as well—and I had another option besides the ordinary sort of flight. An insane option, but still …

I dodged around the Bubble Man, buying myself time by putting him between the monster and me. He turned with me, streaming fresh bubbles from his wand and keeping a protective cloud of them between us. That was all right. It was what I wanted him to do.

Head-tentacle whipping, the creature pivoted after me. Certain I had only seconds at the most before it grabbed me, I studied the curtain of bubbles.

I'd taken enough science classes to know I couldn't be sure of choosing a safe one. Any of the environments inside could have poison air or harbor other dangers invisible to an observer peeking in. But I could at least reject the rocky little asteroid where there was almost certainly no atmosphere at all, the crimson grasslands where a pack of flying faces like living masks were devouring a carcass in the foreground, and other immediately obvious hazards.

My pursuer's proboscis whirled at me, and there was no more time for scrutiny. I lunged and prayed intention would propel me into the bubble I'd selected, and not one of the others floating all around it.

Everything flickered, and then I was on the mountain ledge where I'd meant to go, momentum nearly pitching me over the side before I stumbled to a halt. The place was hotter than I'd expected. Scarlet veins twisted through the purple rock.

Blue bubbles drifted around me. I guessed that while Yog-Sothoth manifested to link places together, the god or devil or whatever was equally present on both sides of any gate.

I wondered what to do next. Then the scuttling thing's head-tentacle swirled out of a bubble. The creature was still chasing me.

From the ledge, there was only one way to flee. I chose a different bubble and flung myself into a plaza in a seemingly abandoned city, surrounded with towers bolted together out of steel and bronze.

From there, I looked for the bubble that would take me back to the boardwalk—but I couldn't find it. Maybe it was lost among the scores of others, or perhaps that one had already popped. After a second, I gave up and chose another.

I jumped eight times in all before I paused. For a moment, I was alone on a misty heath where vast numbers of phosphorescent crickets chirped, seemingly in homage to the comet whose tail split the starry sky. Then the writhing tentacle appeared. I fled into another bubble.

However the monster was tracking me, I clearly couldn't shake it off my trail. Knowing I was going to have to fight it, I started looking for a weapon.

I couldn't spot anything that inspired much confidence, but a swamp shrouded in countless spider webs had a piece of log lying ready to hand. It was small enough to use as a club, so I scrambled into that bubble.

When I snatched my intended weapon up out of mud that heaved and rippled for a moment afterward, I was dismayed at how light it was, either because it was rotten inside or because that was just how wood was in this world. In any case, it might be too light to strike an effective blow.

Then the tentacle appeared, and I decided to hell with it, this was where I was going to make my stand. Trying to hit my pursuer before it could attack me, I smashed at its head the instant it followed the tentacle out of nothingness. And kept swinging.

As I'd feared, the log started to break apart in my hands, but it was also flattening and pulping the monster's head as the creature writhed and flopped. At the end, the beast mastered its pain sufficiently to whip its tentacle at me, and I brought the club down in one last desperate blow. The wood disintegrated into scraps and grit, but the monster's appendage simply bumped me before flopping to the ground.

I'd killed the thing.

I gasped in a breath and then noticed there were more bubbles floating around me than there'd been a moment before. I jerked around.

Standing a few steps away, the Bubble Man dipped his wand in his soap pan and streamed even more of his creations into existence to form a barrier between us. If I rushed him, they'd catch me and hurl me across space and time, as they had the shots from the Luger.

I discovered they were even more of a problem than that when I felt several pulling at me simultaneously. In response to the Bubble Man's will, they were going to tear me apart and scatter me through the universe in pieces.

The only defense was to pick a single bubble and pass through in the second I had left.

I chose blindly, and was lucky. Though the air in the new world seared my airways and set me coughing, it wasn't immediately fatal or incapacitating. I was able to jump again.

In the minutes that followed, I discovered the Bubble Man

was as infallible a tracker as his monster had been, the difference being that I didn't have even a forlorn hope of battling him and winning. I kept looking for a gateway back to Earth but didn't find one.

Evidently I was done for. I'd either flee until exhaustion slowed me and the Bubble Man caught up and tore me apart, or I'd blunder into the wrong world and that would kill me.

Thinking I'd rather die fighting—however futilely—than running like a rabbit, I nearly stopped on a lonely highway with yellow symbols painted on the hexagonal cobblestones. Then I noticed a bubble that offered at least a chance of a better outcome. I lunged onto a hillside where a blizzard raged, where the howling wind blew gusts of snow down the slope and cold pierced me like an icicle dagger. And it was there I stood my ground.

The Bubble Man appeared a moment later, entering the blizzard without hesitation, as he'd chased me all along. Maybe he hadn't taken many science classes back when he'd been in school. Anyway, he seemed not to realize that his creations might partake of the essence of the Blue Knight of the Crossroads, but that they were still soap bubbles, too, and soap bubbles behave differently in a freezing gale.

Some shredded into wisps. Others kept their form but dropped toward the ground more quickly than they would have otherwise. Still others stayed in the air, but the wind swept them downhill. In a moment, the cloud of bubbles that had held me back was pretty much gone. Realizing the danger, the Bubble Man thrust his wand into his pan to make a new barrier, but by then, the contents of the container had already frozen, too.

I threw myself at him. Looking back, it was the right move. If I'd given him a chance, he might have worked a different sort of magic. But that's not the reason I did it. In that moment, I simply wanted to kill him.

I knocked him down, dropped on top of him, and grabbed him by the throat. He squirmed and pawed at my hands, but couldn't stop me. I squeezed until his tongue stuck out of his mouth and I crushed his windpipe.

I then turned my attention to the frozen bubbles lying in the snow. Shivering, my breath steaming, my face so cold it felt like it was cracking, I intended to take my chances with the first gate that looked like it would transport me someplace warm.

Unfortunately, none would transport me anywhere. With the Bubble Man dead, the magic had gone out of them.

That appeared to be the end for me, then. I might as well stop struggling, lie down in the snow beside the Bubble Man's corpse, and let the cold have me. I'd read it was a peaceful way to die.

But I was too stubborn. I clambered to my feet and staggered uphill in the hope that from higher ground, I'd see something that would enable me to survive.

I did. I saw the six colossal crashed airships that make up the habitation of the Mourners of the Butchered Star, and, discerning some ethereal mark my ordeal had left on me, they took me in.

In the years that followed, they taught me their secrets. Those included the mysteries of the Blue Knight, who didn't care that I'd killed another initiate. It was above such trivialities.

Even with the deity's acquiescence, though, it wasn't easy to learn, and by the time I understood how to return to Earth, it was no longer practical for me to live among normal human beings. My appearance would have frightened them, and my urges endangered them.

I still come back occasionally, though, when an adept with greater power and ambitions than the Bubble Man launches some enterprise so potentially destructive that I sense it even from far away. I guess I'm still protecting Beth—and I like to believe my guardianship earns me the right to feed.

KICKSTARTER

Wake Cthulhu!

Change the world!

4 backers

$37
pledged of $400,000 goal

11 days to go

First off, sorry there's no video. Everybody says you should have one. But believe it or not, we're still on dial-up here in Dunwich, MA (AKA the sticks!), and I can't get mine to upload.

Anyway, hello! My name is Hezekiah Whateley, and I'm inviting you to join me on a quest I'm truly passionate about.

Are you unhappy? Do you wish some mighty force would sweep away your dead-end job, your bills, your failed relationships, society's oppressive laws and institutions, and let you start over from scratch?

Do you have nagging questions about the meaning of life and your place in the universe? Would it help if someone showed you the face of God? Or at least the tentacle-waving face of a little-g god?

Have you ever wished the world could be more like a Michael Bay movie?

If any of that struck a chord with you, then this is the opportunity you've been waiting for!

Because according to the wisdom of the ancients, my

bestie Cthulhu is a 'dead' god, dreaming in the sunken city of R'lyeh on the bottom of the Pacific Ocean. And with a little encouragement, he'll rise, smash human civilization, and reign over a blighted planet forever after.

Wow, Hezekiah, that does sound good! But how do I know you can really make it happen?

I come from a long line of cultists dedicated to putting Cthulhu (and entities like him) back in the driver's seat. My Grandpa Squamous (who is also my Uncle Squamous—it's complicated) was reading the *Book of Eibon* and the rest of our family's collection of moldering tomes to me when I was still in diapers. (Well, if my family had believed in diapers.)

It made for a great start, but I haven't limited myself to what I could pick up hanging around the house. In high school, I made several B's in Latin (necessary for many incantations!), carried a 2.8 GPA overall, and scored 1525 on the SAT. Attending Miskatonic Community College online, I earned my Associate's degree in Eldritch Studies (AKA Shit We Know We Shouldn't Teach You, But Nobody Would Take Classes At This Podunk School If We Didn't).

Impressed? I thought so. But I'm just the tip of the cenotaph. I've put together a crack team to make this dream a reality.

Prior to her escape, Aggie Clyburn spent years in an asylum, supposedly being treated for grand mal seizures, violent outbursts, delusions, hallucinations, and an annoying lisp. Her real problem was that she was in telepathic communication with an inhuman consciousness (exact identity TBD). Finally, the doctors did the sensible thing and tried experimental brain surgery. As it turned out, the operation enabled the emergence of several alternate personalities including June Bug, Mary Queen of Scots, Muffin, and A Boy Named Cthu, each with its own special insights into how to wake the Big Squid.

Before fleeing New York (something about child support), Moe Leibowitz bussed tables in Greek and Egyptian restaurants. There, he became fluent in those languages (also necessary for many incantations!) just like I'm fluent in Latin.

Jimmy Hawthorne has served time twice for Aggravated Assault and swears he's "just getting started." A survivalist, his proudest possessions are his 257 knives, his 403 guns, and his complete run of *Tiger Beat*. (I promised to also mention that he's single.)

You and your friends are obviously the real deal! But what exactly are you going to do with my money?

We're confident that together, we've got what it takes to function as Cthulhu's prancing, gibbering, hog-gutting living alarm clock. But the ritual is like Carrot Top's act. It's all about the props, and we still need three items:

The original manuscript of *Al Azif* (AKA the *Necronomicon*), which Grandpa Squamous is "65% sure" is locked in a secret vault under the Vatican.

An Atlantean athame forged of meteoric iron, in the possession of a wealthy private collector (allegedly a drug cartel kingpin) in Bogota.

A ukulele constructed according to instructions left behind by the preternaturally gifted (and arguably cursed) musician Erich Zann at the time of his disappearance. Waiters at Fred's Luau Shack in Scranton strum it when they sing "Happy Birthday" to a customer. (Occasionally with gruesome results.)

Not being master thieves, we can't steal these articles ourselves. So we hired an expert, Larry Bosco (AKA 'The Human Slim Jim'). Your donation will pay Larry's fee and cover his expenses as he jets around the globe swiping what we need.

Risks and Challenges

We honestly believe success is virtually guaranteed. Because we have a contingency plan to deal with the only thing we can imagine going wrong.

It's possible some busybody will decide to go all 'occult detective'/Scooby Doo on us and try to interfere with the plan. It's happened before. (I'm looking at you, Armitage, Rice, and Morgan descendants.) But that's why Jimmy's on the team. I'd like to see some old professor throw pixie dust at him!

Stretch Goals

If we reach $450,000, we'll pop open a Gate and summon Cthugha, another Great Old One, to keep Cthulhu company. With all the volcanoes in the world erupting at once and flame creatures swarming in the sky, every day will be like the 4th of July!

If we make it to $500,000, we'll draw down Azathoth. He's the embodiment of primordial chaos, so his mere presence will pretty much shut down natural law and cause and effect. If (like me!) you loved 'Anything Can Happen Day' on *The All-New Mickey Mouse Club*, then trust me, you really want us to hit this goal!

Backer Rewards

Pledge just $1 and I'll paint your name on the outside of my house in weather-resistant Glidden exterior paint. I admit, the place is kind of a dump, but even so, when Cthulhu returns, it's bound to be declared a shrine or a national monument or something.

Pledge $25 and receive a set of Essential Salte and Peppere Shakers handcrafted of durable Chinese plastic. Even in the nightmare world to come, you'll need to eat, and condiments will keep your rations tasty.

Pledge $100 and we'll send you a pair of inflatable green 'I Love Cthulhu!' water wings. When the god returns, you'll encounter flooding and his fierce aquatic minions, and this stylish accessory can protect you from both.

Pledge $1000 and our alien pals the Mi-Go will take you (well, part of you) on a fabulous vacation to Yuggoth and worlds beyond!

FAQ

How do you know this guy Larry won't just take your money and run off?

No worries there! We found Larry through his classified ad in the back of *Soldier of Fortune*. They wouldn't let him advertise there unless his credentials were solid, and besides, Muffin has a "good feeling" about him.

If Cthulhu makes a comeback, won't I probably die?

Look at it this way. If Cthulhu doesn't return, then sooner or later, you will *definitely* die. If he's on the scene, he just might confer some form of immortality on a chosen few, and who better than those who helped to wake him? It could be a sweet deal, especially if you like swimming!

I heard that Cthulhu will wake when the stars are right. Where do you factor into that?

At the moment, the stars are right*ish*. Cthulhu could wake soon, but he could also snooze for decades longer. Think how sad it will be if he doesn't get his ass up until after you're dead, and you miss all the excitement.

It doesn't have to be that way! My magic and your pledge can goose the process along.

So please, give what you can. It really will change the world—and it will also get Grandpa Squamous off my back.

FLOATER

Frank Campbell gasped when Dr. Harris lifted the gauze pad away from his eye. He'd never had floaters, but he'd expected tiny bubbles or points of light. With its tangled arms snaking from a central mass, the thing seemingly hanging before him looked like a dead, rotting octopus.

"I know it's disconcerting," the ophthalmologist said. "But once you have the follow-up procedure, your vision will be fine."

"I remember," Frank said. Dr. Harris had explained yesterday when he came out from under the anesthetic. The cataract surgery hadn't gone exactly as expected. When the ultrasound pulverized the cloudy lens for easy removal, the sac containing it had ruptured, and now the fragments were floating in the aqueous humor. Frank needed a retinal specialist to get them out.

"Meanwhile," Dr. Harris said, "you'll probably find it less distracting just to keep the eye covered. I'm guessing you can't really see out of it anyway."

"You're right," Frank said. The dead octopus pretty much filled half his field of vision.

"He'll be fine keeping it covered," said Mary, sitting on a stool in the corner of the darkened examination room. "I'm doing the driving."

"Good." Refocusing on Frank, Dr. Harris switched on a bright handheld light. "Look straight at me."

Back at the condo, Frank flopped down on the couch in front of a rerun on the Golf Channel of the 'classic' Player versus Palmer final round. Since he had to make it through the weekend before his Monday appointment with the retinologist, it was a relief to discover that watching TV with just one eye didn't give him an instant headache.

But his thoughts kept returning to the scraps of flesh adrift inside the damaged eye. Had they really looked as weird and blocked out as much of the world as he'd imagined?

The lengths of adhesive bandage whispered as he pulled them loose. The pad itself stuck ever so slightly before it came away. Then he peered, trying to get past the overall ugliness of the object and take in the details of its appearance. After a while, he found he could see it more clearly if he covered his good eye with his hand. That was the attitude in which Mary caught him when she came in with leftover lemon chicken, potato salad, and a glass of lemonade on a tray.

"What are you doing?" she asked.

"Just trying to figure this thing out," he said. "From what Dr. Harris said, you'd think I'd see dozens of separate little dots, and there are a couple pieces like that. But they're floating around a big central … lump. Like back in biology class, where you had the specimens that had been sitting in jars for God knows how long, and a few bits had come loose in the formaldehyde."

Mary snorted. "There's a lovely image."

"I'm just trying to explain what I'm seeing. And to understand it for myself."

Mary set the tray on the end table. "It's just an optical illusion."

"I guess." Although he didn't see how simply applying that label really explained anything.

"And you should leave the eye bandaged."

"Dr. Harris didn't say that. He just said I might be more comfortable."

"Well, that's exactly how I want you."

She fetched fresh gauze and tape. As she started to position the pad over his eye, the tip of one of the octopus's arms quivered.

He jumped and pulled back. "Wait!"

She frowned. "Okay, but why?"

"It moved."

"Why wouldn't it? The pieces are floating in liquid."

"But I wasn't turning or nodding my head, and anyway, it wasn't that kind of motion."

"What kind was it?"

He wasn't sure how to explain, and anyway, it had stopped. "I don't know." He forced a smile. "An optical illusion, I guess, just like you said. Go ahead and apply the dressing, nurse."

In the afternoon, both his daughters called to find out what Dr. Harris had said. After that, he stretched out on the couch and napped.

He dreamed the eye was weeping pus. Dr. Yadav, who'd been the family GP before the Campbells retired to Sarasota, explained that the specks of broken lens were decaying, and the rot was infecting the surrounding tissue like leprosy. He recommended 'daily injections', and then something woke Frank up. He was certain it was something to do with the eye, even though it wasn't hurting.

He raised his forefinger and middle finger to the gauze pad. He half expected to find it as slimy as it would have been if his dream were real, but it was still as dry as when Mary taped it on.

Even so, he couldn't shake the feeling that something was going on with the eye. He sat up, stripped off the tape, and pulled away the pad.

To his relief, though the octopus was as filthy-looking as ever, there was no indication that it had done anything to influence his dreams or wake him. It was motionless.

Or maybe not.

As he studied it, the suspicion came upon him that it was rotating like the Earth turning on its axis, but as slowly as an hour hand turning on a clock face, so slowly that he couldn't readily see the movement, only sense it.

He leaned forward. The tangle of coils loomed larger. When he realized what that meant, he yelped and recoiled.

Mary scurried back into the living room. "What's wrong?"

"I—" His voice was too shrill. He took a breath. "I thought I saw something."

She registered the uncovered eye, the new bandaging

discarded on the sofa cushion, and though her manner remained sympathetic, he sensed the exasperation underneath. "What?"

"I was trying to figure out something about the ... object, and, without thinking, I leaned in for a closer look. And that really did seem to put me closer. Which is impossible ,because the thing's inside my eye. So no matter how I shift my body, it ought to look the same."

She sighed. "Frank, what part of 'Your vision is impaired' don't you understand?"

"I understand. It's just ... freaky."

"It wouldn't be if you'd leave it alone. I'm going to bandage your eye, *again*, and if you take the bandage off, *again*, I'm going to buy some handcuffs."

He dredged up another smile. "Actually, that has potential."

She snorted. "You're getting kinky in your old age."

She sat down beside him to tape on the new pad. He held himself steady against the moment when the octopus-thing would cover her face. That was going to be unpleasant.

But it *didn't* block his view of her. Instead, she partly blocked the sight of it, as if she'd shifted between them. If the tentacles moved now, the thing would have no difficulty wrapping them around her face and throat.

Except that any such thing was obviously impossible when the floating blotch was inside his eye. It only looked like it was on the other side of Mary because ... because ... Frank didn't know why, but no doubt the retinologist could explain it on Monday. Struggling not to tremble, he closed his eye and made the octopus disappear. The soft gauze pressed against his face.

After that, he could tell she was reluctant to leave him alone, lest he remove the bandaging and upset himself a third time. One more time and Mary would think he was doing it just to piss her off. But eventually she had to go to the kitchen to make supper.

Frank told himself to sit, rest, and watch the *Seinfeld* rerun like a good patient. Like a good *sane* patient. But he couldn't keep his mind on the show. It was disturbing to see the floater, but at least when the damaged eye was open, he knew where the thing was and what it was doing. When it was covered ...

He smacked his fist down on his thigh to cut off the string of crazy thoughts. The octopus wasn't anywhere or doing anything, because it wasn't real. He could prove that without even removing the pad—if he could muster the nerve.

He swallowed, stood up, and stretched out his arm. Then, taking small, slow steps, he walked forward and waved his hand back and forth. His skin crawled in anticipation of bumping a greasy length of rotten flesh.

Naturally, he didn't. He stopped when his fingertips were an inch away from Jerry, George, and the flat-screen hanging on the wall, and insisted to himself that now, damn it, was the time to let go of his paranoia.

Surely he could ... if only he could keep from suspecting the mass had *evaded* him. Unfortunately, he could readily imagine it drifting backward or slipping aside. Perhaps it had even made a game of it, allowing his groping hand to come within a fraction of an inch before snatching itself away. Maybe its arms were coiling around him even now, tightening and loosening and making little stabbing motions at his good eye, as it rehearsed his eventual destruction.

He reached for the gauze pad, but then left it in place. Because, clearly, the more he acted on his irrational thoughts, the stronger they became. His hand *hadn't* touched the floating thing, and by all rights, that should have satisfied him. Yet here he stood shaky and panting.

He kept control for the rest of the evening. When the anxiety welled up inside him, and the urge to check on the floater welled up with it, he gripped his glass of Pepsi or simply clutched one hand with the other. Anything to anchor them and keep them away from his face.

In his darkened bedroom, restraint became even harder, and he lay awake until nearly three a.m., with Mary beside him snoring her puffing little snores.

He woke to the dampness of her kiss on his cheek. But the texture of her lips felt different, as soft as ever but with a new raggedness, as if they were fraying apart.

He opened his good eye and rolled over toward her. The gray predawn light coming in the window revealed that she was still asleep.

He jerked up and flailed his arms. His hands didn't contact anything solid.

His thrashing woke Mary. "What's wrong?" she cried.

Frank tore the gauze pad away. The mass looked as it usually did, same size, same position, tentacles motionless. That was good. Only a lunatic would suspect it meant he simply hadn't moved fast enough to catch it in the act.

Mary wrapped her arms around him. "It's all right!" she said.

He took a breath. "I know. I had a bad dream."

"About what?"

He was embarrassed to tell. But at the same time, he wanted reassurance that what he was imagining couldn't be real.

"The crud in my eye. Only in the nightmare, it was a real thing floating in the air. It brushed my cheek with one of its slimy tentacles."

She stroked one of his cheeks and then the other. "There's no slime there now."

"Of course not." He sighed. "Well, I say 'of course', but that's not really how I feel. Jesus, you must think I'm losing my mind."

Mary shook her head. "I've known you for thirty-six years. I can't see why you'd suddenly crack up now. I suspect you're having a reaction to the anesthetic."

"Really?" God, it would be a relief to believe that!

"Really. After I put another pad on your eye, I'm going to call Dr. Harris."

"He won't be in the office on a Saturday."

"He must have an answering service, and if he wants to avoid a malpractice suit, he'd better call me back."

Over the course of the morning she made several calls, her voice getting louder every time. The noise jabbed at Frank, even though the anger was for his benefit.

Shortly before noon, Dr. Harris finally returned her calls. At first, Mary sounded just as irate talking to him, but her tone softened as the conversation progressed.

When she hung up, Frank asked, "What did he say?"

"Well, the literature on the anesthetic doesn't list panic attacks or hallucinations as possible side effects. But he's phoning in a prescription for something to calm you down."

"I guess that's good." *Although if the anesthetic wasn't to blame, what was?*

"It is," Mary said, "and here's something even better. Normally, your Monday appointment with the retinologist would be for an initial evaluation, and then you might not actually have the loose matter taken out for another couple days. But Dr. Harris is going to ask him to expedite things. Depending on the schedule, you might get the procedure done as early as Monday afternoon."

Frank grinned. "Okay, that *is* good." Whatever was really going on, once he became incapable of ever seeing the floater again, surely the craziness would end. "Thank you."

She smiled back. "You're welcome. To tell you the truth, it felt kind of good to give those people hell. Dr. Harris said he'd phone in the prescription right away. Do you want to ride along to CVS?"

"Okay." It might do him good to get out of the condo. He turned toward the bedroom to trade his slippers for shoes and then something fluttered inside his head. He gasped and clapped his hand to the bandaged eye.

"What's wrong?" Mary asked. "Does it hurt?"

"No. But it's weird. Like a clock ticking." A pulsing that fell short of pain but was unpleasant nonetheless.

She hovered, hesitating, and he could tell what she was thinking. She could assume what was happening was real, physical, and spend time trying to get Dr. Harris back on the phone. Or she could proceed on the assumption that it was all in his mind and hurry off to get the pills to calm him down.

"Go," he said. "I'll stay here and rest till you get back."

"Are you sure?"

"Yeah. It's just my stupid imagination."

She kissed him on the forehead, grabbed her purse, and scurried out the door. As he lay down on the couch, the Camry's engine grumbled to life outside.

The drumbeat in his eye tapped on and on. Maybe if he saw the blotch again, and it was just floating quietly, not whipping any of its tentacles around, that would prove it wasn't beating on the inner surface of his eye, and the knowledge would make the pulsing go away.

He reached for the pad and strips of tape and then faltered. If he pulled them off when he was flat on his back, the mass would be floating above him, and that would be creepy. It would be preferable—still not easy, but easier—to see it across the room.

He sat up and pulled the bandaging away.

The floater was flicking one of its tentacles back and forth at a tempo that exactly matched the flutter in his head. He moaned and shut his eyes.

Which was stupid. He'd simply seen what, on some level, he'd expected to see. What the panic wanted him to see. When he looked again, the blotch would be the usual motionless lump. He took a deep breath and pried his eyes open.

The arm was still lashing.

Talking to the blotch might be taking a step deeper into its influence or into craziness. But the impulse was irresistible.

"Why are you doing this to me? You haven't before."

Naturally, the mass didn't reply. How could it?

Yet after several seconds, an answer suggested itself. Maybe it was because the stuff that made up the lump had once been a part of Frank's own body and in some sense still was. At any rate, an idea bled into his thoughts.

Until Mary had mentioned it a few minutes ago, the floater hadn't realized he intended to have it removed. The mass was expressing its displeasure.

"I have to have you taken out," he said. "Things can't go on like this."

The whipping and throbbing continued.

"You're not even real." He closed his eyes and strained to disbelieve.

Finally, brakes squeaking, the Camry pulled up in the driveway. The car door thumped shut, and then the condo's front door opened. Mary was back with the pills to make things better.

When he opened his eyes, she was scowling at his unbandaged face. "Really?" she asked.

He drew breath to explain he hadn't been able to help himself, but just as he started, the octopus floated to the flat-screen TV and wormed the tips of its tentacles around the edges. Maybe it thought he wouldn't be able to keep his appointment with the retinologist if his wife was unable to drive him.

He yelled, "Look out!" and slapped his hand over the damaged eye. Perhaps if he erased the mass from his sight, that would make it less real.

The screws securing the mounts ripped free of the wallboard, and the flat-screen flew across the room. It smashed down on Mary's head like a flyswatter, and she crumpled to the floor. The TV swung up to hit her again.

As Frank jumped up, he opened the damaged eye, and the octopus-thing popped back into view. He charged it with hands extended to grab the flat-screen and wrest it away.

The blotch spun the TV and jabbed the edge of it into his gut. He doubled over, the breath gusting out of him, and the slimy thing grabbed him with a spare tentacle and spun him across the room. He lost his balance and fell down hard.

As he wheezed, the flat-screen crashed down repeatedly. He had to stop the beating, but how? He didn't have a weapon, and plainly couldn't overcome the octopus without one.

Or rather, he couldn't overcome the part of the floater by the front door. But impossible as it seemed, the blotch existed in two places at once, and if he destroyed the half of it lurking inside him, the part that was battering Mary might vanish, too. He raised a finger to his eye.

The floater dropped the TV, and, faster than he'd ever imagined it could move, hurtled at him. A tentacle whipped around his wrist and jerked his hand away from his face. Other arms squirmed under his body to cocoon him from shoulders to ankles.

The tip of one arm jammed itself between his teeth to gag him. He bit down, but there was hard, leathery tissue beneath the cold, putrid mush, and the mass refused to jerk the tentacle out and let him scream for help.

Once it had him immobilized, it simply floated over him like a balloon on a string. Meanwhile, half hidden under the wreckage of the flat-screen, Mary never stirred. In retrospect, it seemed likely the very first blow had crushed her skull before Frank even tried to disarm her killer.

As the days passed, his throat grew raw with thirst. Praying their connection allowed thought to pass in both directions, he begged the floater to let him up long enough to get a drink of water. Otherwise, when he died, it would, too.

No message flowed back the other way, and the mass's coils remained as tight as ever.

At dawn the next morning—Wednesday, he thought—true pain stabbed through the damaged eye for the first time. The organ bulged farther and farther out of the socket, as if it were being inflated. Until finally it burst, spattering jelly on his forehead, nose, and cheek.

Yet the blotch still hung visibly above him. His good eye could see it now because it existed wholly in the external world. The portion that had lived inside Frank had erupted and merged with the rest, in the culmination of some unfathomable gestation.

Surely that meant it had no further use for him! He was going to survive, maimed and grieving, but alive!

But the tentacles still didn't loosen. Instead, the floater opened a mouth lined with yellow fangs, lowered itself onto his face—and fed.

ADVANCED PLACEMENT

Lisa Clarke liked teaching Advanced Placement. When she was *really* teaching, it was fun; when she was drilling the kids in preparation for one of the several State-mandated standardized tests, it was easy at least. Her students were bright enough that several hands usually shot up with the right answer, and then, it was on to the next item.

But a moment came when no hands went up. The new question on the pull-down screen in front of the chalkboard stumped everybody. It read *Sound is to air as vision is to _____.*

Sitting up front with her frizzy black hair and braces, Nikhila asked, "What's the answer, Ms. Clarke?"

Light, Lisa surmised, but to her private amusement, she wasn't sure, either. Fortunately, teachers received the electronic version of a cheat sheet.

"Let's take a look." She touched a button on her tablet screen to display the solution.

Sound is to air as vision is to taint.

"Taint," snickered Jamal, wearing the Orlando Magic jacket he sported constantly, indoors and out, no matter how hot the Florida sun became. Some of the others laughed.

Always serious about schoolwork, Nikhila shot him a scowl and returned her attention to Lisa. "I don't understand."

"That's because it doesn't make sense," Lisa said. "It's gotten garbled somehow. Which just goes to show what I'm always telling you guys. You have to proofread, and when Autocorrect makes a change, you have to double-check it."

After the lunch bell rang, she filled out an online form to report the glitch, though it was a little annoying that she had to. The test developer who'd let the mistake slip through probably made more money than she did.

When class resumed, the practice exercises turned to biology. The screen in the front of the room displayed plants and animals, and the kids had to pick the proper classification from the four presented. The pine was a conifer tree, and the toad was an amphibian.

Then the *National Geographic*-style photos gave way to something murkier.

Nikhila screwed up her face in disgust, and Jamal exclaimed, "Gross!"

The creature certainly was: spiny tentacles surrounding its maw and a ring of glistening black eyes above. What looked like a second slobbering gash of a mouth opened in the center of its body, stalks like rotting tulips stuck up from its back, and spindly, many-jointed legs zigzagged down to the ground. There appeared to be five legs on one side and three on the other.

"What *is* that?" Nikhila asked.

"Look at the choices," Lisa said. When she did that herself, she found *Fungus, Reptile, Insect,* and *Synthetic.*

"Insect!" several children chorused, and clearly, they were correct. Lisa had never seen a creature like this before, but some insect species were notably grotesque, and the other choices were impossible.

Still, when she clicked on *Insect,* the program told her, *Good guess, but no. Please try again!*

Well, then, *Reptile.* It was the only other animal choice. But that wasn't right, either. Nor was *Fungus.*

Synthetic was the only option left. She clicked, and the screen declared her *Correct!*

"But it's not," she said. "It's another mistake. A living creature can't be synthetic."

Nikhila raised her hand.

"Yes?"

"What is it, really?" asked the dark-haired girl.

"An insect, just like you all thought."

"What kind?"

"Honestly, I'm not sure. With some research, we could figure it out, but for now, let's move on."

At the end of the day, Lisa reached Doug Baker's office just as two boys were trudging out. Judging from their hangdog expressions, the pudgy, round-faced principal had just given them a scolding.

With justice done, Doug was fishing a diet ginger ale out of his mini-fridge. When he spotted Lisa, he brought out two. "What's up?" he asked.

She popped the top, and the soda can hissed. "There are problems with the practice tests."

"Like what?" he asked.

She told him.

When she finished, he shrugged. "Well, two items. You have to expect some typos the first year."

"They seemed like more than typos. They were weird. The bug looked diseased or deformed."

Doug smiled. "You know what the kids see online and in video games? I doubt you gave anybody nightmares."

"Still, the answers were gibberish."

"Then it's a good thing you were there to explain that."

"What if the same kinds of mistakes are in the e-workbooks they're going through at home?"

"Then somebody will catch those and fix them, too."

As she walked to her car and drove home, Lisa told herself that *somebody* didn't have to be her. Thanks to Common Core II, educators and parents all across America were grappling with the stupid test. Still, after she rinsed the supper dishes and put them in the dishwasher, a combination of curiosity and a lack of good TV prompted her to switch on her tablet and open one of the workbooks.

The contents were like the in-class exercises. Mostly, they were all right, but scattered among the valid analogies were *Chaos is to strong as mind is to weak; Prey is to curve as predator is to angle*, and *The old are to basalt as man is to dust*.

Sometimes one of the strange comparisons tugged at her, and she felt like she *ought* to understand. But of course it was only her tiredness creating the illusion that the analogies might actually track. She reported each, and the testing corporation website acknowledged that she had.

She then checked the items she'd reported earlier. They were still as she'd first discovered them. The company hadn't reached out across the internet to fix what was on her hard drive.

But though that was aggravating, it wasn't surprising. It had only been a few hours. She switched off the tablet and went to bed. She dreamed that something that resented her calling it an insect was crawling on the ceiling. The drool from its two mouths dripped down to glue her inside the covers.

The next day, the problem with the in-class activities was worse. There still weren't all that many nonsense items, but there were more, as if they were cancer metastasizing through the body of the exercises.

"All right," she told the class, "it's obvious the quizzes are still having problems. So we're just going to skip past the items that are wrong."

With that resolved, she tried to skim text and take in visuals as quickly as possible and, if something was flawed, whisk the question off screen before the students had a chance to process it. That way, she wouldn't waste time or confuse them.

Though really, there was more to it than that. The problem items weren't obscene or outrageous. They weren't likely to titillate, traumatize, or rouse the ire of a protective parent. But something about them made Lisa's throat tighten as if she were about to start feeling queasy. She wanted to keep every trace of the content out of the children's heads.

Sadly, her tactics elicited a reaction. Some of the kids began leaning forward, peering, trying to grasp what was on display before she could snatch it away. She'd given them a challenge, a game to relieve the tedium of the drills.

She told herself that, if it made them pay closer attention, it was actually a good thing. Then Nikhila shouted, "Stop!"

Surprised, Lisa eyed the girl quizzically.

When Nikhila realized she'd yelled out, she looked mortified. Still, she pressed on: "I'm sorry, Ms. Clarke. But the last question wasn't one of the messed-up ones."

Wasn't it? Lisa had been so intent on zipping through the faulty items quickly that, perhaps, she'd made a mistake. With a twinge of reluctance, she called back the screen she'd banished a moment before.

Supposedly, it was a problem in geometry. Too advanced for her class, precocious as they were, but that wasn't the real concern. Though it was difficult to make out exactly why, her instincts told her the shape in the diagram came together in an impossible way, like a tangle of Escher staircases subverting up and down.

Lisa forced a smile. "It's an interesting picture. I can see why you wanted a longer look. But this is one of the bad questions, and the way we know is that there's no way to use the information provided to get to one of the four possible answers."

"But I figured out the answer," Nikhila said.

"She's mental!" chirped Jamal in a bad British accent. Probably imitating some comedian's catchphrase.

"*You're* mental!" Nikhila shot back. "The answer is 407 degrees! Please, Ms. Clarke, check it!"

Although she wasn't sure why, Lisa didn't want to. But she supposed it was necessary to demonstrate her point. She clicked on Nikhila's answer.

Correct! proclaimed the software. *Nice job!*

For an instant, Lisa felt astonished. Then Jamal said, "Lucky guess!"

And of course, it could only have been. Even though two other students sneered at the boy as if they too had solved the problem, and he was the one who was slow to understand. "Retard!" coughed a voice from the back row.

"We do *not* use that word in this class!" Lisa snapped. The room fell silent.

The insult deserved rebuke, but in truth, she was relieved that one of the boys—Edward, probably, he loved outbursts disguised as coughs—had misbehaved. She could focus on that instead of whether or not Nikhila actually had solved the item.

Lisa suspected that a more experienced teacher wouldn't duck the issue. But she was reluctant to argue that the girl hadn't really derived the right answer even though the software backed her up. It felt like something that would eat up an inordinate amount of time and leave only confusion and resentment in its wake.

So Lisa lectured the class on the importance of respect until she had them cowed. When she clicked to the next item, no one dared to protest that he had yet to understand the previous one.

A few minutes later, a graph appeared. It too looked like a subtle optical illusion, the X- and Y-axes curved, the spaces along them irregular, but the initial deviations were so minute that it was impossible to discern exactly where the warping entered in.

Lisa poised her finger to zap the graph away, and Nikhila's arm leaped up. "37!" she called.

Okay, Lisa told herself, good. Once the software declared that Nikhila was wrong, there wouldn't be any ambiguity or lingering bad feeling when her teacher explained that while it was commendable to want to give an answer, it was important to refrain from guessing. She tapped the button.

Correct! announced the screen. *Keep it up!*

What were the odds of guessing 'correctly' twice in a row when all the multiple choices were nonsense in the first place? Lisa shivered and rushed on to the next item.

But she couldn't really run away, not like that, not with other flawed items waiting in ambush. They became more frequent, and Nikhila and the other students who were learning to decipher them grew more excited. They called out the answers as soon as the questions appeared, and they were invariably *Correct!*

So the items couldn't be complete nonsense. Despite all appearances to the contrary, they signified something. Nikhila and her friends understood it, and Lisa didn't. Lisa had a lightheaded feeling as if she were losing her mind. She assured herself that she wasn't.

Still, she needed to stop this before Jamal or one of the other kids from the bewildered half of the class requested an explanation she couldn't provide. That would undermine their confidence in her. She jammed her finger down on the tablet's On/Off button, and the screen in front of the chalkboard turned a featureless gray.

Lisa headed for the light switch. "That's plenty of that for today," she said. "Let's do some history."

Nikhila's hand went up.

"Yes?"

"You said we were going to do all practice for the week before the exam."

Lisa smiled. "But it gets so boring."

"You said the test was really important."

"Don't tell me what I—" Lisa caught the edge in her voice and took a breath. "Trust me, you'll all focus better for taking a break."

Nikhila pouted.

At lunch, Lisa caught up with Doug in the break room, where he was about to dig into a Tupperware of steaming microwaved spaghetti. He cocked his head.

"Aren't you supposed to be keeping an eye on the cafeteria today?"

"Stacy is there."

"Well, if a riot breaks out, it's on your head." He waved her to a chair. "Is this about the practice quizzes again?"

"Yes." She told him about her morning.

By the end of the story, he was frowning. "You shouldn't have stopped doing the exercises. They're supposed to go all day, and that's not me talking. It's the District."

"That's what we're focusing on?"

"If we want to keep our jobs and the school to keep its funding, we'd better. The State is going to use the test scores for all kinds of 'accountability'. But I guess you want to figure out how it is that half your class could solve the bizarro items and you couldn't. And you're hoping for an explanation that doesn't involve early Alzheimer's." He grinned to show the last remark was a joke.

Lisa strained to smile back. "I'm not worried there's something wrong with *me*." Well, not very worried.

"Neither am I," said Doug, "so here's a better theory. Bits of the study exercises are corrupted, just like you told me yesterday. That information got out onto the internet along with the suggestion that students could use it to prank their teachers.

One of your kids stumbled across it, and there you go."

Lisa shook her head. "They're children, Doug. There's no way they could keep it together through some long, complicated practical joke without somebody getting the giggles."

"Have you got a better explanation?"

"Obviously, I don't. But until we understand, we should stop the exercises and delay the actual test."

"You mean, basically tell the education commissioner, the state senate, and the governor to go screw themselves. Even though you're the only teacher who's come to me about any problems."

Lisa blinked. "I am?"

"Yes. So maybe the whole problem is that you got a bad copy. Download a fresh one, and I bet the glitches disappear. If not, just flash past the bad items like you meant to before. Don't *let* the students answer them."

It sounded like a sensible approach, but it didn't work. The strange items were still lurking in the reinstalled software. It proved impossible to keep the eager children from responding to them when they could absorb the gist as fast as she could. Meanwhile, it alarmed her to see comprehension—or its counterfeit—spreading like sickness through the class, the fierce grins that suddenly stretched their lips, the feverish light flaring in their eyes.

Dry-mouthed, heart pumping, she was suddenly certain she mustn't let it infect them all. She turned off the tablet, and children groaned and glowered.

"Reading time," she announced. Her voice quavered, but she infused it with all the brightness she could muster.

The return to normal classroom activity soothed her jangled nerves, and as her near-panic faded, the certainty she'd briefly felt faded with it. The exercises were defective, no question, but that didn't mean there was anything *damaging* about them. Maybe her imagination was running wild.

She was still wondering at the end of the day as she headed for staff parking. On the lawn in front of the school, some students lined up to board the yellow buses in the turnaround while others hurried toward their parents' waiting cars.

Loitering near the flagpole, Jamal was laughing with Diego, the boy who sat next to him in class. Nikhila and her friends Ashley and Mae were scowling at the pair from several paces behind them.

Nikhila reached into her jeans pocket and brought out three ballpoint pens. The girls uncapped them, gripped them icepick fashion, and slunk forward.

Lisa ran toward them. "Stop!" she shouted. "Nikhila, all of you, stop!"

The girls faltered and turned in her direction.

"What were you doing?" Lisa demanded, slightly winded from her sprint.

"Nothing," Nikhila said.

"What were you doing with those pens?"

The girl shrugged. "Just looking at them."

There was probably no way to pressure the trio into an admission of malicious intent. Still, Lisa was unwilling to let go of the situation just yet. "It looked like you were sneaking up on Jamal."

Nikhila made a spitting sound. "Jamal is stupid. He doesn't belong in Advanced Placement."

"That's not true, and even if it were, it would be a cruel thing to say!"

"I was just joking," said the girl, her voice flat. "There's our bus. We need to get on."

Lisa hesitated to let them escape so easily. But pursuing the matter any further would plainly be an exercise in futility, and anyway, the incident was only one symptom of a bigger problem. Until yesterday, Nikhila had been a sweet kid who liked Jamal even though he teased her. The practice exercises were turning her into something different.

Lisa just wished she understood how and, for that matter, why. What would the test developers have to gain by brainwashing innocent children into becoming something nasty and irrational? Unless it was to lay the groundwork for a nasty, irrational future. But really, what did that thought even mean?

Without plausible answers, she doubted Doug would prove

any more receptive to her concerns than he had before. Still, she turned and headed for the front door.

By the time she pulled it open, she was already imagining what to do when he blew her off yet again. Refuse to expose her class to any more of the quizzes, even if defiance got her fired. Talk to the county commissioners. The media. That parents' group opposed to all national standards and testing, even though she'd always considered them a bunch of cranks.

She grimaced at the likely prospect of being considered a crank herself. Then she heard the agitated voices clamoring in Doug's office.

She cracked open the door. Two teachers had squeezed into the little room, and both were talking at the same time. Snaky red braids bouncing around her head, Stacy brandished a tablet, all but shaking it in the principal's face.

Lisa wanted to laugh, cry, hug somebody, or maybe do all three at once, because she wasn't the only worried person anymore. She settled for standing in the doorway and watching her new allies rant and rave.

Then the phone rang. A film of sweat greasing his ruddy forehead, Doug raised a hand to enjoin silence and picked up the receiver.

Lisa sidled a half step deeper into the office. "It took you guys long enough," she whispered.

Stacy gave her an uncertain little smile. "We didn't find anything wrong with our software until today."

"It's a virus," Carlos said wisely, the whistle dangling around his beefy neck proclaiming his dual status as teacher and coach, "and once it's loose on the web, it spreads. These days, everything's connected."

With a tight smile, Doug hung up the phone. "Congratulations," he said. "You all were right."

Taken by surprise, no one quite knew how to respond. Eventually, Lisa asked, "We were?"

"Yes. The test developers admit they've got complaints coming in from all over. They're blaming hackers, but anyway, the governor's pulling the plug." He hesitated. "Apparently, there have even been some incidents that people think are related."

"What kind of incidents?"

"Violent ones. The superintendent told me where to look online for the coverage, but you might not want to see it. I gather it's upsetting."

"I think we ought to see it," Stacy replied.

Doug woke up his desktop computer and found the proper newsfeed. It was coming out of Cincinnati. Viewed from what was presumably a helicopter hovering overhead, the school building looked all but identical to their own. Small bodies lay on the gray asphalt and green grass. Police and EMTs moved from one to the next while their vehicles stood lined up on the turnaround with lights flashing.

Stacy gave a loud sniff as if she was trying to keep from crying. The picture jerked, shattered into a confusion of pixels, and froze.

When it reassembled and resumed moving, the aerial view of the school was gone. In its place, a creature with tentacles writhing around its upper mouth and an asymmetrical arrangement of legs scuttled along a black gravel beach.

Something twisted in Lisa's mind, and afterward, she knew that such servitor beasts were indeed *synthetic*. She even knew what they were called, although she doubted a human being could pronounce the word correctly.

LEAVES

Looking tinier than usual in her puffy vest, Tammy peered at the bare oak, standing with the swing Davis had hung for her rocking ever so slightly in the cool evening breeze. "Daddy," she said, "is the tree ever coming back to life?"

"Yes," Davis said and then, sensing more was necessary, dropped to one knee to look her in the eye. "I mean, it's not dead now. Trees always drop their leaves in the fall. You know that, don't you?"

"Yes." She hesitated. "But I thought this time might be different."

With a pang of anger, which he was careful to conceal, he wondered what she'd seen or heard and who was to blame. "Well, it's not. I promise." He stood back up. "Now come on. We've got groceries to buy. If you play your cards right, maybe even some mint chocolate chip."

As he drove toward Kroger Marketplace, he looked for jack-o'-lanterns, witches stirring cauldrons, and the like, so he could point them out to Tammy. There weren't as many as in prior years. Maybe the neighbors believed the harmless fun of Halloween had something to do with the trouble elsewhere, or maybe they were just too worried to decorate.

If it was the former, they were stupid, and if it was the latter, they were letting everybody down. He swallowed another spasm of disgust.

When they reached the big-box store, two men were gesticulating and shouting at one another in front of it. His graying hair pulled back in a ponytail, the smaller of the pair looked like a scrawny old hippie and was someone Davis had never seen before. Barrel-chested with a Day-Glo orange hunter's cap yanked down on his flushed blocky head, the larger was Charlie Monroe from work. He had a stack of yellow paper tucked under one arm.

Davis passed up a good parking space so he and Tammy could give the altercation a wide berth without being obvious about it. But ultimately, that only postponed his involvement.

A food truck visited Caruthers Ford every day to sell to the sales reps, mechanics, and customers stuck in the waiting room, and just after noon, while Davis was waiting to buy his lunch, Monroe tramped up and got in line behind him. His work boot crunched a stray brown leaf like a dead, dry cockroach.

"I saw you last night," said Monroe.

Davis felt a twinge of guilt even though his better judgment told him he didn't deserve it. "I had Tammy, and I figured you could handle one little guy."

"Sure," said Monroe, "fair enough. But—"

"Next," called Bobbi, the nostril-pierced twenty-something who took orders in the truck.

That put the conversation on hold until Davis had his tuna sub and Monroe his personal pepperoni pizza, but once they made their way to a scarred, rickety table in the break room, the other mechanic took up where he'd left off.

"I was out there to promote preparedness," Monroe said. He took a big bite of pizza, then grimaced as hot cheese seared his mouth.

"You never learn," Davis said. "Wait, or at least blow on it."

Monroe used the hunk of pizza left in his hand to wave the digression away. "I was trying to warn people, and Burning Man there wanted to argue with me. He thinks we can *communicate*. *Negotiate*. Because of what it says in some old book. Can you believe it?"

"Not really," Davis said. "I mean, it sounds pretty crazy."

"Glad you think so. Because the Home Defense League can always use more help. Not just with handing out flyers and shit. With making plans. Stockpiling weapons and training to use them. Are you in?"

Davis tried to think of a graceful way to beg off, then decided only the truth was likely to discourage his coworker permanently. "Honestly, no. No offense, but I think what you and your buddies are doing is a little crazy, too."

Monroe scowled. "How so?"

"Well, for one thing, the ... creatures aren't anywhere near here. When they came up out of the ocean, they went west to attack Japan and Australia and places like that." He tried a smile. "Like Godzilla."

Monroe didn't smile back. "They'll come here someday."

"Then the Army will stop them, and if they can't, how are you guys going to do it with shotguns and hunting rifles?"

"It's better than doing nothing."

"It's been rough on Tammy without her mom." Davis flashed on the eighteen-wheeler skidding out of the rain to T-bone his Fusion, the vigil in the hospital, the funeral. "She needs life to be normal. That means I need to keep her away from anything weird, not jump in the middle of it."

Monroe grunted. "I get why you think that. But when you figure out that's not the really important thing, you know where to find me." He stuffed the last of his pizza in his mouth and stood up. "I've got a transmission to rebuild."

For Davis, the afternoon crawled, a series of oil changes that somehow failed to numb him with the mindless repetition. Instead, they left him free to think about all the things he didn't want to think about.

He drove home under gray skies and found Tammy sprawled on the couch in front of the TV. *Latchkey kid*, he thought with the usual jab of guilt. Then he noticed what was on the screen.

Most likely taken from a helicopter, it was an aerial shot of some sort of warship with bodies in uniform lying among the deck guns. Then the view shifted to men in yellow Hazmat suits about to board the stricken vessel.

Davis strode to the couch, grabbed the remote off the cushion, and stabbed his thumb down on the Power button. The screen went black, and, startled out of her TV trance, Tammy said, "Daddy!"

"Why aren't you watching *Spongebob*? Or *That's So Raven*?"

"*That's So Raven* isn't new anymore."

"You know what I'm talking about."

She hesitated. "I want to know what's going on."

"You don't need to know about things that don't have anything to do with you. Do you have homework?"

She frowned. "Math."

"Then go up to your room and do it."

She pouted, rose, and clumped up the stairs. He turned the TV back on and blocked all the news channels.

Tammy didn't have homework the following evening, which made it a good time to buy her Halloween costume. He considered going someplace other than Kroger Marketplace, in order to avoid Monroe or others like him. But they almost always shopped there, and Tammy was likely to ask why if they went anywhere else.

To his relief, neither Monroe nor anyone else was handing out flyers tonight on the brightly-lit strip of sidewalk in front of the store. He relaxed a little, but only till he got out of the car and heard claws scratching like rats burrowing though a wall. Really, it was just the wind scraping leaves along the pavement, but it still set his teeth on edge.

The fluorescent lights inside the store made people look like wax figures come to life. Quiet, troubled-looking waxworks, shuffling as they pushed their shopping carts around. Trying to maneuver around one such slow-moving obstacle, Davis wondered if the mannequin was afraid that too much speed might break off one of her legs.

Racks of high-collared vampire capes and striped Freddy Krueger sweaters appeared up ahead. Tammy squealed and, taking advantage of her smallness, scurried through the narrow space between the cart and the shelves of Scotch tape, staplers, and manila envelopes to the right of it.

It did Davis good to see her excited, but he couldn't let her get away from him. With a brusque "Excuse me," he shoved the cart far enough to the side to let him through. The waxwork gave an indignant little grunt.

As he caught up with Tammy, she spun around and brandished a fist full of blades. They were part of a rubber Freddy glove that was big and floppy on her hand. He recoiled in make-believe fear, and she laughed.

"That's pretty cool," he said. "But do you want to be something pretty or something scary?"

"Scary!"

No more Ariel or even Merida, then. It didn't mean anything except that kids go through phases, but still, for a moment, he wanted to talk her out of it.

He pushed the feeling away. "Okay. Scary it is."

Scrutinizing and fingering various costumes, picking up items like a necklace of little plastic skulls and pop-in fangs, examining them and putting them down again, she eventually led him to a display of elaborate full-head masks.

He glanced at a couple price tags and winced. The damn things were freaking expensive. Fortunately, they were also way too big for a little girl. So unless she showed signs of getting spooked—with their bloody gashes, crawling maggots, and exposed brains bulging through split skulls, some of the masks were impressively gruesome—he supposed he could let her look as long as she wanted. Whatever it took to make the outing fun.

She tried on a long-eared werewolf mask and the head of the Bride of Frankenstein with its lightning-striped beehive hairdo. Then she pointed at the face sagging between a half human/half robot and a leering clown with pointed teeth. "They were on TV," she said.

For an instant, the green scales and gill slits tricked him into thinking she'd watched an old movie, *The Creature from the Lagoon* or whatever it was called. Then he registered the extra round black eye and the little dangling tentacles that all but hid the mouth. His jaw and neck muscles tightened.

Maybe it wasn't all that terrible, he told himself. He remembered O. J. masks after the arrest, and bin Laden masks after 9/11.

But no, damn it, this was different. He looked around and spotted a stocky woman in a blue Kroger polo shirt at the intersection of two aisles, where she was straightening a display of black lipstick and dead-white makeup.

"You should look at these." Davis took Tammy's hand and led her to a rack of child-sized costumes halfway between the full-head masks and the employee ahead. "Now, stay right here where Daddy can see you. I have to talk to this lady for a second."

Up close, the worker smelled like cigarette smoke. She smiled and asked, "Can I help you?"

"There's a mask," he said, "that looks like the creatures in Japan."

She nodded. "We've got it. I'll show you."

"I don't *want* it! I'm saying you shouldn't be selling it!"

She hesitated. "We just put out what comes on the trucks."

"People—children, especially—are already nervous. Why upset them any worse?"

After another hesitation, she asked, "Do you want me to get the manager?"

He told her he did, and she headed off. Then he turned and found himself looking at 'Burning Man', who gave him a big loopy smile. Tonight, the aging hippie was wearing a ratty old concert T-shirt from a band called Electric Wizard. The picture under the logo was so chipped and faded that Davis couldn't make it out, but he had the feeling that if it were newer, the shirt could serve as a ghoulish Halloween costume in its own right.

"It's really a good idea," Burning Man said. "You put the image out there in a fun context, and it'll make people less afraid."

Davis drew breath to retort that people *should* be afraid. Then he realized that was the opposite of what he'd been telling Tammy, and the contradiction made his thoughts tangle and jam in his head.

"The universe is cycles," the small man continued. "You can't fight the others when their time comes around. But you can go with the flow. The ancients understood. They wrote it all down for us."

Anger gave Davis back his voice. "Bullshit. People *are* fighting."

"Are they winning?"

"*We'll* win if it comes down to it. America is the strongest country in the world."

"The strongest human country."

"Look, even if worst came to worst—which it won't—this is Ohio. We're hundreds of miles from the ocean."

"That won't matter. This is just the beginning."

Davis made himself sneer. "Does anybody listen to your crazy talk?"

Burning Man surprised him with a wry little chuckle. "Not yet. I was naïve not to realize how hard it would be for people to let go of … well, so much. But I keep hoping that if I approach the right person in the right way at the right moment, I can help them. I thought that maybe people who take an interest in the mask—"

"Are you camped out in the store to see who does? Hey, that's not creepy at all."

"Your little girl seemed to like it. I think kids--"

Davis lunged and put them nose-to-nose. Burning Man flinched.

"You don't talk about my daughter. You for sure don't go near her!"

"Okay!"

The hippie's immediate surrender didn't feel like enough. At a minimum, Davis should wait for the manager to show up and get the psycho barred from the store. But he couldn't stand to stick around any longer. He turned and found that this time it was Tammy watching him. He took her by the shoulder and hauled her away.

"The costumes are better at Target," he said.

In the car, she asked, "Why were you yelling at that man?"

"I wasn't. We were just … having a discussion."

"You say it's bad when *I* yell."

The whining note in her voice made him want to yell at *her*. He took a breath and turned on the radio instead. Tom Petty announced that he was "free fallin'".

To Davis's relief, Target was free of real-life monster costumes—and crazy people, too—and in due course Tammy chose a mummy outfit, with shreds of gray bandage dangling off the printed onesie and a withered-looking plastic mask. Davis also bought Hershey miniatures to put in a plastic pumpkin on the porch. And hoped the first kid to come along wouldn't take every damn one of them and stamp on the container too.

He couldn't be home to pass out the candy himself. Tomorrow was his day to work the evening shift. That meant he couldn't take Tammy trick-or-treating, either, and the thought made him feel tight and shivery inside.

For a moment, he wanted to tell her she couldn't go. But that was stupid. Joan from down the street had babysat his daughter a hundred times and could certainly look after her on a walk around the block.

When he drove to the dealership, the wind was gusting hard enough to nudge the car and swirl leaves through the air. They reminded him of jigsaw pieces, like the scene beyond the windshield was just a flat puzzle and now it was breaking apart. He took another sip of hot McDonald's coffee and it seared the loony image out of his head.

At work, he ended up replacing a Focus's evaporator and compressor. Because he had to pull the dashboard, it was a big job, and he liked that. It kept his thoughts pointed in a practical, normal direction. Near closing time, as he carried the paperwork to the service manager, he wasn't thinking about anything except how much chocolate he could let Tammy gobble before a stomach ache became inevitable.

Then, passing by the waiting room on his way back to the service bays, he noticed everyone staring silent and wide-eyed at the TV. Something told him he didn't want to see what they were seeing. He looked anyway.

The image on the screen was jumping around. Davis suspected someone had taken the video with his phone and that person's hand was shaking even though the thing he was shooting was far away.

Something dark was crawling over the crest of a mountain. Davis couldn't tell what. At first he thought it was tongues of black wildfire on the move, and then it looked more like a hundred giant snakes slithering over and under one another. Whatever it was, it had seemingly come out of the gray sea behind the peak. But it was leaving the sea behind.

He remembered *This is just the beginning* and struggled to overwrite that thought with another: *It's Japan, not here!* Which he silently repeated over and over on the drive home.

It calmed him down a little, but not as much as coming through the front door and seeing Tammy safe and sound, even though only a crazy person would even have imagined anything different. Still in the mummy onesie, she was on the couch with her sugary loot dumped on the coffee table in front of her. Deely boppers that ended in little white ghosts bobbing on her head, Joan sat on the next cushion tapping at her iPhone. Texting with friends from high school, he assumed.

Davis scooped up Tammy and gave her a hug. "Was trick-or-treating fun?" he asked.

"Yes. Except Joan says I've had enough candy for now."

"Good job, Joan."

"Daddy!"

"I'll tell you what, though. You can have one more piece if she and I can each have one, too."

"Okay. As long as I can keep all the Andes."

Searching for something he liked and his daughter didn't, Davis inspected the jumble of candy apples, Snickers, and M&M packages. Among the treats was a folded green leaflet she apparently hadn't bothered to look at. Curious, he did.

IT'S A NEW WORLD, proclaimed the caption at the top, BUT YOU DON'T HAVE TO BE AFRAID! Under that was a crude drawing of one of the three-eyed sea creatures, and beneath the picture, blocks of text in which *The Ancients knew*, *Adapt*, and *Darwin's Theory of Evolution* stood out because they were bolded.

He stuck the leaflet in Tammy's face. "Who gave you this?" he asked.

She blinked. "The man from the store. His house was shiny. Like Christmas."

A ghastly possibility occurred to him. "Which treats did he give you?"

She shook her head. "I don't know."

"Then I'm sorry, but we can't keep any of it." He looked around and found the sack she'd used to collect the candy. He raked Baby Ruths and Smarties back into it.

"Daddy!" she wailed.

"Mr. Davis," said Joan, "I checked to make sure everything was wrapped."

He rounded on her. "I trusted you to keep her safe. Get out of here."

Joan hesitated like she was wanted to defend herself or at least demand her pay. But then she just tossed her head and flounced out the door instead.

When Davis turned back around, Tammy was running up the stairs. He almost called out to her. But it would be easier to patch things up after she calmed down. Meanwhile, he had unfinished business, and he wanted to take care of it while the anger was hot and fresh and goading him on. He took his phone out of his pocket.

Monroe answered on the fourth ring. "Hello?"

Davis explained what had happened. "I want you to go over there with me. You and anyone else you can round up."

Monroe hesitated. "Are you sure you can even find the right house?"

"I'll know it when I see it." *It would be shiny. Like Christmas.*

"Well, if you say so, but what are we supposed to do when we get there?"

Davis realized he hadn't thought that far ahead. "Throw a scare into him. Make him see he can't go on doing what he's doing."

"Look, I know the guy's nuts. But I really doubt he poisoned Tammy's candy."

"Okay, maybe not. But—"

"We just can't take a gang of guys and threaten somebody in his own home. How's that going to look if he calls the cops?"

"I don't believe this! Are you the same people who are supposed to fight the monsters?"

"The monsters, yes. Not some funky old hippie who fried his brain with LSD. If we get on the wrong side of the police, that will make it harder—"

"Your League is a bunch of chicken-shits." Davis hung up.

The conversation left him feeling betrayed. By Monroe, Joan, TV, everybody. But he still had to take care of Tammy even if he was going it alone.

Hoping the crisp night air would clear his head, he went out on the front porch. The breeze brought the smell of smoke.

He flashed on the thing crawling over the mountain, the thing that for a moment had looked like black fire, and frantically looked around. But there were no flames in sight, black or otherwise. Most likely, one of the neighbors was burning a pile of leaves.

Once he calmed down, the smell reminded him of the nickname Monroe had given the hippie. Then he realized what he could do.

He dumped Tammy's suspect candy in the garbage. Then he went into the garage and collected his long-barrel grill lighter and the gas can he used to fill the lawn mower.

The drive around the block felt strange, like he was dreaming. He thought about turning back. Then he spotted the house.

Instead of putting up normal Halloween decorations, Burning Man had painted his door and the windows to either side with symbols and geometric designs. They glowed green and purple under black light, just like Tammy said they would.

Davis parked farther down the street and then crept back. Circling the house, he splashed gas on patches of wall and set them alight.

From his car, he watched the bright yellow fires rise and merge and waited for Burning Man to come running out the door. Obviously, he would, and just as obviously, the Fire Department would show up any second to save the house. All Davis had done was deliver a message.

But the hippie never came out. The pump-ladder didn't arrive until the house was one big bonfire, and then nobody tried to go inside. The firefighters just connected a hose to a hydrant and started spraying.

As Davis drove away, he told himself the old guy must have gone out somewhere before the fire even started. And if he hadn't, if he was too stoned or crazy to get himself out of a burning building, well, whose fault was that?

The important thing was that Davis had protected his daughter. There might be terrible things in the world, but this time, he'd kept them from breaking into her life.

He drove to Kroger Marketplace and bought half a dozen bags of candy. He made sure two of them were Andes.

Certain the replacement treats would mollify her, he was surprised when he entered her room and she gasped and started to tremble. He wondered if there was something funny about his expression.

BUG ZAPPER

Baker lost it halfway through the systems check. Already sweating in my Kevlar, steel, and plastic suit, I turned to find out why the technician had stopped talking and saw him sitting, slack-jawed and vacant-eyed, in front of his console.

"Baker," I said, "take a pill!"

He didn't. I walked over, put my hand on his shoulder, and shook him. He still didn't react.

I yelled for help. Someone came eventually, a doctor trotting across the cavernous space that hadn't seemed so huge and echoing back when the building was swarming with scientists, soldiers, and workers.

The physician was a tall young woman in retro cat-eye glasses. Somebody had introduced us at some point, but I didn't remember her name. The syndrome makes it difficult to take an interest in anything, including other people.

The doctor took a syringe from the pocket of her white coat, uncapped and tapped it, squirted a little clear solution into the air, then injected Baker in the neck.

That didn't help, either, and when he didn't respond to the treatment, the doctor sagged like a balloon with the air leaking out of it. "Why are we even bothering?" she sighed.

For a moment, I didn't know, either. Then I snapped out of my funk and shouted, "Pill! Now!"

That startled her into motion. She fumbled open a yellow plastic bottle and dry-swallowed one of the red and white capsules inside.

"Give me one, too," I said. I had my own bottle—I never let it out of my reach—but my gauntlets made me clumsy. She passed a pill through the open visor of my helmet and put it in my mouth.

The floor manager found another technician to finish the systems check. When we finished, I told my team—six armored Army Rangers with SCAR rifles slung over their shoulders—to close their visors, and the reflective ballistic glass erased our faces. Then we activated the resonators built into our helmets.

First, there rose a hum like the hiss of static between radio channels. But only the hum. The snarls, roars, and the gibbering that always seemed on the brink of articulating comprehensible, horrible words had long since fallen silent.

Next, everything started glowing. Some people claim to see the phosphorescence as silvery, like moonlight, or as pale violet; but if they do, that's a defense mechanism. It's really an alien color that human beings can't perceive normally.

The otherworldly light turned mundane objects translucent. Close up, they were mostly opaque. Solid and real. But farther away, they were cellophane. Beyond the walls loomed Cubist mountains with promontories that occasionally rearranged themselves like pieces sliding in a puzzle. Above the roof hung several moons like cracked, misshapen eggs.

A pair of jellyfish drifted ten feet off the floor. One trailed tentacles that writhed without resistance right through the oblivious doctor's face and cat-eye glasses. A scaly bat-like thing hung by its feet from a catwalk, and a giant centipede with an apelike head that was attached upside-down crawled over the arms of a forklift.

One of the soldiers let out a yelp. In a way, I didn't blame him. The monsters the resonators revealed were ugly in a way that mere grotesquerie didn't explain. It was a *transcendent* ugliness that made a person's eyes tear up and bile burn in his mouth.

But it seemed stupid to act scared when there were only four, and none of them were trying to interfere with us. I remembered when they were everywhere, like fish in a coral reef, or the pioneers' descriptions of buffalo covering the plains, or passenger pigeons darkening the sky. *That* was a sight worth screaming over.

The yelper had **MORRISSEY** stenciled on his helmet and vest. I decided to keep an eye on him.

A little jumpiness might not be the worst thing in the world. It showed he still cared if he lived or died. But I didn't need him panicking in an emergency.

The Rangers and I piled into our armored-up Humvee. The demolitions expert settled himself beside his supplies, all secured in their boxes and buckled straps. The machine gunner and another soldier climbed into the turret, and the driver headed for the exit. At first, we hardly seemed to need the door, but as we approached, the wall congealed into something more substantial-looking than a soap bubble.

By the time we got outside, the multiple moons had disappeared. Now, a latticework of colossal bones divided the sky into squares. Closer to the ground, geysers erupted from shimmering spots in the empty air to fill green, steaming pools. Insects scuttled to drink the liquid and vomit forth their wriggling larvae, but not in anything like their former profusion.

Morrissey reached for the keypad on the side of his helmet.

"Don't!"

He froze. "I wasn't doing anything." His youthful baritone voice had a Southern-fried twang.

"You were going to switch off your resonator."

"Well … okay. You got me. But as long as I'm just sitting here, what difference does it make?"

"Probably none. But with so many resonators working, the Humvee exists more in T-space than in normal space. If you deliberately shift yourself out of phase with the rest of us, there's a small but finite chance that it will stop existing for you entirely. You'll fall through the floor and back into the real world."

He grunted. "Wouldn't that be a shame."

"You volunteered."

"I didn't know it would be like this."

I frowned. "I asked for T-space veterans."

"The sickness is hitting the military as hard as it's hitting everybody else. For what it's worth, I'm the only rookie."

The driver called, "We've got a problem."

I craned in my seat for a better view through the windshield.

The highway ran on before us in a filmy kind of way. But we could see right through it down into a gorge that nobody had encountered in this patch of T-space before. Waves rolled sluggishly back and forth in the dark viscous liquid at the bottom. Occasionally streams of the stuff tried to squirm up the stony walls but splashed back down after a few yards of defying gravity.

"The way I see it," the driver said, "we've got three choices. We can go on the way we've always gone before and hope the highway stays real the whole way. We can turn off the resonators and drive in the normal world." A couple of the other Rangers murmured their approval of that idea. "Or we can look for a way around."

"I'm not willing to risk the road," I answered, "and the point of making the whole trip in T-space is to give us a chance to spot whatever it was that neutralized the previous teams from a distance. Go around."

"Roger that." He turned left down a street that ran more or less parallel to the crevasse. A gaunt, eyeless thing like a stretched-out black panther staggered in hopeless pursuit. It was probably too famished to manage its usual flickering lope.

"The weirdest part," Morrissey said, "is seeing two things in the same place. Things that seem like they can't both be true."

"It's because you're seeing normal space with your eyes and T-space with your pineal gland." He looked at me like he wanted to ask what the pineal gland is but was afraid of seeming stupid. "Jesus, kid, didn't they give you any orientation at all?"

"Williams—the guy who was supposed to be here—got sick at the very last minute."

"Then let me tell you what's what." I hoped some chat might take our minds off the shifting, flowing hyper-dimensional chaos outside the Humvee, which was difficult to look at even without a thousand hideous creatures slinking, slithering, or gliding every which way.

"Back in the early years of the Twentieth Century, a crackpot inventor named Crawford Tillinghast enhanced his perception with the first resonator, looked into T-space—which turned out to be the same thing as entering it—and got himself killed for his trouble. No big surprise, right? Considering what we now know about the place.

"And in a better world, that would have been the end of that. But Tillinghast left his notes behind, and decades later, they came into the hands of a physicist whose hobby was fringe and discredited science. He looked them over and, much to his surprise, decided there might really be something to them.

"He built his own resonator, and the modern study of T-space began. The dangers—well, some of them--were obvious, but the potential for new knowledge was limitless, and the scientific community and the governments backing it figured that with the proper resources and protocols, they could handle it."

"But they couldn't," Morrissey said. He raised his visor long enough to pop a pill and wash it down with a swig from his canteen.

"Actually," I said, "while we were *only* studying, things weren't too bad. There were accidents, but nothing completely catastrophic. Then the scientists discovered that to a limited degree, T-space impinges on the normal world even without a resonator field."

"Why?" Morrissey asked.

"Beats me. I've seen the equations, but I can't explain them, or any of the really complicated science. My job was—still is, I guess—to understand just enough of everything to formulate action plans and lead teams to troubleshoot problems in the field."

"Yahtzee," the driver said.

Beyond the windshield, the gorge had disappeared when a different layer of T-space replaced the one we'd been experiencing. We turned right onto a nice, solid, opaque road that ran through a forest of trees with mouths. The trees had torn off much of their foliage and bark and broken their smaller branches as they pawed at themselves in an endless search for the rodents that used to nest atop them but weren't there anymore.

Morrissey considered the trees, made a little sound of disgust, and looked back at me. "So. T-space *impinges.*"

"Yes. In practical terms, that meant some people sensed

the monsters without realizing it consciously. Some of the parapsychologists even claimed their minds touched ours, in a telepathic kind of way. Anyway, research proved that the mere presence of certain creatures promoted the nastier forms of human aggression. Murder, rape, torture, child abuse, you name it. And once we knew that, it was only natural to wonder if we could improve the world by exterminating the filthy things just like we've tried to eliminate the smallpox virus or mosquitoes carrying malaria."

"Did everybody think that was a good idea?"

"Not quite, but as it turned out, everybody who mattered. Obviously, it was a huge undertaking, but by then, we thought we'd learned enough to pull it off, and pretty much everyone who sees T-space creatures hates them instantly. Maybe that made the decision-makers reckless."

The demolitions expert made a spitting sound. "You think?"

I sighed. "The project gave us a few good years. 'On Earth, peace, goodwill toward men.' Meanwhile, the towers we'd built in T-space were working even better than expected, killing off species right and left and breaking down the whole ecology. But who cared? They were monsters, and it wasn't our ecology."

"Except that it really was," Morrissey guessed.

"Yeah," I replied. "It turned out that even though the monsters stimulated some of us in a bad way, all of us need them to stimulate us in a good way. Alien as they seem, they're our symbiotes, like the bacteria in our guts. Specifically, they're vital to human motivation, and if they don't make a comeback, eventually, every person in the world will go catatonic and die of hunger and thirst."

"So we need to shut down the bug zappers."

"Yes, and unfortunately, we can't do it remotely. The towers are self-contained. There's abundant energy in T-space if you know how to collect it—even Tillinghast discovered that before he came to grief—and even if we'd been sure it would work, it would have been dangerous to run a landline or create any sort of permanent link between this place and the normal world."

"So people need to go into T-space to shut down the zappers hands-on," another soldier said, unscrewing the cap of his pill bottle. "But as far as we know, nobody's managed to do it or even come back from the missions. No one in the whole world."

"So we're not going to mess around with the controls inside our tower," said the demolitions man. "We're going to blow the mother up. Fast. In and out before anything bad can happen to us."

"I see it," said the driver, braking to a stop.

Actually, he saw the top of the spire—or bug zapper, as Morrissey and the other Ranger called it—sticking up above some lower buildings on the outskirts of the city. Constructed of bare girders, it looked a little like an Eiffel Tower that some huge fire had heated red-hot.

But the ruddy glow was misleading. The towers didn't actually throw off heat. They emitted a kind of radiation that was only a little harmful to humans but both alluring and highly toxic to many creatures native to T-space.

The Ranger sitting up beside the driver peered at the huge machine through digital binoculars. "I don't see anything different."

"It looks okay from up here," called one of the men in the turret.

"Drive on," I said.

The closer we approached, the more rotting monster bodies we found, and neither the Humvee's chassis nor our helmets did much to block out the stink. One Ranger tore open his visor and retched down the front of his vest. Meanwhile, the armored car veered around the larger husks and bumped over smaller ones.

In due course, we reached the square of tarmac surrounding the base of the tower. The Humvees of the teams who'd attempted this job before us sat among the scores of alien corpses. But there was nothing to tell us what had actually happened to our predecessors.

"We can search the other vehicles," said the Ranger who'd thrown up.

"No," I said, sneaking a glance at the name stenciled on the demolition specialist's gear. "Ramirez has the right idea. He sets the explosives, the rest of us stand guard, and then we get the hell out of here."

Four of us climbed out of the Humvee, although the driver and the men up top stayed where they were. Ramirez trotted toward the tower. He'd studied the blueprints back at the base and knew where to place the charges.

Picking my way among the decaying bodies, I prowled some little distance away from the utility vehicle. Like everybody else, I was looking for signs of trouble.

But for that first minute, I didn't see any. Though a few blue-green flies the size of rats were crawling on the dead things or flitting above them, they couldn't hurt a man in body armor. Their rocky faces sliding, the distant mountains opened to reveal the vistas of galaxies and nebulae they held at their cores. But that had been going on for years and was no threat to us, either.

"One down!" Ramirez called. Then the light changed, the red glow of the tower giving way to another alien color no one ever sees in the normal world. This was one I'd never seen before, either. For an instant, my brain tried to perceive it as an electric white, then surrendered and accepted the otherness for what it was.

Lifting my rifle, I spun around. At first, I couldn't tell where the new light was coming from. Then, suddenly, the source appeared. I had the sense that it had emerged from around a corner or behind a barrier, even though there was so such object nearby.

It was a haze of otherworldly glow almost as tall as the tower itself, and within the cloud was a Tinkertoy skeleton made of lines of glare. Shifting like the shapes in a kaleidoscope, the lines danced to form a series of patterns. Once again, my brain tried and failed to turn what I was seeing into something more tolerable. Even though I could barely make them out, I recognized that the angles and congruencies would have been impossible if I were back where I belonged.

The thing was closest to Ramirez. Inside it, lines and triangles rotated or formed to point at him.

As soon as they did, he became almost unbearable to look at, too. I could still see the outside of his armor, but also both his naked body and the bones and organs packed inside it, and all of that from multiple angles at once.

Screaming, fumbling to unsling his rifle, he floated up into the air, broke apart, and dispersed like a puff of smoke. It only took a moment, but there was still a wisp of him twisting above the ground when the rest of us opened fire.

Was there any hope that firearms could hurt an entity like Ramirez's killer? Maybe, because of those of us who were left, Morrissey was the closest to it. But it ignored him to focus elements of its internal structure on the Ranger blasting away with the M2 heavy machine gun, the most powerful weapon we had.

Cursing at the top of his lungs, he clung to the gun to keep the entity's attention from floating him up out of the turret. He disintegrated anyway.

His partner up top took over for him, but only for a second. Then the creature pointed again and dissolved him, too.

"Turn off your resonators!" I bellowed. "Turn off your resonators!" Raising my hand to my helmet, I typed in the code.

Nothing changed. Apparently the luminous thing was a kind of resonator in its own right and could hold us in this reality if it saw fit.

"Get in the Humvee!" I cried.

Firing as we went, we all retreated in that direction. Morrissey made it through the door. Then the entity focused on the vehicle. The Humvee somersaulted slowly upward and broke apart into nothing as it rose, along with the two men inside.

"Run!" I screamed. "Scatter!" Maybe that way, someone could escape.

No, wrong again. Changing position for the first time, the entity shot over the corpse-littered asphalt like a bishop sliding across a chessboard, and it gave chase faster than any man could run. Wailing and thrashing, the Ranger it was pursuing drifted upward.

As he disintegrated, I could only think of one thing left to try. I dropped my rifle, threw away my helmet, and pulled my Beretta M9 from its holster. I reached around behind my head, pressed the pistol's muzzle against the lower portion of my skull, and put my thumb on the trigger.

I knew where the pineal gland was, tucked away in a groove between the two halves of the thalamus in the center of the brain. I knew where surgeons go in when they have to biopsy it or excise a tumor. Still, what I was intending was crazy, suicidal, and I froze until the last Ranger was gone. But when the shining thing focused on me, and my feet left the ground, I screamed and fired.

The next thing I knew, I was here in the hospital.

I've learned that while the bullet didn't kill me, it pretty well ruined me. I can't walk or see, either. But my memory's all right. I know I've already told this story a dozen times. Still, I keep repeating it, even when I doubt anybody's listening. Because everyone needs to understand what I saw and what I've figured out.

The mathematicians say T-space in infinite, and we've only explored the nearest parts of it. I think that when we killed so many of the monsters in the bit that's right next door, we opened up that territory for creatures from deeper in to colonize it, and now that they've moved in, they're not going to let us put things back the way they were without a fight.

I want to believe we can beat them. But the hospital's quiet. I've been pushing the call button for a while now, and the nurse hasn't come.

It makes me wonder who's left to go to war.

THE BODY SHOP

One man is black, good-looking, and lanky; the other, white, homely, and squat like a bulldog. Yet in the ways that matter, they look alike, both dressed in urban camouflage, both carrying M4 rifles they may have scavenged from the corpses of Army Rangers, and both still holding on to anger. I see that last item in the way they carry themselves.

In other words, not my typical customers, who tend to be ragged, hungry, and desperate. Some are downright twitchy.

So right away, I start wondering. But I have a successful business and the comforts it provides, in a time when most people live like savages or rats, and I keep it going by trying to accommodate anybody who walks in the door. So I pull the buds out of my ears—I give good value for iPods and such if they have plenty of New Country on them—smile, and stand up to greet the newcomers.

"Clark Davis," I say, extending my hand.

The black man takes it in a strong grip. "Bill Pryce. My friend is Paulie Larocca."

Larocca looks around the front of the store. It was a tattoo and piercing parlor before the aliens came, and the outer area still is, give or take. "You've got electricity," he says, envy in his voice.

"I have a generator," I reply, "and I accept gasoline as payment. So that's one way we might be able to do business. If you want to tell me how I can help you?"

"I'm not sure," says Pryce. "I mean, obviously, we've heard *something* about what you do, or we wouldn't be here. But I don't know if what we've heard is exaggerated or ..." He shrugs.

"And you don't want to put yourself in my hands until you

do know," I say. "I'd feel the same way. I'll tell you what, why don't I give you the tour? That way, you'll see the full range of services I have to offer."

Pryce nods. "That sounds all right."

"Then we can start right here." I wave my hand at the walls. Before the invasion, they were hung with flash and photos of work I'd done on customers. They still are. But not the same flash or the same photos.

"I guess you understand the basics," I continue as they move in for a closer look. "Since the invasion, some people have changed. Sometimes the monsters take them and experiment on them. Other times, the changes just happen. It could be poison in the air or water. Or maybe the king alien, the god that's moved into—"

"It's not a god!" Larocca snaps.

It's possible he hasn't yet glimpsed it in his dreams. Anyway, why argue? "Sorry. Or maybe the *thing* living in the Macmillan Center affects the city just by being here. No matter why it happens, the fact is, once a person is altered, the aliens are less likely to attack him."

Pryce grunts. "Less likely."

"There are no guarantees," I answer. "But if somebody wants to play the odds, that's where I come in. Maybe you've heard about the dead rising or seen some of them yourself? Then take a look at this."

The imitation zombie in the photo has a gray cast to her skin, shadowing under her eyes and cheekbones, and what look like little rotten patches spotting her face like acne. The customer heightened the illusion with a slack mouth and empty stare.

"Yuck," Larocca says.

I smile. "I'll take that as a compliment. But really, this is only the most basic kind of disguise. If the customer is willing to take the next step, we can do something like this." I point to a different photo.

Larocca winces. "Her nose!"

"And her left ear, part of her upper lip, and the last joint of her left pinkie. Obviously, I don't take anything the person can't manage without, but short of that, the more the customer is willing to part with, the more convincing the results."

It's Pryce's turn to point. "But these are better still?"

He's indicating the picture of a shirtless middle-aged man. I inked the suggestion of blue scales into his skin, cut a long horizontal scar onto his chin, and melon-balled pieces of flesh out of his chest so the hollows march down from shoulders to waist like a double row of buttons. He looks like his body was trying to develop the second mouth and extra eyes of a Subway Howler, but the change didn't take.

"Yes," I say. "The aliens are less likely to bother a zombie than they are a living person, but less likely still to mess with a person who looks like his body is trying to mutate into one of their own kind. I have to warn you, though, there's no way to get to any version of this without a fair amount of cutting and shaping."

"But afterward," says Pryce, "it's at least *near*-perfect protection?"

"Sure," I say, "from a block away. Closer than that, though, and all these options start to run up against the same limitations. The creature may recognize the tattooing or scarification for what it is. Or maybe its sense of smell comes into play. Who knows? But if you stick to the parts of the city where there aren't as many of them—which is what smart people do anyway, right?—it will definitely improve your chances."

"But what if you have no choice but to get up close?" asks Pryce. "Is there anything more?"

I eye him for a moment but don't pick up on any clues to what he's got in mind. I tell myself it's none of my business anyway.

"There's more," I say. "Follow me."

We push through the beaded curtain that separates the front room from the next one. I flip on the fluorescent lights, and Larocca mutters, "Shit!" He isn't the first. It's a pretty good collection if I do say so myself.

Writhing slowly, a severed tentacle floats in an aquarium. Across from it, the head of a Laughing Cyclops grins from its own jar of alcohol. I've opened the torso of a Black Kid and sawed away the tangled ribs to expose the glistening organs that crowd the chest cavity.

The specimens are impressive, but their only purpose is to convince people I really can deliver the goods. This is all material that I suspect—it's hard to tell for sure—has passed its Sell By date. The real merchandise is in the freezers.

"This is the next level," I say. "Instead of giving you fake monster parts, I give you real ones. Real spurs on the backs of your legs. Real Cold Moth wings attached to your shoulder blades. A real set of Blind Dog feelers on your face. The face is always the best if you can stand it. Take a look at these." I gesture to the photos on the wall.

I think the work on display in the front room is pretty darn convincing. But when a person lays eyes on what I can do with real parts, he sees the difference. And occasionally throws up in his mouth a little.

Or resists believing the pictures of the human form blended with things from beyond can possibly be real.

"These are fakes, too," Larocca says. "Just better fakes. A *real* doctor couldn't graft alien body parts onto a human. The human's system would reject them. And this guy—"

"Is only a tattoo artist," I finish for him. "Except, not anymore. Would you believe, the aliens themselves taught me how to do this."

"Convince us," says Pryce.

"Okay. Do you know that during the first hours of the invasion, the Burning Flyers snatched up a lot of people and carried them away?"

Pryce nods. "They nearly got me."

"Well, they did get me and took me to one of those domes that popped up all over downtown like mushrooms. Inside was a kind of creature most people still haven't seen. Like a lot of the invaders, they're hard to describe. But if you imagine smoke crossed with a pile of maggots, that's in the ballpark."

"Why did they take you?" asks Pryce.

"They wanted information," I say. "Not that I knew anything that mattered. But like you saw, they were grabbing people at random. Anyway, the important thing is that when they look into your head, it's a two-way street. You see what's in their minds, too."

Larocca sneers. "Bullshit. They wouldn't let a human know their secrets."

"It's not a problem," I reply, "if they kill the human when they're done. And as far as I know, I'm the only person who ever went through it and got away afterward."

"How?" asks Pryce.

"Since it was the first night, America still had a military. Bombs fell on the base and blew it apart. The explosions killed the monsters and all the other prisoners, too, but I got lucky and survived."

"And came away with the knowledge to do what you do?"

"At first I didn't know I had it. I couldn't understand most of what I'd taken in and didn't want to try. I was pretty sure that if I didn't forget it, it would drive me nuts. But over time, the medical knowhow started making sense. Maybe it piggybacked on the skills I already had."

"Right," drawls Larocca, "because really, what's the difference between a tattoo artist and a doctor?"

Pryce gives his friend a look that tells him to zip it, then turns his attention back on me. "And after that you started disguising people?"

"Well, not for a while. It took me about a month to accept that the monsters really had won and we'd lost. Then the idea had to come to me. And *then* I needed tools, medicine, and parts. I was able to dig the tools and drugs out of the same bombed-out base where I'd been a prisoner. As for the organs, you've probably noticed that these days, the aliens sometimes fight each other—and luckily, they don't always bother to haul the bodies away afterward."

"All right," says Pryce, "I believe you. Just how effective is this?"

"I already said there are no guarantees. But one customer told me he turned a corner, came face to face with a Cyclops, and it ignored him. Another was sneaking along in the dark, stepped in a patch of Leopard Mold, and it didn't poof out any spores. You wouldn't think that stuff is even aware, but apparently it is."

Pryce smiles. It's a cold smile. "Then this is what I need."

"Believe me," I reply, "if we can make a deal, I'll be happy to sell it to you. But first I have to warn you about the downside."

He shakes his head. "That isn't necessary."

"Yeah, it is. Early on, I had a couple dissatisfied customers come back here screaming that they hadn't understood what could happen. I don't need that. These days, I spell everything out."

Pryce shrugs. "If it will make you feel better."

"First off, you'll almost certainly get to where you can't stand looking in a mirror."

"I don't do a lot of that anyway."

"Fair enough, but other people may not be able to tolerate looking at you, either. Even if they care about you. Even if you keep the deformity covered up most of the time. Even if they're carrying similar grafts themselves. I transplanted pieces of Window Crab shell onto the faces of a father, mother, and their little son and daughter. You never saw a family that loved each other more. But when I ran into the dad later, he told me they'd all gone their separate ways. They just couldn't bear to be around one another anymore."

"Still not a problem."

"Okay. But this could be. Maybe you know that after the monsters change the outside of a person, he sometimes changes on the inside, too, until he basically stops being a person. Well, what I do is more or less what they do. For a different reason, and without any deliberate fooling with the customer's brain, but still, once or twice my work has pushed people down the same slide."

"You mean once or twice *that you know of*," Larocca says. "In the long run, maybe it happens to everybody."

"Could be," I say. "But you know the saying: 'In the long run, we're all dead.' And when has that ever been truer than now?"

"He's got you there," says Pryce. "And I know you don't like any part of this, but I believe what Mr. Davis is telling us. So let's move ahead." His eyes shift back to me. "Have you read me the entire warning label?"

"Pretty much," I say, "and if it didn't scare you away, we can start negotiating. What do you have to offer?"

"Freedom," Pryce replies.

I blink. "What, now?"

"You're wrong about the Army," he says. "There's some of it left outside the cities, and it coordinates with the resisters inside."

I hold up my hand. "Stop. I don't need to know about this. I don't want to know it. I do what I do to take care of myself, and that's that. Tell me if you've got something real to trade."

"Don't you want the human race to rise up and defeat the invaders?"

"That sounds like a no." I sigh. "Look, let's say that whatever your little scheme is, it works thanks to the disguise, and you kill a hundred aliens. Hooray for you. Naturally, everybody would be happy to see it. But it wouldn't change a thing. There are just too many of them."

"But we're not after them," says Pryce. "The Army gave me a canister of what's supposed to be the deadliest nerve gas ever invented. I mean to carry it into the Macmillan Center and turn it loose on the king alien. There are scientists who think that if you kill it, its servant creatures will die, too. Or at least their social organization will fall apart."

Larocca gives me a leer. "That should make sense to you. You're the one who thinks it's a god."

"You're out of your minds," I say. "The military already tried to kill the king aliens. They tried with everything they had."

Pryce shakes his head. "Not this gas. Not from up close when the alien's not ready for it. Or so my contact tells me."

"Then your contact's full of shit. And just to be clear, I don't care if you come back here with every luxury item left in the world. I am *not* going to do anything that might draw the king's attention." I imagine the huge eye from my dreams rolling toward me, the double pupils dilating. I shudder.

"Whatever else the gas does," Pryce tells me, his tone gentle, "it will kill me instantly. So there won't be any way for the creature to know you were involved."

"Really?" I say. "What if it already knows who disguises people as monsters, but up until now, it hasn't cared? What if you being dead doesn't stop it from pulling information out of your brain? What if it can see through time like you and I see across space and it backtracks you to my shop?"

Larocca makes a spitting noise. "You're letting your imagination go crazy."

"It's dangerous to assume that these things have human limitations," I reply. "If the last year hasn't taught you that, then you're the one who's crazy."

With one sure, sudden motion, he points his M4 at me. I freeze.

"Let's cut through the crap," he says. "Bill's right. I *don't* like any part of this. But if he says this is the plan, then I guess it is. Meaning, if you don't operate on him, I'll shoot you. Simple as that."

I look to Pryce. "Is it?" I ask. "As simple as that?"

He looks regretful but not enough to matter. "I didn't want it to go down this way. I hoped you would want to help. But yes, if we have to do it like this, we will."

"If you kill me, that's the end of your stupid plan. Nobody else can perform the surgery."

"But if you refuse, what's the difference?"

"None to you, maybe. But other people will come here. Not with some insane plot but because they need my help to survive for a little while longer. Are you going to take that away from them?"

Larocca laughs. "A minute ago, it was all about what's good for him. Now all of a sudden he's a saint."

Pryce ignores that to stay focused on me. "I am willing to let those few people suffer," he says, "just like I'm willing for you to die if you won't cooperate. It's not right or fair, but Paulie and I are fighting for the future of the whole human race. Once we win here—"

"But you won't!" I explode. "Hell, forget the god itself. Have you seen the Macmillan Center? It's *covered* in barnacles, and it's got monsters wandering in and out of it all the time. If just one of them gets suspicious, you're toast."

Pryce smiles. "That sounds like a reason for you to do your best work. Because the way you live through this is if you get me to the target and then the gas turns out to be everything it's cracked up to be."

"Shit," I say.

Pryce claps me on the shoulder. "You'll see, you're doing the right thing. And afterward, nobody has to know we twisted your arm. You'll go down in history as a hero."

"Let's just get it over with," I answer.

The preparations are pretty straightforward. I take the parts I'm going to use out of the freezer to thaw. When they're nearly ready, I have Pryce strip, and then we both wash at the bathroom sink. It probably doesn't get us perfectly clean, but the aliens' sterilizing spray kills whatever germs the soap and water miss. I park Larocca in the corner, and he hunkers down to glower and point his rifle in my general direction.

He keeps it pointed, too, through the administration of the anesthesia and the hours of cutting, grafting, and laser-splicing—I call the beam a laser but it may be something else—that follow. The gun makes it that much harder to keep my hands steady.

I manage, though, and when the job is done, I give Pryce the shot that will wake him up, pull down my surgical mask, and peel off my latex gloves. My hands tingle and ache. I go back into the bathroom, bend down to the faucet, and gulp my thirst away.

Behind me, Larocca yells, "Hey! Hey! Talk to me, Davis! Tell me how it went!"

I wipe my mouth with the back of my hand. "Look for yourself. And ask him. He'll wake up in a second."

Larocca moves to the surgical table. Then his mouth pulls into a grimace. He already had some idea of what I was doing. But watching from across the room isn't the same as seeing the results up close.

Pryce's human eyes flutter open. Larocca tries to hide his revulsion but isn't fast enough.

"I guess our friend did a good job," Pryce croaks.

I bring him some water and hold the glass while he sips through a straw. "How do you feel?" I ask.

"Not too bad."

"The anesthesia's still wearing off. There'll be more pain later. But I can give you pills."

"Thanks." He tries to sit up, and I help him. "Let me see what's got Paulie so shaken up that he can't look at me straight on."

"You should brace yourself." I bring him a hand mirror.

Give him credit. Unlike Larocca, he doesn't flinch, even though it's his own face he's looking at and even though I've given him what he asked for: my best work ever.

Mottled black and yellow like a bruise, oily hide covers his head and neck completely, and, together with the lack of external ears, the three extra eyes bulging from the forehead, and the serrated mandibles framing his mouth, nearly erases any trace of humanity. Thanks to the implants, even the shape of the skull is different.

The same slimy new skin covers his shoulders, from which flop the flabby tubes a Barnacle Man uses to connect itself to the inside of its shell. From there, the hide runs downward to make sleeves for his arms and mittens for the hands that now resemble flippers with thumbs.

"It's perfect," says Pryce. His voice is almost steady. "How could the monsters *not* believe I've turned into one of them, physically and mentally both?"

"Glad you like it," I say. Waiting, but hoping the resistance fighters can't tell that I am, I move to the instrument stand and start cleaning up.

Meanwhile, Pryce looks to Larocca. "Can you grab my clothes? Davis, leave that. Just pack a bag. We're moving out as soon as I feel up to it."

"What?" I say.

"You're coming with us," he tells me.

"That wasn't the deal!"

"I know, and I'm sorry. But you said it yourself. Nobody else in the world knows how to do what you do, and the human race needs you to do it over and over again until all the aliens are dead."

"Then the human race is out of luck."

Larocca hands Pryce a ball of tangled clothing, then aims

his M4 at me. "I don't believe you," he says. "Bill's about to give his life for the cause. You just need to work for it while the rest of us do everything we can to keep your safe. So get with the program, you cowardly son of a bitch!"

For another moment, I wonder if I really will have to. Then Pryce jerks, sways, and makes a retching sound.

Larocca turns back toward his friend. "What's wrong?" he asks.

Pryce's mouth moves, but nothing comes out except drool.

Larocca looks back at me. "What's happening?"

I could tell him. It gets back to what I said before, about how you shouldn't make assumptions about an alien, even one of the lesser monsters, based on what's true for human beings.

A Barnacle Creature doesn't have a brain. But it has strings of nervous tissue running through its skin that serve the same purpose.

Normally, I lobotomize the brain web when grafting Barnacle-Man hide, and lobotomized or not, I don't connect it to a customer's own nervous system. But Pryce isn't really a customer.

Of course, I don't *want* to tell Larocca any of this, and Pryce—or the thing that used to be Pryce—saves me the trouble of lying. By throwing its arms around Larocca and pulling him in close.

Larocca shrieks and tries to get his rifle pointed at the Pryce-thing. But before he can, the hybrid's scissoring mandibles find his neck and puncture the left carotid artery. Blood spurts in an arc.

By then, I'm scrambling for the other M4, the one Pryce carried into the operating room. The creature either recognizes the danger or just wants to make sure I don't escape. Anyway, it shoves Larocca away, jumps up, and lunges after me.

I snatch up the rifle and lurch around. The Pryce-thing is nearly on top of me, but not quite. I fire and fire until it falls down, then shoot it three times more.

Afterward, my ears ringing, gasping like I've run a mile, I realize my half-assed plan worked better than I had any right to expect. Yet what I mainly feel is ashamed.

That's stupid, though. Because while there may be a tomorrow, there won't be a day after tomorrow. And if you let the fools who think there can be call the shots, they'll rob you of the last little piece of life that you have left.

HOPE

Like most of his crew, Perez was asleep when the alarm started hooting and the lights in his cabin flared on. He snatched his headset from the little table beside his bunk and slipped it on. "Bridge, report!" he snapped.

No one answered.

"Computer, report!" he said.

"Working," Athena, the AI, replied. Then the next several seconds crawled silently by—when it should only have taken her an instant to assess the status of the ship.

Perez grabbed his coverall and boots. As he was pulling on the latter, another female voice came though the headset.

"Captain? This is Michaels."

"What's going on?" asked Perez.

"It's the K'Maarja, sir. They ... we're still trying to sort things out, but it looks like they've taken control of the bridge. Ohayashi and Nader are dead. Maybe others."

Perez ran his hands back from his temples as though that could press his yammering thoughts into some sort of order. "Where are you now?"

"Aft of the bridge."

"I'm coming."

As he raced through the cramped spaces of the ship, vibration rattled the metal deck. The green readouts flickering on the bulkhead monitors were nonsense. He stumbled as his body suddenly took on extra weight. Then another stride nearly slammed his head into the ceiling when he became light as paper.

By the time Perez reached Michaels and the three crew members with her, the artificial gravity had stabilized. The deck was shaking harder, though, and any nearby readouts had gone black. Plainly, everything was still going to hell.

Short and auburn-haired, her heart-shaped face white as porcelain under its countless freckles, Michaels hefted a wrench. "Sir, I suggest we storm the bridge."

Perez looked at the other crew members. They were holding tools, too.

"We need the weapons from the locker on C Deck."

"The K'maarja got there first," Michaels replied.

That was that, then. The only other weapons locker was on the bridge itself. The *Hope* was a military vessel of a sort, but nobody had seriously anticipated a battle inside its passages and compartments.

Nor would there be any need to contemplate one now, if Perez hadn't conceived the scheme to lure the K'maarja aboard. But then how could he or any of the crew have borne the guilt?

"If we don't have firearms," he said, "or even the flashbangs and Tasers, there's no hope of retaking the bridge by force."

"Then what is the plan?" Michaels asked.

"I go forward and talk to them."

"Sir, considering the situation, what can you possibly say?"

"Gebmorn and I have spent a lot of time together. He won't just kill me on sight." *He hoped.* "You're in command until I get back."

The hatch leading onto the bridge was shut. He could try the keypad, but the aliens on the other side might react badly to the steel panel sliding open unexpectedly. He turned the headset's mike back on.

"Gebmorn, are you monitoring communications? I'm just outside the bridge, alone and unarmed. I want to parley."

After a moment, the hatch whirred open to reveal the two K'maarja on the other side.

Perez was no biologist, but his hazy notion about evolution was that humans achieved intelligence because they lacked the physical strength and natural weaponry of wolves and tigers and such. The K'maarja, however, were blessed in both departments. The gray hairless centaur bodies were thick with muscle, and the four writhing tentacles had rows of retractable claws.

Fortunately, the hooks stayed in their fleshy pockets as the aliens grabbed Perez and jerked him inside. There they patted him down and divested him of the headset.

Perez glanced around. Using the pull-down menus, some K'maarja were inputting commands into the various consoles, presumably at random. Others had forced open access panels and were yanking equipment apart.

It was scarcely expert sabotage. It couldn't be when the saboteurs hadn't built the *Hope* or trained to fly her. But it was getting the job done.

His captors shoved him toward Gebmorn. Perez had spent enough time with the chief envoy to recognize him by the puckered scar on his shoulder and the pattern of warts on the forehead of his chimp-like face.

"Are you here to surrender?" Gebmorn asked. Like the rest of his kind, he had a startlingly high alto voice, and warm, swampy-smelling breath that tingled in a human's nasal membranes when he or she caught a whiff of it. "We'll spare you if you do. *We're* not murderers."

"I'm here to parley," Perez reiterated. "Can your friends stop tampering with the ship while we do? We wouldn't want to reach an agreement only to find out they'd crippled her beyond all hope of repair."

"I also wouldn't want to order a stop," the alien replied, "only to discover I'd given your people time to prepare some sort of trick. So if you believe there's another way to resolve this, talk fast."

Perez wanted to. But suddenly he felt like Michaels had. There was nothing to say, nothing that wasn't damning.

Playing for time, he asked, "How did you find out?"

"Doctor Votyakov told us. He thought we deserved the truth."

Perez winced. The ship psychiatrist, responsible for helping the rest of the crew keep a lid on their feelings. And meanwhile, nobody had been helping him.

"At first," Gebmorn continued, "we thought he was joking

or had gone insane. We couldn't imagine that a race advanced enough to cross the stars had done so because you're terrified of a primitive superstition."

"Whatever else you think of us," Perez said, "believe this: It's not superstition. Cthulhu is real. He's about to wake, and then he and his creatures will overrun my world. I've seen the proof. If you'll let me use one of the terminals, I can show you video."

"Votyakov already showed us. The images were disturbing. But even if no one faked them on purpose, they're too murky and blurry to prove anything."

Metal clattered as a K'maarja ripped another access panel off its mounts.

"You can't see the images clearly," Perez said, "because you're not attuned. Surely Votyakov explained that, too. Let me guide you through the meditation."

"I understand it takes several hours," Gebmorn said, "during which time your crew will attempt to turn their situation around. And if they fail, if the ceremony actually reaches its conclusion, I risk being left as brainwashed as you evidently are. That isn't going to happen."

"You've gotten to know me, Gebmorn. Do you honestly believe I'd be a party to this if the threat weren't real?"

The K'marrja hesitated. "The man, the people I *believed* I was coming to know would have fought a danger that threatened them and fought it honorably. They wouldn't have sought to transfer their misfortune to the innocent."

"We tried to fight," Perez said. "God only knows what all the nukes we dropped in the Pacific would have done to the environment if they'd detonated. We might have wiped ourselves out and saved Cthulhu the trouble. But they never went off. We had to find another way. We had to study the strange old books that warned about R'lyeh, the Great Old Ones, and all the rest of it."

The end of one of Gebmorn's tentacles tied itself in a knot, a gesture indicating skepticism or derision. "Did the books tell you how to construct a starship?"

"Not really. They told us we *needed* to construct one.

Because it was the stars, moving into a certain alignment, that were waking Cthulhu up."

The talons contained in the alien's writhing tentacles rippled into view, then slipped back into their sockets. That was a sign of impatience. "That's preposterous. The light leaving my sun today won't reach your planet for a hundred years. You and I both know that."

"The problem isn't the light," Perez said. "It's the gravity. It warps spacetime in our part of the galaxy in a way that Cthulhu finds—I don't know, stimulating? Nourishing? You'd have to ask someone who understands it better than I do. Anyway, once we figured it out, the whole world worked together to invent an interstellar spacecraft."

"Plus a bomb capable of blowing up a sun."

Perez swallowed. "Yes. Destroying a star in the pattern will disrupt the balance that allows Cthulhu to wake."

"And if you commit genocide in the course of saving your own precious species, that's simply the way it has to be."

"When we chose to come here, we didn't even know your star had planets. Our astronomers hadn't detected them. Once we arrived at the edge of the system and picked up your radio and TV transmissions, we were horrified."

"Just not horrified enough to travel on to the next star in the pattern."

"We can't. The others are all too far away. It's not like Earth was on the brink of inventing interstellar travel anyway. We had to combine hypotheses we didn't even know how to test with ancient lore we only half understood. The result was a miracle, but a miracle that had lots of unexpected problems and barely made it this far." He shivered. "Subspace is rough."

"Not rough enough. You made it out the other side."

"At which point, time was running short. Still, after we discovered your people, not one of us was willing to launch the missile immediately." That was an exaggeration, but Perez was trying to convince the K'maarja that humans weren't monsters. "We knew we had to help you."

"By lying, kidnapping a pitiful few of us, and exterminating the rest."

"It wasn't entirely a lie. You *will* come to Earth as honored guests. We *do* want to learn about your culture. And as far as 'a pitiful few' is concerned, we crammed in as many as possible. There are twice as many of you onboard as there are of us."

"That isn't working out very well for you."

"The point is that we wanted both civilizations to survive instead of only one!"

"If that's all you want, then do it the other way around. Surrender, fly the ship back to my world—under close supervision--and you and your crew be the last survivors of *your* race."

"I can't do that."

"Consider that at least we know my race is still alive. You can't say the same for yours. For all you know, Cthulhu, if indeed he exists, has already risen. Your kind may already be extinct."

"Not if the calculations are correct. Do you understand that if that if your friends damage the ship beyond a certain point, everyone aboard, human and K'maarja alike, will die?"

"Compared to the destruction of our entire planet, that's an acceptable outcome. If it's not acceptable to you, you know how to forestall it." With the flowing brush of a tentacle, Gebmorn pushed Perez back into a corner, then turned to help with the ongoing lobotomy of the AI and demolition of the hardware.

Perez glanced around. The K'maarja had raided the weapons locker on C Deck. Maybe they'd left a pistol or shotgun within reach.

They hadn't, though, and after a moment, he recognized the possibility for the false hope it was. In these close quarters, he might gun down one or two aliens, but then the rest would overwhelm him.

Still, there had to be something he could do! Eyes closed, twitching at every sudden distracting bang and clank, he strained to think what it might be. Eventually, he hit on a single possibility.

He'd read selections from the *Necronomicon, The Book of Eibon,* and a couple other weird old texts to prepare him for the mission. Someone had thought it would enhance his understanding of the physics that made the *Hope* possible and of the rationale for blowing up a star.

Maybe it had. But it had also exposed him to the prayers the ancients used to petition the entities that dwelled at the bottom of the sea, in outer space, and in the hyperspatial chaos beyond.

It was absurd to think Cthulhu might help him. But if the passages he'd read and the briefings he'd received were true, the Great Old Ones and Elder Gods weren't all allies or invested in one another's schemes. If he called out to something else, it might answer. But only if he could remember the flowery convoluted language of the lengthy invocation.

Unfortunately, he hadn't even attempted to commit any of them to memory, and after a minute of fruitless struggle, he nearly despaired of dredging anything up out of his subconscious. But then, a word at a time, a prayer started articulating itself inside his head, revealing itself so facilely that he felt like it wanted him to remember. Or like something was whispering it to him.

Perez whispered, too, to keep the K'maarja from hearing as he recited the lines that came to him. "Nyarlathotep! Pharaoh with a thousand visages and none!"

For a while, nothing changed. Then it did, but the transformation was only inside Perez himself. Gradually, it became sickening to murmur the words, like eating filth or sticking a needle under his fingernails. Meanwhile, the aliens continued their sabotage the same as before.

He told himself that *something* was happening. He needed to keep going even if it was torture. "You take the lonely multitude in your shadowy hand and crush us into a single raging joy. You drink the river dry and bring the desert."

A K'maarja working at one of the terminals started to chuckle. Over the course of several seconds, the chortling swelled into raucous laughter that continued even when the alien could barely catch her breath.

Perez felt a surge of excitement. Because the K'maarja *didn't* laugh, not normally. They had humor, but they expressed their mirth by coiling and flicking the ends of their arms.

Two other aliens gathered around their stricken friend. She peered at them with wide yellow eyes and then, still laughing, whipped her tentacles up, bared the claws, and flensed her face off the bone beneath.

One K'maarja grappled with her in an effort to restrain her before she could do herself further harm. The other giggled. Then he hooked his claws in the shoulders of the male who was trying to help the female and ripped gory trenches down the length of his back.

Any human would have dropped. But the wounded male turned to fend off his attacker, and for a couple seconds, they flailed one another to shreds. Then he who had been the last sane one of the three began to laugh. He curled a tentacle around his own neck and jerked. The claws lodged in his flesh spun his head all the way around as it came off.

By then, other K'maarja were laughing, their high voices like blaring trumpets. Mostly, they concentrated on tearing themselves to bits, but when someone tried to stop them or any of their fellow self-mutilators, they were happy to turn on the meddler instead.

Still rational, Gebmorn rounded on Perez.

"Make it stop!"

Perez spread his hands to signal that he, the unarmed prisoner held incommunicado away from all the I/O devices, obviously had nothing to do with what was happening. He also kept reciting under his breath. "I beg you, debase and obliterate my enemies. For I am your groveling servant, now and forevermore."

Claws out, Gebmorn's tentacles reared like cobras. Then the alien rushed in, and, pent in the corner, Perez couldn't even try to dodge.

But he didn't have to. A demented K'maarja looped a tentacle around one of Gebmorn's front legs and jerked it out from under him. Bone cracked, and the chief envoy fell down. His attacker lashed and rent him until the broken leg flew off and tumbled halfway across the bridge. Then, with a howl of mirth, Gebmorn started attending to his own destruction, and, satisfied, his assailant resumed his own.

When Gebmorn exposed it, the structure of bone and cartilage analogous to a rib cage looked like a spider web. As he caught it in his talons, the K'maarja managed to quell his laughter long enough to gasp, "Please don't. Please don't." Then he was roaring once again. He tore the web loose and ripped at the glistening organs beneath.

The aliens finished killing themselves before Perez finished the prayer. He gritted out the rest of it anyway. Something told him it was the safe thing to do. Then he puked, and, after that, opened the hatch for the crewmen waiting outside.

Michaels peered about in a combination of horror and relief. "Jesus Christ! What happened?"

Even though the slaughter had been necessary, Perez realized he couldn't bear to explain. "They just went crazy. Something about our air, maybe. The tests said it would be all right, but possibly there was something they didn't catch."

"Maybe." She shook her head, perhaps to clear it. "Now we can get guns, and the K'maarja weren't all on the bridge. We need to make a sweep of the ship."

"You're right." They had to go through the motions. But his gut told him that Nyarlathotep had killed every last one of the aliens, and that turned out to be the case.

Though it took hard, dangerous work as well as considerable ingenuity on the part of the engineers, the crew succeeded in repairing the ship. They were able to slingshot around the K'maarja's sun, release the bomb, and race outward. They reached the fringes of the system, where gravity was feeble enough to permit entry into subspace, and made the jump just ahead of the explosion.

Now that they knew what to expect, the journey home proved somewhat less arduous than the outbound voyage. Occasionally, Perez had time to think, and then he found himself pondering the possibility Gebmorn had suggested. What if Cthulhu had already destroyed humanity before the *Hope* launched the bomb?

Eventually he decided that in a way, it didn't matter. His world was dead to him either way. He couldn't stand to live among the human race, given the crime that had been committed to save it. It didn't matter that they hadn't made the choice; he had. They would have done the same.

And if he was wrong, then they deserved better to have him lurking among them, polluted, groveling servant of death that he was.

He waited until it was 'night' onboard, and most of the crew was asleep. Then he took the belt of his dress uniform from his locker. As he looped it around his neck, he thought of the K'maarja's tentacles.

ABOUT THE AUTHOR

Richard Lee Byers is the author of forty fantasy and horror novels. He has also written dozens of short stories, scripted a graphic novel, and contributed content to tabletop and electronic games. A veteran fencer, he lives in the Tampa Bay area and is a frequent program participant at Dragon Con, Gen Con, and Florida SF conventions. He invites everyone to connect with him on Facebook, Google+, Ello, and/or Twitter.

BIBLIOGRAPHY

Deathward
Fright Line
The Vampire's Apprentice
Dark Fortune
Dead Time
The Tale of the Terrible Toys
X-Men: Soul Killer
Caravan of Shadows
The Ebon Mask
Dark Kingdoms (includes The Ebon Mask and completes the story that novel began)
Netherworld
On A Darkling Plain
The Enemy Within
Called to Darkness
Blind God's Bluff
This Sword for Hire
The Things That Crawl

Ire of the Void
Joy Ride (The Nightmare Club, Book 1)
Warlock Games (The Nightmare Club, Book 3)
Party Till You Drop (The Nightmare Club, Book 6)

The Black River Irregulars Series

Black Dogs
Black Crowns

The Dead God Trilogy

Forsaken
Forsworn
Forbidden

The Imposter Series

The Impostor #1: Half a Hero
The Impostor #2: Blood Machine

Forgotten Realms Novels

The Shattered Mask (Sembia, Book 3)
Queen of the Depths (The Priests, Book 4)
The Black Bouquet (The Rogues, Book 2)
Dissolution (War of the Spider Queen, Book 1)
The Reaver (The Sundering, Book 4)

The Year of Rogue Dragons Series

The Rage
The Rite
The Ruin
The Year of Rogue Dragons

The Haunted Land Trilogy

Unclean
Undead
Unholy

The Brotherhood of the Griffon

The Captive Flame
Whisper of Venom
The Spectral Blaze
The Masked Witches
Prophet of the Dead

The Shadow Guide (forthcoming)

Curious about other Crossroad Press books?
Stop by our site:
http://store.crossroadpress.com
We offer quality writing
in digital, audio, and print formats.

Enter the code FIRSTBOOK
to get 20% off your first order from our store!
Stop by today!